Wayward School

Thomas Gondolfi

Rianna,

Squeamish is for the other person.

TANSTAAFL ⬩ PRESS

Thomas Gondolfi

TANSTAAFL Press
891 PH 10
Castle Rock, WA 98697

Visit us at www.TANSTAAFLPress.com

Wayward School

First printing TANSTAAFL Press
Copyright © 2018 by Thomas Gondolfi
Cover illustration by

Printed in the United States
ISBN 978-1-938124-42-6

Cover illustration by Roslyn McFarland (www.RoslynMcFarland.com) - Far Land Publishing
Book layout by Hydra House

To all of those people who have had the courage to go against the advice of your trusted advisors because it was the right thing to do.

October 13, 2050

"Elizabeth, learning your troubles might just spark the moral character inside another girl and save her from your fate," says my court-appointed priest, a gaunt, long-haired Amerind.

I think it is a crock, but why not. I've got nothing much better to do until they put a bullet in my brain, or something equally glamorous. I can't explain where I went wrong without telling the entire story, so this is it, crayon on butcher paper and all.

I think my fatal error is believing that people have the same intrinsic value. "We hold these truths to be self-evident, that all men are created equal—" is a very poetic line at the base of American society, but it is so patently untrue as to be criminal. Teaching it should be an offense punishable by death. Blame the teachers, not the students. But this is supposed to be about where I went wrong, not a diatribe on the failure of society.

When I was in grade and high school, guess who was one of the last picked for teams? Yes, that's right. I was. Oh, there was always a good reason for not getting picked: too fat, too smart, not the right social class, or even the wrong color. With me standing alone on the court, field or gym, some team was eventually forced to take me. I remember the burning in my cheeks when there were only four or five of us left. I didn't care about the shame of the person chosen last, just so long as it wasn't me.

I would chant to myself under my breath, "Please God, don't let me be the last chosen." But my guess now would be that God had forsaken me long before that.

There is an aphorism that if you dye a monkey purple and put him down in a cage with normal monkeys, the normals would tear him apart. I felt purple staring out at a mob of brown simian faces. I can't fault the girls who didn't pick me. Society taught them how to behave. I grew up wanting to be the same as they were. I wanted to be able to choose whom I wanted to be with. I wanted to be a snob, too. Later I did exactly the same thing when the opportunity presented itself. Maybe I am even worse because I knew the cruelty of it.

I know this sounds like nothing but the whining of a preadolescent or even someone trying to excuse her actions. I put it here simply to tell the story—my story.

Yes, I was the dumpy cauc girl from the wrong side of the monorail. Po' white trash, went one idiom. My family was too poor to afford new clothes for me so I wore my three older brothers' hand-me-downs: jeans, undershirts and flannel shirts with holes in the elbows. My face almost burst into flames when I would see the yellow satin dresses, fitted silk pants or even the designer frayed shorts most of the other girls displayed. Every day the same old passively hurtful faces in a sea of new clothes battered my soul even further into submission.

The best I could manage with my meager wardrobe was some retro look back to last century with a T-shirt tied up under my breasts or a torn-up undershirt to give myself a punk look. No matter what I did, though, they were still my brothers' hand-me-downs. I held my head high against the constant snickers and giggles of the others, both boys and girls alike, but that derision heaped even more abuse on my miniscule ego. As the ugly duckling I had no chance to become the swan.

Oh, some might say I was just being over-sensitive, but it all added up. The priest said I should be thorough.

The only things I ever had of my own were my bras and panties. The peeking of the first spring sun to an Inuit could not have brought as much joy as these did to me. When my mother took me shopping it was all I could do not to swoon with delight as the one time I got clothes not worn by anyone else. I carefully took the ones at the back of the rack. I didn't want anyone to have even touched them—I was rather fanatic about it. I always chose the most lacy and silky under-things that my mother would allow. The bright colors and fancy cloth reminded me briefly, every morning and night, that beneath the grunge I was a woman. These items delighted me. Had I known the word orgasm, I might have used it.

Oh, I wanted to be loved, adored, and worshiped. What girl

at that age didn't want to be a cover-girl model? I would have even settled for being an object of lust like the Playboy holo girls my brothers hid in computer chips between their mattress and the box springs. I'd have given up my brains just to have someone love me, even one person.

On those occasions I took the trouble, I could be presentable with my lumpiness almost hidden beneath my long, almond-brown hair after a good washing and hours of brushing. This never got me anywhere. Boys of that age are only interested in a skinny waist, big tits, round ass, pretty face and how quickly a girl will fall into bed with them. I didn't have enough of the first four to matter about the fifth. If I were a boy I'd be called stocky. For a girl, the only single word that came to my mind at the time was "unlovable."

Maybe all of this explains why when dreamboat Jimmy Hendsen asked me, Elizabeth Zimmer, to the Spring Dance in my sophomore year, I stood speechless for nearly a minute. He even had to repeat himself. I fell over myself accepting, literally. I tripped on my rolled-up pants. Only Jimmy's big muscular arms saved me from sprawling on the floor. I remember that young girl's thought that she could die happy. How ironic that seems now.

Every parent who cared wanted Jimmy for their daughter. He wasn't captain of the football team, but one of the running backs. Long, blond hair wreathed his head and big, powder-blue eyes stared deep into your soul. That his shoulders were wider than mine didn't hurt. His family owned the principal recycling center for the entire state of Minnesota. Playing his cards right, Jimmy could have become someone important—a senator or maybe even governor—and Jimmy never missed anything.

Since I turned five, no boy had ever looked at me twice, unless it was as the punchline of a joke. That a member of the football team asked me to the dance should have set off alarm bells. I was too far gone. My intelligence shut off with the soft baritone of his voice. My emotional fantasies covered up everything else. I was going to be Cinderella, no longer held back by her wicked family.

I envisioned a fairy-tale night full of dancing and social chatter as the belle of the ball. Late that evening I would receive a chaste, or maybe not quite so chaste, peck on the cheek from my knight, just before he escorted me to the door of my home. Jimmy and I would then go steady for the rest of our high school days, choose the same college to attend together and get married shortly after we both had been awarded our BS degrees. We'd have four lovely children in a middle-class suburban house with a neatly mowed front yard. Maybe Jimmy would go into politics. But no matter, my fantasy of the white picket fence kept any logical reasoning from flowing around in my brain.

I decided that my mother wouldn't convince me to wear one of her out-of-date disco dresses. Cinderella needed to be properly attired. I pooled all the money I'd made from babysitting over two years. I should amend that. I pooled the amount I'd managed to keep hidden from my father and brothers' sticky fingers, and bought a dress and shoes for the dance. I spent nearly twelve hundred on that gorgeous and classy dress—black net stretched over a translucent, periwinkle blue nylon/satin blend in the current style of too short and too tight. For once I would be in vogue. Almost as sexy as what the other girls wore, it showed off my one decent attribute—my legs. Oh, they were, and still are, a bit too thick, but they did make me look and feel like a woman when I wore the matching knee-high, five-inch-heeled boots and the seamed stockings.

It's funny that I worried about being embarrassed by Mom's dress. That dance, or should I rightfully state, the circumstances surrounding it, started me on the road that ended here, sitting here waiting for . . . How did the judge so eloquently put it?

"For the cold and callousness in which you perpetrated your crimes, the law mandates the maximum sentence I can impose. That maximum and your sentence is 'death.' Though, in truth, Ms. Zimmer, I can't rightly think of any appropriately heinous punishment for the despicable acts you righteously claim as being for the public good. This just shows how far you have fallen from a lawful and moral path."

He hadn't even concluded with "May God have mercy on your soul."

Yes, the dance that I never quite got to. That night all my dreams and hopes blew away like the seeds of a dandelion puff in a tornado. An interesting question begs. How many times does a girl have to be victimized before she becomes the victimizer? I think society has given me its answer. I'm not so certain.

The big night came. My family, as usual, didn't pay any attention to me as I hovered by the door waiting for Prince Charming. Jimmy picked me up at 6:30 sharp. When I saw his neatly combed hair framing his huge shoulders in a sapphire-blue tux, I wanted to faint into his arms. I *would* be just like that mythical Cinderella, taken to a waiting coach on the arm of a masculine man who wanted nothing more than to protect and please his lady. If I had only known how wrong I was, I would have run screaming in terror even into the arms of my not-so-loving family. I allowed Jimmy to escort me to his tomato-red Chevy pickup. Just like that princess, I maintained an aloof and cool demeanor but deep down I bubbled with excitement. Half an hour later, my fantasies shattered with all the romance of the Tuesday smell of a Friday fish dinner.

Jimmy didn't take me to the dance. He took me out to McGuire Lake. My dream world clouded my judgment so far that I hadn't even noticed we weren't going toward Bear Creek High until he wove in amongst the trees. Jimmy's song and dance about picking up his friends adequately allayed anything resembling a warning flag in my fantasy-soaked brain. Once in the dark, wooded, and seldom-traveled area of the lake's north shore, we met up with three of his friends, Bill Loder, Jr., Don Nunes, and Tom Bazley.

Oh, why go on with all the details. I could give them all, right down to the cologne Jimmy wore: English Leather, his Calvin Klein underwear, and cinnamon Scope mouthwash. I even remember looking over at the Pirelli "Jackson Lowrider" hoverboots of his truck.

Cutting to the chase, they raped me, not once but twice each. They'd planned it from the beginning. Jimmy had set me up, and I had been such an emotional fool to allow it. All I could focus on through the ordeal was the torn knit netting of my expensive dress—ruined. I clung to that thought through the conscious-shattering acts that followed. It seemed such an inappropriate thought for such a violent crime. Through it all I did nothing. I didn't fight. I knew it was useless against four big football players.

I also knew my chance of getting justice afterward in the one-computer town of Bear Creek never rose high enough to even see zero. It would come down to the story of an "ugly girl" allegedly raped by four of the most handsome boys from the best families—boys who could have probably snapped their fingers and had any girl fawn at their feet. "Preposterous," would be the only comment from what passed for law enforcement in our town. George Bunn, our corpulent sheriff, a beer buddy of Loder, Sr., would dismiss my story faster than he could down a six-pack of Coors on a Friday night.

Oh, those boys knew it as well. I could see it in their animalistic eyes and their grunts of lust. They used me with impunity. It wasn't just a fuck that they sought. They got off on the power they wielded over me. Three nearly interminable hours later, they finished with me. Their thirst for rape abated. The boys pulled up their pants and laughed as they floated off in Jimmy's big pickup and Don's bright-green Toyota Celica. They discarded me like a puzzle too easily solved. From their attire, it seemed they would attend the dance anyway, the proof of their crimes covering their privates as they danced with other girls. I heard their mocking voices many miles off in the distance.

I had done nothing during the assault and I did nothing afterward. They had murdered Cinderella and any hope of normality by their one final abuse. The princess would never come out again.

For hours I lay in the dark, totally numb. Eventually, as the dampness of dew deposited itself on my body, I picked myself up and walked the four miles home, hiding with shame from any passing car. I even avoided a remote police drone. Why did I feel guilty? I kept asking that question to myself. Was it because I was foolish? Was it because I hadn't seen through Jimmy and his criminal intent? I'm not sure to this day.

Looking back, I did all the wrong, stereotypical things. When I got home, I sneaked in through my bedroom window, tore off the remains of my clothes, and immediately scrubbed my skin in a biting hot shower. I soaked there in self-pity until my father bellowed something about the cost of hot water coming out of my hide. The next day I threw away my dress and everything else I had worn. In place of my usually frumpy clothing, I buried myself even more in the degradation by wearing one of my father's loose work shirts, long enough to hide my bruised wrists deep in its stained sleeves.

For weeks, nighttime taunted me. I couldn't close my eyes without seeing their leering eyes stained with the craving for violence and dominance. I couldn't be in the dark without seeing Jimmy blowing me a kiss as a vile reminder of what they had done to me. Each night I relived my personal hell of the Spring Dance. Each morning I had to wash Jimmy's sins from my body in the hottest shower I could tolerate. Self-pity soaked in with the heat.

My humiliation continued daily at school. Every time I passed Jimmy, he smiled and licked his lips. I cringed and my cheeks flamed. I feared him and detested the shame I felt. Even his friends got in on the act. I wanted them dead but I told no one. In fact I can't ever remember telling anyone the whole story until now. The legacy lives on with me to this day in this very jail cell. I still bear the marks on my back from gravel rubbing repeatedly into already torn skin. My psyche carries even more significant scars.

Oh, don't get me wrong. At the time I was trying not to be whiny, blubbering woman. I thought I was being strong keeping myself going in a situation where I couldn't win. Throughout my life, whenever I felt put upon, my mom would twist up her face and say, "Life isn't fair. Get used to it." I didn't understand her words until that excruciating night. I wonder if her life had been unfair this way also. Maybe Father did this to her. It didn't matter.

On second thought, I was a sniveling twit—but despite all I endured, as an object of violence, neglect, and apathy, I think I could have licked my wounds and gone on had not the unthinkable happened twelve days later. I missed my period and then again twenty-eight days after that. My situation had quickly gone from worse to impossible.

October 15, 2050 (Evening)

Sorry for the delay, but on death row in Alcatraz, you eat when told, you exercise when told. You do what you're told and when, or you get hurt. I'm still nursing the bruise from when I insisted to a guard, in court, that I had to use the ladies' room. She delivered her counterpoint with a nightstick in my ribs.

That old fraud of a priest, with the Amerind name, is something of a pest. He visits me every day. Peter IronSky seems to know what I'm feeling half the time. What is his story anyway? A Catholic American Indian? He is such a dark little man—obsessed with my death. No, to be fair, he is concerned about my soul, not my body. He wants me to confess my sins to God and seek forgiveness for my transgressions. I told him to stuff it. God never listened to me throughout my entire life. To ask forgiveness now would be the worst hypocrisy on my part. Who was it that said, "The definition of insanity is doing the same thing and expecting a different result"?

Even in light of that, I'm finding some measure of peace in writing this account. I am surprised at the emotions I evoked in myself by telling this story. Last night I relived that rape once again. I thought I'd buried any connection to that dirty laundry years ago. Instead I see that it lurked in me like a starved panther awaiting a long overdue meal. Perhaps that old fart of a priest isn't as much a fraud as I thought—but I still don't think this will help anyone but me.

Where did I leave off? Oh yes, I was pregnant.

My family was oh-so-understanding. I managed to find a time when my whole family was together, at a rare after-dinner TV session. I had hoped that my father might just be a bit more reasonable when everyone was there. Can a person be more wrong? My father's face went red as lava as he erupted. My mother got a sad, faraway look on her face and didn't speak. For over an hour the mildest thing Father called me was "slut." I don't recall him ever repeating himself. His command of the darker side of English was as powerful as his weakness in its normal use. Every time one of my brothers would attempt to interject something, for good or bad, my father would turn on him with a few choice comments and intimidation. I think my father ended his tirade not because he had finished but rather due to fatigue.

Oh, didn't I say? I wasn't even given the chance to speak. No one heard my side. Neither of my parents even gave me the chance to explain. I've never had the chance to tell the story to anyone. First because I wasn't allowed, and later because it was too late to matter. Everyone had some preconceived notion as soon as I got to the word "pregnant." I gave up trying that very day, that very moment.

Maybe now would be a good time to mention that I wasn't in the greatest family. My father's response lived up to my worst expectations. I was nearly twelve before I knew that my family defined the word "dysfunctional." It came as a very slow realization as I saw acquaintances get a minor scolding for something that would have gotten me a week's worth of verbal abuse and a strap across my back.

I still wince when I remember one incident, when I was seven. An almost-friend and I swiped a pair of skates from the backyard of another girl. I was going to give them back. But my friend and I skated most of the day until each of our fathers came and took us away. My father said nothing to me at all. He wouldn't even look at me. When we got home he picked up the handiest item, a heavy oak stirring spoon, and started disciplining me with it. Through bleary eyes, I lost count around fifty welting strikes of that spoon across my ass. I blacked out not long after that. After he dowsed me with water, Father informed me that I also would not be allowed to eat for a week.

Don't get me wrong. I deserved a beating. I didn't deserve to have bruises that took nearly a month to heal nor did I deserve enforced starvation. Worse, I realized then that he didn't do it to keep me from stealing, but because he had been embarrassed.

My father was an out-of-work carpenter. He always managed to be out of work. He was proud that he was smart enough to know he had to work thirty hours a week before he would earn any more money than the checks welfare gave him for doing nothing. His favorite pastime was to get liquored up and bowl with his buddies. They complained ceaselessly how niggers, frostbacks, and slanties had the same rights as white people. I think that in another age and place he would have been the Grand Dragon in the KKK or maybe a commandant of a Nazi death camp. I never really understood his views and have never cherished anything the man ever said to me. To be honest I can't remember a single thing he ever did that made me care for him in any way. My most vivid childhood memory of him is his sharp, biting hatred of everything.

My three older brothers, Frank, Tommy, and Joe, all had some kind of minor criminal record. In my opinion, each of them was well on his way to being on the next *World Class Scum* or *Interpol Events*. They all three lived at home and seemed interchangeably useless. Father threatened to throw them out on the street at least three times a day, usually at mealtimes. I think if my father's version of "justice" had extended to the boys, they might have turned out better. They got away with anything and everything. But then at the same time, look at where I turned up with Father's heavy hand.

Mom, I couldn't figure out. At times I thought she deserved better than the life she ended up with. She wore sad brown eyes under a barely kept mop of gray and brown hair and a figure that clearly showed she had borne four kids. She might have been a looker in her day, but not now. Father barely tolerated her presence most of the time and at others he would throw a fit and demand that she do something. She just meekly accepted his dictums. Once she even confided in me that she had learned the best way to avoid his attentions was not to be near him. I think Father felt resentful that she allowed herself to get pregnant with Frank. Did Mom trap Father? I doubt it. It wasn't her style. Did Father decide to take responsibility for his unborn child? It was another doubtful situation knowing his life and choices. The only thing I could think of was that perhaps it had been a shotgun wedding. Grandpa Tilsen did have a temper and never seemed to like Father at all.

As a child I never remember things being happy when my parents were in the same room. Tension always filled the air with them together, like waiting to see if the grade you received on the calculus test you didn't study for was as bad as you thought it would be.

My mother showed her maternal streak infrequently. At times she could be a most compassionate woman. As a very young child, I remember her picking me up after a nasty tumble off my wagon. She soothed my hurt palms and elbows with kitten kisses, comforting words and warm arms. She could also be the coldest, most heartless bitch I'd ever known, especially when anyone even thought of interrupting her bingo night, apparently her only true love. Our relationship bordered on tempestuous, tiny moments of great empathy within a sewer of apathy.

On the fateful night I had confessed my condition, Father ranted and my brothers smirked. I knew my siblings' feelings about me echoed what my father spewed out of the toilet he called his mouth. I never got to put two coherent words together. Every time I did, my father brutally rebuffed me. "Lizzy, don't you even think about say'n nutt'n, bitch. You're a whore and won't ever amount to nutt'n."

By the time he had fully run down, I knew nothing I could say would make the least difference. My father had the answers to all of my rebuttals before I'd even voiced them. Each of his answers involved copious amounts of profanity and humiliation. I kept my mouth shut. Hoping to avoid the worst of whatever he planned seemed to be my best option. Mother left the table in a snit. In fact she never said another word to me . . . ever.

October 17, 2050

Lights-out is a bit abrupt in the Alcatraz Women's Maximum Security Prison. I'm sorry that I cut off, but that's prison life. Part of it is the food. Unlike the complaints I continually hear from the other inmates, I almost relish institutional kitchen food. I mean I didn't eat much else after I turned sixteen. When I did go back to eating real food, it gave me severe digestion problems.

Father Peter and his flowing, gray ponytail visited this morning. It was pleasant talking to him again, even if he has a sharp tongue. You don't get much human interaction on death row.

"God will forgive you if you allow him that opportunity, but you have to go to him. He won't come to you," he said in a light baritone that belied his slight stature.

"Why should I repent to God? If he even exists, he abandoned me years ago."

"That is not true. He has always been there; you just didn't reach out to him."

"Oh, I didn't? How about each time I prayed to him when my father abused me? Or the time I begged to be delivered from my rapists? How do you explain these things and nary a word or act from our Father who art in heaven."

"That is a question I have never had an answer for, Elizabeth. I don't think any honest priest has that answer. I can only hope to plant in you the thought that we can't fathom the ways of God."

I snorted.

"Just because I cannot honestly give you an answer doesn't give you the right to do the things you've admitted," he said looking down at his rosary.

"So, Father, you want me to ask for forgiveness from a God who you know allows horrible things to happen? Why don't we ask God to beg for my forgiveness? I think that would be more appropriate." Father IronSky rubbed his rosary against the thigh of his black pantsuit. I watched him count out the beads with his fingers. "Besides, what do I have to confess to God? I have saved lives."

"You don't consider the murder of . . ."

"That is where we differ, Father. In my book, murder is the taking of someone with value. I either took something that wasn't wanted or that was put there specifically to be used. The greatest good for the greatest number, is the philosophy that it took me years to obtain." The wrinkled old priest sat almost still for several moments in what I had to assume was contemplation of what I had just said. His lips moved as his fingers worked his rosary.

"I will pray for you, Elizabeth, even if you will not," the short man said as he stood and walked down the hall toward the guard station.

Court occupied my day yesterday. Thirty of us, including eight heavily armed guards, loaded into a tiny black-and-white prison launch at daybreak. We suffered through thirty minutes of four-foot swells out on the bay. They didn't even have a hovercraft to take us, possibly to prevent an escape if we managed to overpower the guards and the sealed pilot's compartment. I grinned at the ridiculousness of it.

Three of the inmates took to feeding the fishes and even a couple of the guards looked troubled. I felt a bit green, but after seven pregnancies, nausea is something you learn to live with. I could do thirty minutes of that while eating salt pork and reading Browning.

Robert Kafka, the lawyer thoughtfully supplied to me by the government-funded branch of the ACLU, and I had a long talk. His current plan wasn't to reexamine the evidence, but to reopen the penalty phase of the trial to get my sentence changed. We both were honest enough with each other to never even broach the topic of innocence. I was guilty as hell of breaking the laws of the land. Robert litigated hard because he morally didn't believe in the death penalty. He pursued his vocation with a passion, but for me personally he felt little but contempt. I knew it. He knew I knew it. We didn't pretend.

I spent the rest of the day with my feet chained to a wall. Enough klieg lights to start a new solar system and more TriVid cameras than were at the '36 Olympics recorded my every move and facial expression. Six hours later the police matron ushered me into the courtroom. Court held no surprises. Without even as much as looking at me, the judge, fair and grand arbiter of all disputes, pronounced his ruling. I knew what it would be before that worthy said a single word. My original trial had been a grand gesture to get a certain governor enough spotlights to run for president.

"Request for reopening of the penalty phase of the trial of State of Southern California v. Ms. Elizabeth Zimmer is denied. No sufficient cause has been brought forth to warrant such an event."

Bob whispered to me, "Don't worry, Elizabeth, I'll keep up the fight. We have several other avenues to approach."

I feel Robert's sincerity but I'm not really expecting anything out of his efforts. It is only prolonging my life by days. With the Judicial Reform Act of '28, the longest they can stay my execution for appeals is thirty days.

No longer is the waiting time on death row measured in years. Did that solve the problems of the United States? Our high school civics class taught us about the '28 JRA in great detail. It had been a cry of pain from a nation that had endured too much from the criminals who abused the system. JRA cited a mandatory death sentence for anyone convicted of a violent crime. It helped. The number of jails dropped to an all-time low. Crime rates dropped to their lowest point in over a century—at least until they took away the death penalty for most crimes with the United Nations' Liberalization Concords of '34. Thirty-four's UNLC was the greatest boon to crime since the invention of the gun. It decreed a worldwide court system that prohibited the death penalty for all but the most brutal and savage of murders. The required number of jails in the USA alone surged by a factor of 20. Crime became the employment method *d'jour* either in committing it or controlling it.

November third is the day I die unless God smiles upon me. The thought earned another snort from me.

I didn't have contempt for Robert Kafka. As an honorable man, he pursued what he believed in with all the tools he had in his bag. I did hold his views in scorn, even if they might keep me alive.

But this is not supposed to be a dissertation on the penal

system in the United States today.

Let's see. Oh, yes, I was talking about Father and the Three Days of Penance. If you will pardon the cliché and the sick pun, it was quiet as a tomb in my home. I don't think anyone from my family talked to me for that entire three days. My family wouldn't allow me to attend school. They disconnected computer service in my room. Any conversation that was taking place stopped abruptly at my entrance. Dinners became a special hell. The rest of the family would eat before me, leaving me nothing but scraps and glaring at me as they retreated as if my presence alone polluted the entire room.

On Saturday the Coventry treatment just about had me reaching my breaking point. As an outsider even at school I didn't have much human interaction. The zilch I received during the Three Days made me itch. Not only that but I suspected some Machiavellian plan involving my condition festered just beyond my perception. Sometimes my foresight and imagination tortured me.

At ten o'clock on the third day, unusually early for him, Father roused and dressed in his old, off-brown leisure-suit. He always looked ridiculous in brown with his balding, graying head of red hair like a not-quite-ripe strawberry on the top of a pile of dung. He climbed into our brown and white '22 Chevy. White had been its original color but now you couldn't tell the deep brown dirt from the salt-induced rust that held the body together. It even still had tires and rolled on the road. With no declaration, he drove off.

Lunch passed without his presence. My tension level ratcheted up. Father made it a point never to miss any meal.

"Boys," as he would say with his chest puffed up when he was about to impart some of his timeless, sage-like wisdom, "skipping a meal isn't a crime, but it certainly is stupid. You never know when your next bite will show up." In my lifetime, he never missed a meal that I can recall. As a first it made me even more nervous. What kept him so long?

As the clock edged around each hour I looked out the front window up and down Ashland Drive. It maddened me to know who shaped my future and to be absolutely impotent about it. Each hour ensured that something ghastly lurked. Each hour insisted that no matter how horrible a fate I imagined, Father had come up with something worse. It loomed larger than Pinocchio's nose would be after running for political office.

The family's corroded Cavalier screeched its marginal brakes as it pulled into the driveway, just in time for dinner. I ran to the door like this was some dark, reversed Christmas where I didn't want any presents but had to know. Father flashed me a smug look as he went directly from the door to the table, leaving me standing in the entry like a fool.

I followed him to dinner. For once I wasn't shooed away. Father actually pulled out the chair for me to sit. I think a beaten puppy would have taken the seat more readily. The rest of the family sat down and immediately dug into Mother's fried chicken. All eyes bored into him. One hand he used to stuff a biscuit into his mouth and the other held a chicken leg. He looked like a modern Henry the Eighth, two-fisted eating, with manners a pig would shun. He held power over me that Satan himself would covet. I remained quiet. Everyone knew something was about to break loose but not what.

"Well, Lizzy," he said as he bit into the chicken leg, his other hand reaching for something else. The food he talked around muffled the rest of his sentence. "I think I finally have a solution to your *problem*." The last word he slurred into profanity. As soon as he cleared enough room in his mouth he crammed in another whole biscuit.

One of my brothers snickered. They knew something. A naval cruiser sailed in my stomach. My food went untouched. I feared he might make me get an illegal abortion.

"You are going to a school for wayward girls in Southern California," he said casually as he put the remains of his chicken leg on his plate and scooped up a heaping of mashed potatoes.

I'd never been farther than the hundred-three-mile monorail trip to Fargo, so Southern California seemed like half the planet away. I shook uncontrollably. Yes, my family wasn't a loving family, but it was the only one I knew. And to go away when I felt so vulnerable made me even weaker inside than the mild morning sickness I'd had of late. I ran to the bathroom, barely making the toilet. I relieved the weight in my stomach with six or seven sticky brown heaves.

I shuddered as a sweaty chill flowed over me, still kneeling by the bowl. I stayed where I was, trying to regain my composure. The threadbare floor mat chafed my knees, but I didn't care. I heard loud, raucous laughter from the other room. I knew the butt of those guffaws was me. I slumped forward and cried against my arm over the toilet. For nearly an hour I sobbed, dripping salty tears and snot down my face. Each time I tried to buck up and make a move to rejoin the world, I'd relapse into whimpering chin-quivers and then more weeping.

Some interminable time later I managed to finally stem the flow from my eyes. I guess the practical side of my personality finally decided to come out and lift me up.

I took the time to wash my face in the sink. Blush-pink surrounded my eyes and mottled-red covered my cheeks. I hoped it would disappear so my tormentors wouldn't know I had been crying. I cleaned up the spots where I'd not quite hit my porcelain target earlier.

I returned to the living room. A small, covered plate sat alone on the dining table. It had to have been my mother's doing. As sympathetic as the gesture was, it also was a tiny but pointed reminder of my unclean status. Everyone else had finished eating and was off doing whatever it was that amused them.

My father's abuse on me as a child had accomplished its mission. Did I throw a fuss? Did I speak my fears? Did I run away? No. I quietly, meekly packed my bags to go live out my disgrace. I was that brainwashed. "It was for my own good." Little did I know back then that it wasn't anything of the kind.

I have to interject here for a moment. I know now that a girl can perform an abortion fairly simply by taking too many birth control pills. Not only was and is this illegal, I didn't know about it back then. Remember, I didn't have any friends who would share such black information, nor would that have been in any books or magazines, or even on the underage web. I'd been terribly naïve, but then weren't we all at the age of sixteen?

Two almost silent days later my father drove me to the Amtrak station. He didn't say a word as he pulled up to the front of the building. He didn't look at me as he handed me a ticket and a ten-dollar bill. I got out with my one small, red, beaten-up American

Tourister suitcase. He'd already explained it in very head-shrinking detail. Someone would meet me in Los Angeles and take me to the School. I would remain there until my *problem* was resolved.

I climbed out of the car with my case. Father sat there watching me from the car. I waited near three other families on the platform. I tried to calm the jitters in my stomach but had little success as Father stared at me. I felt like a lemming in fear of a snowy owl pouncing. Part of me had wanted to believe I was going to someplace better. What could have been worse than my family? But I couldn't put out of my head how smug Father had been. I shivered, not in the spring breeze but at how my *problem* had him going from anger to joy. I looked back and saw him doing nothing but observing me. I shivered again.

His eyes didn't see me. They looked like he watched nothing more important than a weed in his yard. Had I any presence of mind I would have run. Repeated beatings over the years drove initiative from even the heartiest of souls. After a lifetime of that environment the thought of resistance of any kind doesn't even form in your brain. I could no more run away than a caged animal, even if the bars were psychological.

The monorail, one of the only mass transport forms that still traveled on land, finally arrived. Its mass of graffiti actually livened up its tired exterior.

"All aboard for all points west. Fargo, Bismarck, Billings, Salt Lake City, Reno, Sacramento, San Francisco, Los Angeles and all connecting cities," called out a crackling, tinny speaker above the pneumatic doors. I had no connections. I was to stay on to the end of the line—Los Angeles.

"Please fasten your seat belts against the acceleration," the automated train said mechanically. I felt the gentle swaying as the train levitated on its magnetic cushion.

I turned and looked at my father. I waved weakly at him. He didn't wave. He didn't even see me. He waited just long enough for the train to start moving before he backed the car out of its parking stall. Even the loss of something bad can be painful. Exactly three tears leaked down my right cheek as I watched the station wagon pull away.

The acceleration of the mono pulled me back into my seat.

Having only experienced it once, it still felt new and it took my thoughts off my destination and problems. For a very short period the excitement of making a long trip to somewhere I'd never been took over.

The mono took me through rolling fields of fresh earth and green-gray wheat as far as the eye could see. Every thirty seconds so the mono would flash by a faded farm house in various stages of disrepair compared to those simply abandoned to heaps barely discernible from neglect. With most of the farms owned directly through conglomerates, the need for these artifacts of a bygone era had evaporated.

While it only seemed a few moments, the train raced past an industrial area with the pipes of the Dakota Petrochemical Cracking Plant dominating the view from ground to sky. I caught a glimpse of the Keystone pipeline that fed it. Then, just as quickly, the area snapped to suburbs of apartment complexes flying by at over two hundred miles per hour.

"Please fasten your seat belts against the acceleration." The mono slowed rapidly to a stop in another station. Look as I might, I couldn't see anything new or exciting. It might as well be the same group of faces getting onto the train and the same backs of the folks departing. I couldn't even see the newly built spire of St. Alexius Medical Center. The station looked barely different than where I'd gotten on.

With nothing to look at, the wait seemed endless before the same announcement repeated over the speakers. Seconds later the force of the train pulling out of the station pushed me back into my seat. For the next few hours I sat back and allowed the spring's green growth to mesmerize me with its sameness before drifting off to sleep.

Around noon someone sat in the adjacent empty seat, waking me with a start. I still remember the handsome, twenty-something Amexican. The slick, dark-haired Hispanic man wore a real leather jacket sporting a stylized globe and the legend "Earth—the only all-natural breath of fresh air."

From the moment I opened my eyes, he struck up a conversation. Jesus Mendoza revealed that he was from the "Banana State," Yucatan. We chatted amiably about the condition of Mexican states. He talked about his home in Valladolid and how much better it had been since the annexation of Old Mexico by Los Estados Unidos.

Our history books talked about how bad the quake of '28 had hit old Mexico but it was just another dry fact. According to my companion his parents talked about it constantly. Before the annexation in '29 civil unrest, starvation and repression dominated their lives.

The talk eventually drifted to movies and the latest James Bond flick, "Red Planet Blues." He tried to guide me into conversations about my home, my family and my dreams. Jesus listened attentively to any word I'd share. It didn't take a Rhodes Scholar to realize he hoped I was a runaway.

He kept trying to get me to go to dinner with him. After repeated comments of concern for my health, I let him buy me a fully wrapped tuna fish sandwich at the train's kiosk. I may be naive, but I'm not dumb. I know some of the new designer drugs they have can hook you faster than my father could fly into a rage and still others made you as pliant as clay.

The only way Jesus would shut up was when I talked. As I wasn't about to tell him anything personal, it meant he babbled and never relented. I thought my ears would eventually give out.

Oddly, after all these years I wonder if I'd have been better off with him as his whore or mule, hooked on junk or even sold into slavery. I think, though, that he would've been surprised when my belly started to grow. Back then I didn't even know how long it took before I would start to show. Who knows, maybe he would have rejoiced at having gotten two for the price of one.

Well, the point is academic as I wouldn't have jumped into something I felt certain would end up badly. Instead, I continued on with the course laid out for me, much as I had the rest of my life.

I think I vexed the dark Mr. Mendoza when the train pulled into the Tom Bradley train station. I'd failed to sleep on the entire trip and I never gave him the opportunity to get into my head. I think Jesus might have tried something more coercive had there not been a rather imposing black man with my name in bright pink letters on a large white sign. I stared at this new person's skin, shiny and black like enamel paint without a hint of brown.

When I acknowledged his sign, he said in an accent so deeply southern as to have fried okra dangling from it, "Y'all cum wit' me."

While I wondered if he were Creole, he didn't take his eyes off the oily Hispanic man who had insinuated himself as my traveling companion. The black man's jaw clenched tightly as Jesus fingered something in his gray jacket. The black man pulled me behind him.

For just a moment I thought there would be an old-fashioned shoot-out. I mean, I didn't see a weapon on either man, but it did remind me of two gunfighters facing off down a long dirt road, pulling their long range coats back to reveal revolvers. Instead, the intense moment faded as Amexican shrugged and walked off, writing me off as the one that got away.

As soon as the other man disappeared around the corner, but not a moment before, my nominal protector turned to me. "Ya got any bags?"

I pointed to my one American Tourister, the one that dragged my arm off every time I moved it. He lifted it as if it contained feathers. As he glanced cautiously over his shoulder in the direction of the departed man, I noticed my guide's rather large, onyx nose in profile. The ripples down the bridge showed it'd been broken in at least three places in its history. Its questionable past, combined with the pockmarking of acne scars over his cheeks, gave him a distinctive face that many would call ugly. Instead, it comforted me.

My new guardian took me out to the parking structure to a beaten-up, white Ford Aerostar with one of the oldest lift conversions I'd ever seen. The African American opened the side door and carefully set my bag inside, motioning for me to get into the back seat. In spite of my nervousness, the odd man was doing a good job of making me feel better without saying so much as a word. He climbed in and fired up the vehicle's old internal combustion engine. It ran fairly well in spite of its age.

Eventually, my companion's silence got the best of me. I started talking. Maybe babbling would be a better choice.

"This is my first time to Los Angeles. Do you still sometimes get acid rain here?

"Are we going to be anywhere near Hollywood? I'd like to see Mann's Chinese Theater and Universal Studios." No response was forthcoming. "How about the Hollywood sign?" By this point I was becoming irate. Not only had my rambling failed to provoke a response, I was almost out of my small supply of chit-chat. "Disneyland? LA Spaceport? Did the Yankees win yesterday?" Finally, I couldn't stand it anymore. It was like a pressure cooker boiling over. "WHERE ARE WE GOING?!" I took a deep breath. "Look, do you have a name?"

"Abe Boxner. But call me 'Box.'" Now that he brought out the comparison, he did look like a big black box, imposing and almost square in torso. The man who called himself Box smiled. The white beacon of his teeth against the night of his skin made him look younger than the thirty I had tagged him, maybe twenty-five.

"Pasadena is where we head'n."

"Isn't that a slum?"

"Yes. And t'Yankees won nine to five."

Pasadena, the worst of the LA slums. A chill ran through me. I didn't know what to think or do. I got quiet for the rest of the forty-minute drive. I still had questions and no answers. I still had fears and no comfort.

Mr. Box turned off the levitation skirt and settled the big van in front of a complex of red-brick buildings that looked big enough to hold a football stadium. Weather-battered thirty-inch white letters announced "Bertion Enterprises" with the B dangling from only a single support. A plastic "Condemned" sign, obviously from all the way back to the '23 Watts quake, lay on the ground covered with muddy footprints in front of a rusted-iron double door. The graffitied masonry held cracks that you could throw a baby through, with the left-hand side of the closest wall leaning precipitously out over another parking lot.

As soon as the engine stopped I got the shakes. My belly twisted into knots that wouldn't ever come undone. I wasn't a wreck, I was a four-car pile-up. I worried as Box opened the decrepit van's door and took out my beaten red suitcase. What would I find inside? What horrors waited? I couldn't have guessed that it was worse than I could ever conceive in my naïve teenage brain.

October 18, 2050

"But Elizabeth, if you are truly repentant, God will forgive you," Dr. IronSky reassured me again today in another of his attempts to bring me to the light. His animation belied his age. His speech reminded me of my own musings about death. It's one of those things that you can't know until after you experience it and then it's too late. Is there a heaven or a hell? I know conventional wisdom has me going directly to hell. Do not pass GO. Do not collect $200.

"But even if I believed in an afterlife, which I don't at this point in my life—"

"Is that better, Elizabeth?" he interrupted. "Is having no afterlife a better alternative than there being a heaven and a hell? I personally believe that is truly sad—truly sad. You are about to cease to exist by your own admission so what does it matter to you?"

"No, it does matter, Father, probably because I am a proud woman. That is about all I have left. Besides, how can confession be enough? If I'm honestly guilty of these moralities then how can I be assured of eternal salvation by just saying a few contrite words?"

"That is not the point, Elizabeth. Your admission of guilt and request of forgiveness is enough for our God."

"Father, what is your doctorate in?"

He didn't blink at my radical change in subject. "I hold two PhDs—one in philosophy and the other in metaphysics. Why do you ask, Elizabeth?"

I could see the Catholic Church had chosen well by sending Peter IronSky to me. "Curiosity. I guess they reserve you for the hard cases."

Father Peter chuckled before he spoke. "More like the intelligent and stubborn ones, Elizabeth."

"Call me Beth, sir," I said, softening my crusty exterior just a bit.

"I will if you will call me Peter."

"Only if you agree not to try and change my opinion."

"Then you had better stick to 'Father' then, Elizabeth. I can no more let you throw away your immortal soul than a surgeon can intentionally let a patient bleed out on his table."

"Bad choice of analogies, Father."

"Hmm. Yes, I guess it is.

"I'm sorry, Beth, but I must leave early today. I have another appointment this afternoon."

"I understand, Father."

The old man stood, his rosary in one hand and a Bible in the other.

"I'm scared," I whispered. Adrenaline chose that moment to race through me.

"I know, Beth. I really do know."

I know there are those out there who would deny that I even have feelings. Most of that is media hype. I'm not heartless, not soulless. I knew that one priest saw through my façade.

The police arrested me at the order of a single man. My trial had been a planned media circus. If I even bother to turn on the TriVid set in my cell I can't help but see my face plastered all over the news, talk shows, or even "Real Justice." I'm the greatest boon to news and tabloid programming since Sean Penn III was arrested for killing his girlfriend, Penny Rapport. Of course, he managed to get off by spending more than the GNP of multiple small countries on legal fees and, I suspect, bribes. My arrest was to further a political career, so I was convicted before I even got to give my side of the story. It wrapped up what my father did to me some twelve years before like some neat, evil bow.

Well, anyway. Where were we? Bertion Enterprises.

As Box opened it, the dull brown door creaked low and ominously like the lid on a casket in some hokey old B-grade horror flick. Maybe I should've listened to the omen of that portal and fled. I'd been given so many portents but so few real chances. My father's fist still kept me on the course that led me here.

From within the portal I could hear a murmuring of a multitude of female voices. There is nothing quite like the sound of a hen party. It frightened me in a new way. I'd never been welcome where there was a large group of people, much less a large group of women. I never fit into a crowd.

Without thinking I had wrapped both of my arms around Box's nearest arm. Maybe it was "any port in a storm" mentality, but for some reason I trusted him.

Box led me into a barely lit hallway. The building had obviously once been a manufacturing facility. Now it formed one great room—one I eventually learned in intimate detail. It is three-hundred-sixteen-feet long by one-hundred- ninety-two-feet wide and nearly forty high to the open metal truss construction, or at least it was until they tore it down after my arrest. The room had once been painted a grim white that had faded over time to a dirty yellow. A large skylight of Plexiglas, marred into opacity over years of gritty wind and acid rain, let in just a smidgen of sun. I learned later that the skylight leaked during the rains. Not that there ever was all that much rain in Southern California, but when drops fell on your head during the night it woke you up. Cots lay end to end in this huge expanse—row upon row of them. But even that didn't grab my attention.

The room overflowed with women, all apparently in some stage of pregnancy. Some barely showed, but most bulged like someone trying to shoplift a bowling ball in their blouse. There were millions of them. Well, what I thought was millions at the time. It averaged twelve hundred in the School. They crowded together tighter than the refugees of the '35 Twin Tornadoes in the Freemont High School gymnasium.

The women came in all shapes, ages, and social background although at times it was difficult to tell because all the pregnant girls wore the same white muumuu-like hospital gown and white slippers.

My mouth gaped open as I panned around the room. The women milled about; clustered into groups; slept; complained of various pains; jogged; just sat and stared; or stood in lines. It seemed like a room full of cattle. There was, as I found out later, no privacy at all. If you whispered, people heard you. If you cried, someone saw. If you masturbated, people knew how long it took. It seemed worse than prison to me at the time. Actually, death row isn't nearly as bad if you ignore its fatal outcome because the food is decent, there isn't overcrowding and you have your own toilet.

I guess I didn't know what to expect of a school for wayward girls. Romantic notions of a convent high up in the Alps with nuns in black habits and the girls in white novitiate robes ran through my head like something out of the Sound of Music. The girls would spend each day on their knees quietly pledging their devotion to God and praying. Instead I saw a few men and women in red tunics walking among the white-gowned pregnant women like lords amongst the peons. Their manners and bearing said everything. The women in white scurried to be out of the way of any crimson tunic and when spoken to all but curtsied and genuflected. It wasn't really that way, but first impressions are hard to shake.

Box led me beyond the pandemonium to a windowed office that overlooked the floor with the milling masses. It was up two sets of perforated steel stairs, about thirty feet above the main floor. Originally, it had obviously been designed for the plant manager or floor supervisor. I wondered, as Box held the door open for me, if it now held a more sinister tyrant. When he closed it behind us, the remarkable din below dropped down to a whisper. I gulped as I was now trapped within yet another unknown.

The room held two occupants. A matriarchal, butch, mulatto woman with short dark hair seemed enthroned at a utilitarian desk signing papers. She weighed no more than sixty kilos, and half of that was her gigantic bosoms. They had to be an E cup at the very least. Maybe it just seemed that way because of her small frame. The other woman, passing papers to the seated one, was a beautiful Latina with flowing brown hair in one of those ubiquitous white gowns. The Latina wasn't yet bulging, but she couldn't hide it, either.

For nearly a minute the tiny woman with the big presence thankfully ignored my existence. I needed that long just to collect myself. Only the shuffling of papers, the scribble of an old-style ball pen, and through the thick Plexiglas windows, the ever-present din of people sounded in the room. The pregnant lady quickly stacked together the signed papers and made a hasty exit through another door. Briefly the harsh sounds of the floor below clanged against my nerves. The stern woman examined me up and down with an expression dearth of emotion. I wanted to back away. I wanted to run home. I wanted to be anywhere but here. Box seemed to know what I was feeling and put a reassuring hand on my shoulder. It buoyed me enough to stand my ground, although barely.

"Name?" the masculine woman asked in a deep, businesslike manner. She looked right up at me with big brown eyes that reminded me, for some reason, of my mother. I wasn't sure if that was good or bad. I swallowed hard and absently hoped under my breath that it wasn't bingo night.

"Elizabeth Zimmer." The woman turned around and typed my name into an archaic desktop computer even older than students get in grade school.

"Zimmer, Elizabeth, your father writes you were born April 13, 2020." She turned back toward me before leaning back in her dilapidated office chair, all business. "Miss Zimmer. Have you had a pregnancy test yet?"

"One of the drugstore kind, ma'am." I just thought it was the right thing to say. "Ma'am." She seemed to expect my obedience, like a grammar school principal, a junior-high vice principal, or my father.

"Box, when we are done, I want her down to the examining queue immediately," she said directly to the large black man. The words were an imperial command that didn't require an answer. She was definitely used to being obeyed without question. She turned back toward me and leaned forward. For some odd reason I noted how her large breasts spread across the desk almost as if someone had poured semi-solid green Jell-O there (green being the color of her dress). It distracted me.

She had been speaking directly to me and I had to catch up. She had obviously given this speech a great number of times as she did it mechanically, without even slowing down between sentences. Most people in her position would have been bored, but instead she used the time to intently study my face. I had a feeling she could look right down into my soul, measure it with a micrometer and tell me what sized halo or pitchfork I'd need. It unsettled me even further, especially as I honestly tried to listen.

". . . will have a lockbox for your personal effects, a cot, a pillow and a blanket. We provide clothing and undergarments.

We also keep the dorm warm enough so that more is not needed. You will get biweekly medical exams. Drugs, other than dispensed by the physicians, are not tolerated; that includes alcohol and cigarettes. Food is served three times a day, don't miss it. All of your expenses will be paid for by the School. As you are under eighteen you will attend school while you stay here. You will not leave the School until you deliver. If you leave the grounds, you will not get a second chance. Administration and Discipline is dealt with by any person wearing a red tunic. I am the absolute arbiter of the rules. I am the last and only appeal, but I will say that I've never yet overturned a single one of my Ay-Dees. We are professionals here. You may have any correspondence sent to the address on this card. Mail call is every evening after supper. Absolutely no visitors are allowed. Do you have any questions before I assign you to a bunk?" Somehow, she seemed to spit that all out with one breath. It impressed me.

"What's an Ay-Dee?"

"Ay-Dee is short for Administration and Discipline. Letter 'A,' letter 'D.' They wear red and carry my authority with them. Don't cross them, Miss Zimmer. Any more questions?"

"I wouldn't think of it, ma'am; and not right now, ma'am." She gave me a measured look and then returned her gaze to the papers on her desk. Other than her voice, she seemed to give me no more attention.

"If you do have questions in the future, address them to any of the Ay-Dees. There is no such thing as a stupid question, Miss Zimmer, only stupid mistakes. You will tentatively be assigned to cot E, like Edward, one-twelve. Do you need me to write it down for you?"

"No, ma'am. Edward one-one-two." The headmistress hooked Box with her eyes. A flash of communication flowed in that one look. Words that I was not privy to.

Box took me by the arm and turned to leave the room. "Excuse me, ma'am?"

"Yes, Miss Zimmer."

"I do have one question. What is your name?" I think a mouse walking across the floor would have been loud.

"For your sake, Miss Zimmer, I hope you never have to address me directly again—but for the record, my name is Margaret Fox. But, I assume you will soon be calling me 'Spouse' behind my back like all the other girls do. That is all." Spouse was an unusual nickname, I thought, momentarily taking my mind off my current situation.

This time Box was successful in leading me from the room, down the steel stairs, and back into the blaring sounds of the main room.

"T'at was a brave question, Lizzy," Box said with a slight squeeze on the arm he still had a hold on. I winced at the short form of my name.

"She didn't introduce herself, and I thought that was rude." As I walked with my chaperone I muttered my cot assignment under my breath, "Edward one-one-two, Edward one-one-two, Edward one-one-two." Box didn't say another word before delivering me to a short but very robust woman who nearly was as black as he. Her skin was not midnight black but the velveteen black of velour cloth. Robust would have been kind. Rubenesque would also have been merciful. She was huge. I couldn't tell if the steel support girder she leaned against held her up or the other way around. If she weighed less than three hundred pounds, it was only by what she had gotten rid of in the toilet that morning. Her bulk prohibited me telling if she was pregnant. She wasn't wearing a red tunic but rather the white all the rest were wearing so I had to assume she was expecting. For all her size, she had a very kind and pretty face, under a short mat of curly black hair.

"Anita. This is Elizabeth. She is fresh caught. Spouse says she needs a pregnancy test."

"Yeah, sure, Box. I'll take care of Elizabeth."

With the most words he had yet put together, he turned my shoulders square to him and looked deep into my eyes. His gaze reminded me of Spouse's measuring stare. "Lizzy, I want ya t'behave. Ya will be a'right with Anita. I'll be 'round watchin' ya."

"We'll be fine, won't we, Missy?" Anita said in almost a sing-song voice, slipping in and getting an arm around my shoulder. I felt like I'd been hugged by a marshmallow. I nodded much more enthusiastically than I felt. "All right, you big nigger. Get on with it. I won't eat her. Off with you." I watched with some trepidation as Box let go of me and walked off. I'm not sure why Box made me feel safe when he was near me—maybe because he would listen. Maybe because he seemed to know me better than I did. At that moment he was the closest thing I had to a friend even if he did hand me off to a proxy.

Box went directly back toward the long cement block corridor that led to the door out. I looked at that passage with longing a great number of times over the next seven months. It was unguarded. Only an overwhelming dread and an apprehension of being totally cut off from even this place kept me from leaving through that doorway to freedom. I later learned that it was a common misconception among all the women that anyone leaving through the door was hunted down and killed. I don't know if the management fostered the rumor to keep the girls in line without actually imprisoning them or just something they dreamed up themselves. None of the girls I ever heard of violated the virginity of that dark exit.

"Well, Lizzy, we had better get you into the Medical queue," Anita said with wavering tones that held some warmth in them. She took me by the hand and guided me toward a long line of girls and women against one wall. Looking back over my shoulder I watched in a daze as Box opened the large iron door in a blaze of early morning sun. I couldn't help wondering what I would be like when I got back on the other side of that door.

October 19, 2050

Sorry, I never was a very fast writer, without a computer, that is. As a death row inmate, I don't get much in the way of anything. I have no computer, only crayons to write with, and only soft paper to write on. Ironic, really. "Don't give a 'dead woman' anything she could hurt herself with, so we can kill her the right way." What a joke.

Maybe it's just sour grapes. I don't want to be here. I don't want to be quietly awaiting execution. I want to scream, rant, and rattle my cell door. I want to kill the politicians who really put me here. I want to shout at the world, "I don't deserve to die!" I only ever really meant to help people and myself. I didn't get credit for the people who I saved, only those I supposedly killed.

Anyway, back to my story as it were.

Anita looked at me rather softly before speaking. I gathered from her tone that she really knew how I felt being new there. "I know the first few days are a bit much, Missy, but I'll get you through 'em. Do you have a cot assignment?" I remember staring at Box leaving. I was caught up in the fact that I was going to be alone again. It took me a moment to realize she had asked me a question. I felt like a tiny elm leaf cast upon the Niagara River. I'd been over the falls and survived thus far but there was still the rapids and a whirlpool to drag me under before I reached the calm waters and relative safety.

"Oh, yeah. Um, Edward one-one-two."

"Good. Now, if you want to have even the slightest chance of seeing the Doc, we'd better get you in line, girl," she said, pulling me by my arm. My other arm tugged along my luggage. She put me in a line that nearly covered the short side of the building. Anita then began to talk my ear off. She seemed to be the female counterpart to the Hispanic man on the train . . . conversationally speaking, that is.

"What is it like on the outside? I've been cooped up here for almost five months. Goddamn that boyfriend of mine. He keeps knocking me up. I wish the man could pull out in time, the fucker. I buy him rubbers and he won't use them. I tell him I'll get him an implant, but 'Oh, no!' That might just bring down his virility. Can't have him being less than a stud, can we now, girl?" She nudged me with her elbow. "Any new movies with Denzel Washington, Jr.? I love his ass. Oh, baby! I'd kill for just a pinch of that. I heard there was a new one. Something about a plague wiping out Serendipity Base and then the rest of the Lunar Colony. How about the soap, *Southern Nightfall*? You do watch *Southern Nightfall*, don't you? I wanna know if Mark and Amanda's son, Lane, got married to Mark's illegitimate daughter, Nancy." Anita just kept barraging me with questions she never gave me the chance to answer. Between them she interspersed irrelevant comments.

For two hours she kept her mouth moving. I think I managed to get in about a dozen words and most of those being "Uh-huh," or "Yup." She talked incessantly about the other women in the School, about her boyfriend, who she hoped wasn't cheating on her while she earned them a good living, and about the vagaries of Ay-Dees. She never quite managed to repeat herself. I've never been able to see how people can talk constantly like she did. My jaw usually numbs after five minutes. A soft gong saved me from permanent listenitis.

"Oh, there's dinner. I'll go and fetch it, girl. Don't you dare move or you'll have to start all over again." Anita disappeared in a haste that belied her bulk. I looked back. In the two hours I'd stood there, I'd crept forward in the line about twenty feet. It had managed to grow behind me by thirty. So much had it grown that I thought it would have taken another two or three hours to inch up to my current place.

I waited. I had begun to learn that the most important virtue at the School was patience. In fact, I learned patience helped in every aspect of life. I learned it, but I hated it. The line inched forward ever so slowly. I waited some more. On the walls were all types of graffiti, mostly of the "Marigold was here, June 2035" type. There was an occasional request for mates, "Petite blond looking for couple to form troika-style marriage. Contact Suzy at bunk R45," which shocked me just a bit. I knew that multiple-partner marriages had been legal for years, but we never saw any of it back home. Oh, some of the girls at school would giggle and gossip about how sexy it would be to have two husbands, but it never happened. It always turned out to be one guy and one girl. Maybe Southern California was different. I always heard they were a bit strange. Of course, I thought I was only a temporary one of them.

Some of the scrawling just confused me totally. "Enod speaks for Wanda. No sipli need call." Was Enod another woman, a man? And more importantly what was a sipli? It went completely over my head. How about, "Outerbun to Arthur Express. Rigger required. See Mac." Mac is a man's name . . . there? And where was Outerbun? Or Arthur for that matter? Another confusing scribble was "Ovot player needed. Will spot fingers or any other Var." Just call me clueless.

Worst, though, some of the writing on the wall fascinated and repelled me. "Butch brunette Six wants feminine Four or less for mutual pleasures. See Helga at G56." The Sapphic lifestyle never appealed to me. My fantasies were always about boys or men. Don't get me wrong, I don't think lesbians are wrong for who they sleep with, women just didn't excite me. Come to think of it, neither did the thought of men at that time.

How about the scribble, "Have someone in your life who needs to be removed? Get in touch with Toni at B14." Had that been a blatant murder-for-hire request? By the time I decided that I didn't want to know, Anita showed back up with two loaded fiberglass trays, just like the kind we used in high school. I hadn't expected to eat on the run, or on the crawl, rather.

"I didn't know what you like, girl, so I just got a bit of everything." The tray she all but dropped in my arms held a chef salad, with a reasonable amount of ham, cheese, egg and croutons over a rather large helping of lettuce. A small plastic cup held a very thin buttermilk dressing and another larger cup had diced peaches. A large baked potato was steaming next to the rest. At the apex of the tray stood a tall glass of milk. Anita loaded hers the same except that in the place of a baked potato she had potato chips. It was probably better eating than I got at home and a much larger quantity. I guess it made the most practical kind of sense. I was eating for two. I had to get used to it.

"Thanks, Anita," I said, salivating over the prospect of food. With the exception of one sandwich, I'd starved for more than twenty-four hours.

"No problem, girl. We gotta watch out for ourselves. Damned Ay-Dees aren't going to. Probably the one good thing in this place is the food. They gotta feed this right," she said, pointing to her belly. I assumed that she meant her baby and not the excess of fat that was around it. "I'll stand in line here. You sit over there and eat your food. When you're done, I'll eat." Fortunately, there was nothing on her plate to get cold or I might have protested her generosity. My legs and feet silently thanked her for the rest as I plopped onto someone's nearby bunk. As I hurriedly ate, I hoped I hadn't broken some taboo by sitting in someone's bed.

Anita jabbered on while I shoveled food into my mouth. In spite of her diarrhea of the mouth, I listened to her closely just in case a nugget of valuable information would drop. She could seem to talk endlessly about anything and then, when it looked like she would run out of steam, she would radically change topic and start all over again. Taxes, travel, catty women, fashion, cars, interplanetary politics, civil unrest on Mars, and even xenobiology. Her list of speaking subjects never bottomed out. She needed no response from me. She just kept right on babbling. I ate and ate some more. Before I knew it, my fork hit an empty plate. I felt I had vacuumed the food rather than eaten it. At least my middle didn't feel like it was best friends with my spine anymore.

I exchanged places with her, thinking she would have to quiet down to eat. No such luck. She still managed to talk most of the time even to sometimes waving a fork full of food at me to make a point about animal husbandry or lithography. Anita returned our trays before sitting tailor-style on the floor next to me. I decided to do the same because I started to get just a bit tired. I shouldn't have eaten such a full meal, especially with so little sleep the previous nights.

When my own loud belch brought me back awake I realized that Anita had stopped talking in deference to my snores. Anita woke me from time to time to move along with the line. I couldn't believe I just dozed off, sitting on the cold tile floor and leaning against the wall, but I had. Each time I stopped moving, I slipped right back into sleep. The trip and stress had obviously taken its toll.

I finally reached the beginning of the line some seven hours later and still had to wait.

"Name?" a testy looking nurse asked.

"Elizabeth Zimmer."

"You aren't in my system. Are you new?"

"Yes, ma'am."

The nurse pushed a clipboard into my hands. "Answer these questions completely front and back return the forms into this box when you are done NEXT," she said in one breath.

I answered the ten million medical questions about myself. "Have you ever had rubella, chicken-pox, mumps, diabetes, hypoglycemia, heart disease, neural galflexism (a.k.a. Yoko's Disease), tissue transplant, blood transfusion, embryo implantation, HIV, ectopic pregnancy, D&C . . ." The questionnaire went on for no fewer than ten pages. I wrote a book on myself. When I finally finished, another woman in a white gown took it from the box without a word and pointed me to yet another line. Anita already held my place for me. Her thinking ahead probably saved me another hour.

Only ninety minutes later I managed to get into an examining room. The doctor, an older balding man, took a blood sample, a Pap smear, and a dozen other cute little things. What little hair he had left was in a silver crescent around his shiny head. He clucked when he did the vaginal exam. I wondered if, as part of their training, male doctors should have one of those vaginal spreaders (I didn't know its proper name back then) placed into a freezer and then shoved up their asses. It might just make them a bit gentler. I didn't know any better as I'd never had an exam before. The whole process hurt. And while it wasn't as humiliating as what I'd suffered at the hands of Jimmy and his cohorts, I still felt exposed and ashamed. I have since learned why gynecology exams are so important, but it doesn't make me like them any better, nor keep me from cramping every rotten time.

Anita continued to be a big help. I think had I been alone I might have tried to slug the old man. She stayed with me the entire time, nattering away and holding my hand. She made soothing noises as the doctor did his worst. I don't recall that she said anything that really mattered, other than a general overview of how things worked at the School, but her presence settled me. She was a good soul who just hadn't learned to close her lips.

As doc took off his cold latex gloves he announced, "You are pregnant."

Boy, that was the shock of my life. He didn't wait for a response.

"I'm going to give you a shot for . . ." and then listed off two or three dozen sundry things that I don't remember half of. "You should have a sonogram to determine how far along you are and follow-up examinations."

"I can tell you exactly when I got pregnant."

"That isn't the best indicator. A three-dimensional sonogram will give us much more precise information."

"Too many girls lie, Elizabeth," Anita assured me. "Just let them get their own answer."

I just shook my head.

When the doctor finished placing his medical benediction upon me, Anita took me to my bunk. E112 was right in the center of the room. Hunger gnawed at my middle again and my eyes drifted in and out of focus. As food wasn't to be served again that day, tired won out. I pushed my red suitcase, which I had lugged all the way from Minnesota, under the gray-green army surplus cot. I didn't even change. I curled up onto the folding bed and pulled up the covers.

A horrifically large screech owl accompanied by lights four times brighter than the surface of the sun woke me up. Through my watering eyes my watch proclaimed it 7:00 a.m. To someone who wouldn't have gotten up before noon, even for the Second Coming, I found this a bit more than annoying. When I grumbled, turned over, and pulled the covers over my head, one of the girls in a nearby bunk whispered sharply to me.

"Hey, fresh meat. You better get up before the Ay-Dees catch you. You won't like it if they do." I peered out to see the shiny, sincere face of the "girl next door." She was extremely far gone in pregnancy and stood with one hand in the middle of her back to help counterbalance her huge abdomen. While I had no conscious recollection of a decision, I wisely got up. Two cot rows over, C row, I think, I witnessed what happened to those who didn't. A red-jerseyed matron applied a wicked-looking, black shock-rod to the sleeper's exposed feet. Several days later I learned, through my own stupidity and laziness that the Ay-Dees applied the prod to whatever appendage just happened to be sticking out. If none were handy they just randomly stuck it under the covers until they hit something. The voltage couldn't damage but it sure hurt like hell, especially when it hit . . . Well, let's just say I stood up for my morning meal that day.

"Thanks. I'm Elizabeth Zi—"

"No surnames or hometowns, Elizabeth. Here, it's rude. Learn that now. I'm Stacy. I'm an Eight."

"Eight?"

"You really don't know nothing about nothing, do you." It was a statement, not a question. "Here, you are the month of your pregnancy. Your status is directly linked to that. I'm in my eighth month. My guess is that you are a Two." The brown-haired girl turned her back and began folding her blanket and fluffing her pillow. I remembered thinking a long and hard few seconds about status being directly related to month of pregnancy and eventually shrugged it off. She had not been directly rude, but neither had she been kind. Well, on second thought, maybe she had been— rude, that is.

"Yes, I guess I am a Two, Stacy." I now got a quick look at what my little area had in it. It wasn't much. Two and a half meters by two meters of space held a cot and a small lockable chest. I decided to empty my suitcase into the chest. A place for a lock meant potential theft. I couldn't imagine anyone wanting to steal my clothes or the couple of pictures I brought, but as "fresh meat" I should be prudent. I gazed about at the sea of women who were all folding their cot blankets. I decide to imitate the Romans. While I was still folding, Anita showed up at my side.

She looked up and down at my jeans and flannel shirt, the same ones I'd worn the day before and had slept in, for that matter. I was too damned self-conscious to change in front of the other girls. "We'll have to get you some proper clothing. That won't do around here at all. But first, breakfast and a shower. Ready for some eats, Lizzy?" I bristled.

"Sure, but you know what? I hate Lizzy. Call me Beth."

"No problem, Beth. We'd better hurry. I heard that they are going to serve bacon and eggs. Real eggs, again. Usually we only get those reconstituted things." We scurried over to an already overlong line of women. I found it difficult getting used to seeing not only just women, but vast numbers of pregnant women. After thirty minutes of standing, I had a heap of scrambled eggs, three strips of bacon, wheat toast and fruit jam all deposited onto a large white molded plastic plate on the orange fiberglass tray. A large glass of milk was thrust into my hands before I managed to escape. It was just like high school, or as I am now learning, very much like jail as well. The small dining area had already filled with loud, talkative women. Anita led me away to a relatively quiet corner underneath the perforated steel stairs—the same stairs leading up to Spouse's lair. That is where Anita and I ate every morning, lunch and dinner. It became a ritual in both our lives up until she wasn't there one day, sometime after I'd become a Six. I sat and cried for almost the entire day because I never saw Anita again.

Oh, but that was months later. Even when I learned everything there was to know about the girls there, I knew even less about her. I hope she did well with her life. It's funny. For all her talking I never did really learn that much about her. She never talked of her family, her home, or her life, although if anyone brought up theirs, she ploughed into advice about loved ones. Anita possessed a soul that would match any saint. She helped me in a time when I had no one to turn to. As a giver she nurtured everyone who gave her the chance. If there is a heaven, I hope she goes there.

During the meal on that second morning I quizzed her on all the white gowns. I had begun to notice some with personalized markings, rolled sleeves. They were the same base dress but with tiny modifications. "Girl, you can paint 'em for all Spouse cares as long as it comes out in the wash. We get 'em fresh each day, same as underthings."

"Why doesn't everyone wear their own clothes? I think that would be much more comfortable."

"Aye! How would they get washed, girl? And where you gonna

get maternity clothes when you get fat? You just can't run down to WalMaCo no more. Spouse, she lets you bring your clothes if you want to, but she doesn't guarantee that the laundry is going to bring 'em back." The light was beginning to dawn in my thick skull. "I mean, I've seen gals sporting sequenced gowns but they get lost sooner or later. Either that or the gal gets too fat. No. I'm not bringing my own duds, girl."

After our breakfast, Anita led me to the showers. We stopped long enough to gather our clothes for the day; the same off-white hospital-style gowns as everyone wore and a dull pair of cotton panties and bra. The bra didn't fit right. I wasn't surprised. I always had to experiment to find the right size.

Another line greeted us in front of the shower stalls. It only took a small sledgehammer for me to learn that queues were a way of life there. Anita didn't seem to mind. She just got in at the end and turned to chatter some more. An hour later we managed to get into the water. While I had to admit that the hot water felt surprisingly good, I hated the whole experience. Just like a locker room shower, the open communal nature allowed everyone to see. I was so self-conscious that I could hardly stand it. I showered in record time, not looking at anyone nor taking place in the almost gossip-like atmosphere of the place. The women, whose bellies were in all different stages of waxing, chattered on like they were at a garden party, oblivious to the fact that they had no clothes on. The main topic seemed to be a pair of girls who had been caught in each other's bunk. It seemed to be a popular topic of discussion.

I don't think I've cleaned up so quickly in my entire life. My face was a beet-red that extended down well below my breasts. It took me weeks to get used to communal bathing, each time ending up with a redder face than I went in with. Sometimes I would skip the shower just to avoid the embarrassment. It was always a struggle because I did so enjoy the heat soaking into my skin in the morning and also to have the clean spread across me. The feeling of fresh was especially important because one, I was still having Jimmy nightmares and two, I don't perspire like a socially correct lady. I sweat like a horse. For that matter, I probably stink like one, too. Although, being an endangered species, I've never been close enough to a horse to know their particular odor.

The School's school was the next change in my life. Anita didn't go as she was well over the age limit, but she took me the first day. The School was three converted office rooms at the far end of the building. It was nothing lavish as we all sat tailor-style on the floor. The classes were generally broken up into three groups: those who were learning to read, those in middle grades, and those who really belonged in high school or beyond. I was in the latter group but wasn't the youngest by several years. Some of the girls were exceedingly young, but their bellies proved that they were at least physically women.

That brought up an interesting group of statistics about the School's population that I haven't mentioned yet. The average age of the girls hovered at eighteen years. Two-thirds of us were between sixteen and twenty, but that certainly didn't count the oddballs. We had one eleven-year-old, a twelve-year-old and three thirteen-year-olds. At the other end of the spectrum, we had a forty-year-old grandmother of four and two mothers in their mid-thirties. The upshot of all this was the "Wayward School for Girls" wasn't just for girls. I didn't understand this myself. How could a mother or a grandmother be sent away in disgrace? As personal questions were discouraged there, I didn't ask. It took four more months before I began to learn the truth about the School and its operation.

I carried an A-minus average in school before my family sent me away. I particularly liked mathematics and computer programming. The only class (except gym) I ever had trouble with was home economics. I could bake tolerably. I could put together a well-balanced meal, but keep me away from a sewing machine. They are the evil contraptions the devil himself inhabits. I never did manage to figure out the difference between a cross stitch, a stretch stitch, a zigzag or a zipper stitch, or what a serger is for. I nearly failed the class for my inability to sew together a simple dress pattern. Seeing the pretty blond cheerleaders (with brains that competed in size with small nutmeats) not only producing the most beautiful clothes, but also making modifications to the patterns to produce even more startling results, drove me mad with anger. My teacher, Miss Audrey, only had one comment about my misshapen finished product. "I wouldn't wear that, if I were you."

I got a D for the class.

The school (small "s") within the School was an odd one in that there really weren't any texts, there weren't any desks, there weren't any classrooms—just teachers telling the How and Why of Things. The teachers were no meaner or nicer than in any school in the world. Take your own school and pick a handful of teachers at random and you probably had close enough to our group for a general description. Why is it that all teachers are about the same? Take any twenty teachers and you have one exceptional one, a good one, two bad ones, two who couldn't teach a baby to suck a nipple and fourteen average ones. Three of the twenty will be male (usually in the science or physical education areas), one will be a writer and another will raise cats for show. Are teachers all this predictable?

I guess all in all the only other thing odd about this school was that we were taught more practical things—like how to cook a meal, how to sew a pair of pants (I messed it up again), comparison shopping, and about our pregnancies. I note specially the information about the last one. We were told about symptoms and ways to deal with them. I mean who knew that you could abate some of the morning sickness by eating a cracker a few minutes before you got up in the morning? Or how about eating a banana if you have frequent leg cramps? There was obviously a whole world out there that I didn't know about. We were also taught about cravings, and when they were abnormal. I couldn't understand why anyone would have the craving for dirt, or laundry detergent, until it happened to me. I can't describe the overwhelming desire to chew on the end of a bar of soap. It amazes and sickens me to this day. We never learned about childbirth or how to raise a child. It wasn't mentioned. I noticed the lack but I didn't understand why.

I don't mean to imply that all we were taught about was pregnancy. We actually spent no more time on it than any other topic. Our curriculum was much of what you would expect from any high school, although much more emphasis was placed on the practical rather than the theoretical. I mean courses like mathematics, history, home economics, English (as a first or second language), computer use, programming, and chemistry were fairly standard and what you'd find anywhere. But there were some of our courses, like civics, physical education, and sex education that had a bit of a twist.

Sex Ed was what many parents had been lobbying for years to get but because of an extreme group of lobbyists it was one we would never see in the normal school system. We learned about STDs, contraception (legal and illegal methods), abortion (extremely illegal except in the very specific condition of the mother's life being at risk), OB/GYN disorders, and even the care and feeding of men-folk (and I don't mean their stomachs, either). That last one was quite a fun topic, with a great deal of giggling amongst the girls, even among the butches and dykes.

Physical Education was the most different from what I was used to. No push-ups and no sit-ups. The closest we came to conventional Phys. Ed. was walking laps around the main room. Boy was I glad! I hated gym, for reasons I've already discussed and won't repeat. We mainly learned and did things directly related to our conditions including, but certainly not limited to, posture. They were like: best sleeping positions, ideal-sitting positions, the pelvic rock, Kegels, and even how to get into and out of bed. Trust me, for those who have never been pregnant, getting out of a cot when you have an extra twenty-five pounds of bloat on your front is a challenge equal to building the Pyramids—twice!

The only class that I'm going to spend any time on is Civics. For some reason I paid extremely close attention in this class, although before coming to the School, my interest in such things approached nil. Civics was taught by a rather handsome, but not precisely pretty, Hispanic woman in her thirties. Donna Hernandez was the only teacher who was extraordinary in any way. It wasn't her down-home looks, it was because Donna had once been in our place. She had been a . . . what should I call it? Inmate? Client? Well, whatever. She had been in our shoes some ten years before. The only time she would bring it up, however, was when we were perfectly unwilling to listen to her. She would loudly slap the floor with her hand and say, "Ladies, if you want to be nothing more than baby factories, get out of my class for I have nothing at all to teach you. If you want to make something of yourself then you had DAMNED well better listen up!" Her voice never changed pitch, but its intensity sure did. Most of us listened intently from that point. The rest at least pretended to pay attention.

Donna taught us so many things that I don't even know where to begin. I remember one day we were discussing Roe v. Wade and how that led the country to the Kennedy Act of '28 outlawing abortion (except if the mother's life was in jeopardy). Ms. Henandez's tone told us how very little she cared for that law.

"Carrie, can you tell us how the Kennedy Act came to be law?" Carrie had never been one of the best students and she faltered rather badly. She hadn't read her lesson. "Andrea?" Ms. Henandez asked, picking another victim.

"Well, basically a group of anti-abortionists, known as the Abortion Equals Murder Coalition, or the AEMC, told President Joe Kennedy III that if he didn't put this bill to the floor they would kill his son. Uh, I think they had kidnapped him some days before."

"Don't stop there, Andrea. That's only half the story."

"So he did?" Andrea said hoping that she could get away with that trite little line. Ms. Henandez pushed her long brown hair back from her face and glared briefly at Andrea.

"Liz," she said, pointing at me. "Continue from there."

"President Kennedy was a staunch pro-choice advocate. He abhorred the proposed bill but didn't think anything would come of it. He did as they asked. What he didn't know was that the AEMC had bribed, blackmailed or otherwise subverted enough votes in the Senate and House of Representatives to get the bill passed." I felt a bit smug. I had read about this entire historic event as it did somehow relate to my situation at hand. "Kennedy's son, James, was released. It brought a new era of terrorism to lawmaking."

"Very good, Liz. That's exactly right. To continue, despite repeated attempts to overturn the law, there have always been enough votes to keep it in place. Worse, the AEMC was never prosecuted for their actions."

We also learned about the Cloning Prohibition of '28, totally ending all scientific research and exploitation on cloning. All governments placed it on top of the capital crimes list and it remains there to this day. We had a long discussion of that in class. The popular opinion of the time was that there were too many ways to abuse clones, and the people they were made from. The popular misconception at the time was that cloning produced a duplicate to organism cloned—excellent for science fiction but totally false. Cloned organisms had the same genetic structure as the donor, but they had to grow just the same way as the original. A cloned human adult would produce a baby without memories, not a duplicate adult. That baby would then have to grow up just as any normal child would, adding to the already overpopulated world.

The UN passed the CP209, creating a body of enforcement officers who had the power to seek and destroy any facilities, equipment, subject, and/or result of said experimentation. It put an end to legal cloning of humans. Oh, it still happens illegally, but the punishment is severe enough and the cost high enough that it is extremely rare, not to mention rather difficult to hide.

One obvious lack in the Civics class was instruction on our rights as women under the laws. I asked Donna about this one day. She shocked me with her answer. "You have no rights, Ms. Zimmer." She was quiet for a moment, looking right into my eyes. "I can't give you the real answer. Beth, you are a good student. I don't know how you ended up here, but make sure you don't come back. Most of the rest of these girls have nothing else to offer our world other than making babies and sucking down the IQ average. You could be someone, Beth. Just don't come back." Ms. Henandez turned away and fell silent as she pushed tests to be graded into her briefcase and walked off.

She never talked to me that way again. I think she might have been ashamed of it because of the way she avoided being alone with me. I think I came a little too close to getting her real feelings and it scared her.

I don't mean to tell you that all these things happened the first day at school. Not at all. These are just some of the highlights over seven months. School (small "s") was a breeze for me. On the whole I ended up with good monthly grades. Those who passed were actually awarded General Equivalency Diplomas before their delivery. I can't say that it did me any specific good.

The School had a library that they encouraged us to use

liberally. It contained eight closet-sized rooms of standing bookshelves sporting uncatalogued books. Books were so crowded in each room that there was barely room for a Nine to move around. A small staff of volunteer girls kept the books in their right section but it would have taken a miracle to keep the books in any type of real order. Reading was one thing that highly nourished us all so books came in and out all the time.

I have to admit that one of my great loves is reading. I might almost call it an addiction. I would read nearly anything and the library supported a large number of titles, in spite of its small physical size. I read fiction, nonfiction, romance novels (this was the largest section by far), biographies, science texts, science fiction, spy novels, gardening books, tag lines, music lyrics, programming languages, famous quotations, or even cookbooks. The list seemed endless. I never did begin to touch one part in a thousand in this huge collection, not even in the ten or eleven years I had access to it.

I spent most of my time reading. But even one's favorites can pall over time. Ever eaten three banana splits in a row? What tasted great the first time around was cloying and even a bit nauseating by the third. Books helped, the school helped but it wasn't nearly enough. There was very little to do in the School and it was dreadfully boring. Boredom was my biggest enemy at the School during that year.

October 20, 2050

Well here we are back in the glorious Chez Alcatraz. Seating for one, almost no waiting, with a lovely view of the "gallery." Yes, that is my attempt at sick humor. Sorry if it offends you. Well, on second thought, I'm not sorry. I'm the one who is going to dance the long-neck-limbo here. You have nothing to beef about.

I might as well continue. Not much to do in my enamel twelve-by-twelve-foot cage but write or sleep. I guess I could go over and use the pot. Back to the School.

After about a week, life at the School settled into something akin to routine. Settled was too weak a word—try solidified or maybe concreted. The days varied as much as the apathy of the world—that is to say, none at all. The monotony started by waking up at seven. Get in line for breakfast. Eat breakfast. Attend school for three hours. Queue up for lunch. Three more hours of school before we mustered for supper. Then hit the showers to wash away that ladylike stench. Gossip until lights out. Granted not all the women did these things at the same time, but enough did that it was always slow to get anywhere except the bathroom. The only place you didn't have to wait in line for was the bathroom. Oddly, the bathroom held the only slightest bit of privacy at the School.

One might wonder what we had to gossip about in our own little closed world, but you would be surprised. There were several basic topics. We discussed how our symptoms affected us today, who was doing what to whom for how many Oreo cookies, who had or was going to deliver, who had just made Nine (or Eight or Seven, etc.), and the ever popular what was the first thing we were going to do after we delivered and were on the outside. I found this less than intellectual level of conversation boring. I'm sure everyone else did as well, but there was nothing else to do. The School was much like prison. You hurry up and wait to do anything, hoping your waiting would hurry up.

Through most of my first time, Anita shared my loneliness. I don't know what drew us together but we became strong friends. Her sharp and constantly wagging tongue had me wondering at first. She could put a tease into anyone. One day, in the first week, when my long brown hair draped into the food and I found several small pieces of egg in the very split ends, Anita giggled and said, "Girl, if I got my locks dirtied like that, I'd never get laid. O'course maybe, just maybe, you're sav'n some of that for later." I frowned angrily at her. The frown almost immediately changed as she mimed pulling several food items from my hair and eating them. I gasped for breath as I held my side for the stitch my laughter put there.

Yes, Anita did much to alleviate the boredom with her quick wit and easy manner—but even her highly unusual and effusive personality only dulled it.

We weren't allowed to go anywhere and we weren't allowed visitors, not that I thought my parents would show up. Who else could I possibly expect? Jimmy? I couldn't decide whether to laugh or flinch at the thought.

The orderlies taking away a Nine or an Eight provided the only excitement that punctuated our dreariness. It happened about two or three times a day, although we might miss one if it happened on the other side of the room. Never fear, though, the gossip tree would get us the information almost as fast as a loudspeaker announcement could. Sometimes the woman would have sudden pains or contractions and be whisked away on a stretcher before anyone could say "postpartum." Other times, women would walk through a special door marked "Deliveries" and never return. That was the only thing that broke up the monotony most of us faced. Day after day for weeks and months at a time; 253 to 303 days, the almanac says.

The boredom tore at our souls. There were only so many things to do, so many people to talk to, so many times you could play Monopoly missing the Ventnor Avenue property card, and only so long you could read any book. You couldn't sleep during the day as the lights were so bright from the overhead skylights. As all of us did, I thought only of the things I couldn't do. It became almost a mantra. I would sit there and list all the things I was effectively proscribed from doing: walks in the woods, fishing, petting puppies, movies, my soap—*Southern Nightfall*, boys, bowling, snowball fights, counting stars, lazing in bed on a Sunday morning, any color other than gray or white, making cookies, talking on the telephone, watching my mother knit, milkshakes, boys, the news, shopping. Every time I thought I had exhausted the list another prohibition leapt to mind. Every minute that wasn't otherwise occupied somehow managed to dredge up something that I didn't get to do at the School.

In an effort to combat the seemingly endless hours that needed filling, I explored the entire building from one end to another. Oh, I don't mean I poked into every room to see what was there. I was much more thorough than that. I looked in every corner, found every hiding place, and even found every single item ever hidden in the School's history. The list included forty-two love letters, fourteen various drug hordes (including three growing cannabis plants), thirteen vibrators, sixteen weapons (three handguns, twelve knives and a police baton), sixty-five candy bars in various stages of consumption, eighty-six different money caches (totaling over twenty thousand dollars!), one copy of *Mein Kampf* and one copy of *Trump: The Art of the Deal*. There were a lot more "secret things" that no one would think necessary to hide, but they were there. Every nook and cranny of that place seemed to hide something. I never took anything, leaving it the way I found it. I probably shouldn't have been snooping in the first place, but with nothing else to do I became a snoop.

Over time I grew to loathe each of the rooms in that building. I knew them all, all except for Spouse's office and her assistant's private bedroom. I wasn't jealous of those rooms because I knew that if I were able to get to them, I would hate them just as intensely. I walked around each room, sometimes as many as ten times a day, following the perimeter, counting each of the off-white linoleum tiles. Each one of those tiles became an individual to me; the wrinkled one, lifting just a bit in the middle just before the entrance to the kitchen; the one in the examination room with the broken corner that looked like a finely cut diamond; the brown one in the third bathroom stall that was used as a replacement; and the tiles with the color of an old smoker's teeth that led to the exit door. I knew them all and despised each and every one. The yellowing, stained, cracked and broken one-foot by one-foot floor coverings became the enemy personified.

Each tile I walked marked another tic of time closer to when I could escape that prison. It was like I had to mow each down with another step, like a tank through a field of wheat. The floor coverings offered no resistance except to the sweep of the second hand. It became maddeningly simple. If I walked faster around the room, then time would speed up and I would breathe fresh air sooner. Seven months, times thirty days per month, times twenty-four hours per day, times sixty minutes per hour, times sixty seconds per hour, yields eighteen million, one hundred forty-four thousand seconds, give or take a few hundred thousand. Close to eighteen million seconds from the time I arrived until I should get to leave and each stained, over-waxed, ivory-colored tile became half a second. So if I managed to cover those thirty-six million tiles faster, my time there would come to an end all that much sooner—at least it was what I'd convinced myself.

I would walk faster, the tiles becoming less individualistic, becoming just their imperfections of the twelve-by-twelve-inch mold: this one with a black groove in it, that one covered with a stain of excess wax, and the other one with a cracked corner just waiting its chance to be free from the floor. Faster I would go, my head still firmly looking at the floor. The tiles became only lines on the floor I passed and seconds of an imaginary clock that ran between my feet. Ten, twelve, fifteen flew past at a time. I would begin to jog, or before I got too heavy, run. I obsessed at making those tiles go by under my feet. And while I covered thousands each day, at lights out I would fall into bed breathing in the same stale smells of too many women in one place: urine, perspiration, hair spray, spearmint gum, flatulence, sexual release, nervousness and the smell of hospital style disinfectants trying to mask them all.

I can't begin to explain the pure sameness of each day. The Chinese water torture had nothing on our agony. Each second that would slip by, another aged tile would fall on my forehead and shatter. Ever notice that there is no other word for tile? Check it. Pick up any thesaurus and check: "Tile, n. see tile." I even got to hate the name. I walked the square-covered floor each night before bed, hoping that the clock would magically speed up to match my feet, praying that it would be over sooner. The only change from day to day was the likelihood of a new symptom, a new ache, or a new way that my body could protest its condition.

October 23, 2050

While I've been laid up in the infirmary, I've managed to look over that last bit I wrote. Wow! Was I on a downer trip or what? Well, I guess the truth does hurt to a certain extent; it had been a very depressing and lonely time.

I'm in the hospital with a stab wound in my left side. It still hurts like hell to move around, but the doctor said I was well enough to go back to my cell, especially with all the other wounded that they have to treat.

I'm getting a bit carried away with myself and not keeping things in their right order. There was a riot here in Alcatraz. I still don't quite understand it all. The prisoners are complaining of overcrowding and substandard living conditions. Fuck, it's a jail, for God's sake. What do they expect, the Ritz? Anyway, I didn't see as if the riot could have any meaning. Is it me or do most people have "stupid" written across their foreheads? I mean they seem to have the IQ of a dim carrot—most people anyway. Did they expect that Southern California's governor would just throw up his hands and say, "Sure, have whatever you want"? I doubt it. I guess I'm just a bit more realistic.

It was like when I was arrested. I knew who set it up. I knew then that I was going to be convicted. There isn't really anything to do except relax to the inevitable—kind of like being raped. The only difference is that this time I can fight back. I may not be able to prevent what is happening to me, but I can make sure this rapist is castrated. But that is another story.

Anyway, very shortly after the first alarms sounded, forty Coast Guard Cruisers surrounded the Rock with orders: "Shoot to kill." At least that is my assumption. Several of the general population hit the water swimming only to have gauss guns from the Cruisers chop the water to red foam right where the swimmers had been. Anything large enough left to bury just offered another morsel to the sharks.

My interest in the uprising approached zero. Even the reasons the other inmates rioted are meaningless to me. I don't expect to be here all that long so I don't see as prison conditions can be a big deal to me. Of course being on death row does have its advantages. I have my own cell and it is rather clean and cozy compared to the conditions that the ordinary decent criminals have to endure. I don't really feel one way or another about their plight. Some deserved it and some didn't. Just like the hand life deals us, some are winners and others are losers. Just look at my life. Just when I get a good hand, someone changes the game.

One of the young women looked unfavorably at my passive stance on prison life. I ended up with two feet of cement-sharpened Plexiglas through my left side, just below the bottom rib. Doc says I was lucky that all it did was punch a hole through my intestine. That young lady made one mistake. When I went down to the floor she thought me dying or dead. About two minutes later, I returned the makeshift knife by burying it in the base of her skull. I guess now I'm really a murderer. Above and beyond what they said I've done, that is. Maybe I am the heartless animal that society has branded me. I didn't even feel remorse at the woman's death. My killing her was something I did to make sure she didn't come back for me some other time. Hell—I didn't even know her name.

The death toll among the inmates that day seemed excessive—a number of the dead seemed for no apparent reason. No one has ever connected me to my murder or has had the moxie to bring it up. I figure the outside world really doesn't care what happens inside here. Realistically, they are right as long as we stay in here and they stay out there.

I wonder what the inmates thought they would accomplish. It only had one impact on the world at large. It made the governor/presidential hopeful, look like a hero. On the second night after the riot he ordered the entire island gassed.

The sleep agent brought everyone in the entire place down. Fortunately for me, I was lying on my bunk trying to live with a hole in my gut. The Gov made his mark again. I knew him well. He had made his mark on me long ago. Of course that was much later in my story. But I will get the last laugh.

The ruckus here reminds me of something that happened the

third week after I arrived at the School. It was over something so trivial. But when you are in such close quarters with so many people, trivial doesn't exist. Even the most minor things take on an importance beyond themselves.

It was a hairbrush. A simple hairbrush. Stacy, the Eight with the bunk at the head of mine, walked up to another woman, a Five I think, and snatched the other girl's brush up off the Five's lockbox. Stacy always was an arrogant bitch. She turned her back and began combing her hair with it. The Five, Denise, let out a yell and leaped at Stacy. It was like watching All-Star Wrestling because in less than the wing flap of a hummingbird, dozens more girls got into the fray, pulling hair, biting and kicking. In an even shorter time it spawned a general free-for-all. Everyone got into the action. One Hispanic bitch even took it as an opportunity to play Tarzana with my hair as a vine. This got me into it, so I wasn't little Miss Lilly White, either.

Cot poles were swung as clubs, hard bound books thrown, heeled shoes used as daggers, and even the occasional shock-rod wrested from the hands of an unconscious Ay-Dee. The "scuffle" involved over two hundred girls and resulted in smashed lockers, torn blankets, bloodied faces, blackened eyes, broken bones and severely twisted noses. Stacy, I heard, miscarried. Of course that could have been a "standard line." I mean I know the School used it as a standard "break it to 'em," but I'm not sure in her case. No one in the area escaped without at least minor scratches and abrasions, and that included me. I still have a scar across the back of my neck where one woman caught me with her claws.

It took twenty-two Ay-Dees and nearly four hours to break up the riot. Most of the Ay-Dees were called in from off duty. The bedlam of the fight had acted like the steam valve on a pressure cooker. It popped open just long enough to bring the strain down to a manageable level. Maybe it was something we needed. It didn't seem so at the time. It broke the boredom for a time.

The entire fight provided gossip material for weeks. And if you think we wouldn't talk about something so demeaning, you would be very wrong. Someone would remember landing a sweet hit or kick. That would remind someone else of biting a hunk of flesh out of some other tramp. It would feed on itself.

What made the fight extremely significant for me happened toward the end. A black woman, about a Six, who held a grudge because I wouldn't switch bunks with her lover halfway across the room, tried to break a board across my face and head. Instead I saw big, burly Box race forward and throw a very illegal block, at least in the World Football League, underneath the Six's chin. The Six fell back into a heap with, I learned later, her jaw broken in three places and a severe concussion.

By this point the Ay-Dees had managed to get the fight down to a mere whisper of its former glory. I didn't know what to say to Box, but I squeaked out a windless, "Thank you."

I thought that would be the end of it, but the next week Box showed up in the evening, just as I was starting to walk the tiles.

"Lizzy, ya like t'play a game o'chess?"

"Sure, I love chess. None of the other girls will play me," I said, eager to do anything but face the boredom of yet another evening on those tiles. "They say I'm too competitive. They won't even play Uno with me." We set up a board in the almost-empty dining area.

"Check," was the only word I heard Box say in the entire next hour of play. A crowd of watchers formed around us. There were no fewer than fifty spectators, all whispering amongst one another—and I don't think the topic was my brilliant strategy. After I checkmated Box, he stood and shook my hand. "T'ank ya, Lizzy. I enjoyed t'at." Without fanfare, he left. Even before he was out of earshot I heard snide comments from the girls near me.

"How does she rate?"

"I can't even visit my own husband and that little tart has 'em delivered."

"Sucking up to the owners—literally."

"You go, girl."

I personally didn't know what to think. It had been just a game of chess. The only time we even touched was when he shook my hand. I didn't see what the big fuss was about until Anita sat next to me as I was putting away the pieces. She was still sporting a yellowing bruise on her cheek from the fight.

"Well, congratulations, Beth."

"What are you talking about?"

"Box is what I'm talking about, girl. He likes you."

"All we did was play a game of chess," I remarked, not even looking up from the white and black plastic pieces jumbled in an old cigar box.

"Do you know how many pussies that man has had waved under his nose? He never even gave them the time of day. Not only does he save you from getting your pretty face looking like mine," Anita said, making a show of gently brushing her injury, "but he takes the time to play a game with you."

"Hell, my father would throw a hissy if he knew I even talked to him. In his crude idiom 'ain't got no use for niggers.' Besides, I'm not even interested in Box," I objected.

"Girl, don't you know that's the fastest way to attract a man who shows any interest at all."

"Ah, 'Nita, you are just blowing things out of proportion," I said, as I got up to return the chess set.

"We'll see."

I continued to get spiteful comments and dark looks from some of the girls, but surprisingly, many more of them seemed to be cheering me on. I'd get a wink or a thumbs-up from women I'd never even met before. More than once a pair of girls would point in my direction and bust up in giggles. I went back to my tiles to try and make my time shorter. I found that being the target of gossip was not as easy as being its spreader. Soon, though, some other tidbit of scandal pushed out my unprecedented visit with Box.

I thought nothing more of it for several days until Box showed up the next Thursday evening and invited me to play a game of Uno. Anita and the other girls seemed to think this meant something, but I wasn't sold. Once again we set up in the dining room with a smaller but more intent group of spectators.

"T'Cowboys beat Detroit Monday night, twenty-one t'twelve," Box offered unsolicited.

"Really? Who was staring quarterback? Draw two."

"Carter Dura," he said as he drew two cards. The conversation took some effort as Box was not gregarious by nature. Several times during the next two hours I had to all but pull his teeth to get him to talk as the discussion drifted from football to world politics to undersea colonization. His breadth of knowledge fascinated me. But soon, all too soon, Box stood up and announced his departure.

"T'anks fer t'company, Lizzy." While I winced at the nickname, I decided not to correct him as I didn't want to give him any reason for not returning. While I had no romantic interest in my visitor, I certainly enjoyed his company a lot more than hundreds of tiles. "I got somet'ing for ya, girl. I know ya din't get ta see any of ta sights, so I brung ya this." He handed me a five-by-seven-inch flat picture of the Queen Mary.

"Thank you, Box. You didn't need to do that."

"G'night, Lizzy." The onlookers found intense activity somewhere away from Box as he strode out. After putting up the game I sought out Anita. She was braiding the hair of another friend, June.

"Why?"

"Whacha talking about, girl?"

"I still don't know . . . Why?"

"You mean Box? Shoot, girl, I told you last week. He likes you," she said, tying off the end of the braid with a tiny hairband.

"But that doesn't answer the question. I'm not attractive. I'm not the soul of wit. Hell, I even fumble through small talk."

"Maybe he's just out for a piece of your white ass," June piped up from her sitting position on the floor. June yelped as Anita pulled a double handful of the troublemaker's hair.

"Hush up, girl. You don't know nothing neither. Look, Beth, I don't know what the man wants but it is obvious that you may be it. Why ask? Just enjoy."

I couldn't just enjoy. I needed to know why he paid attention to me. Maybe he believed in love at first sight. I couldn't come up with an answer that seemed to hold water. At the same time, while I needed to know, I didn't have the courage to ask outright. But understanding or no, it didn't stop Box from coming to visit. He rarely missed a week after that.

Box always showed up on Thursday nights. He would show me that tiny glimpse, the merest peek of the outside world with something trivial like a flower, a handful of M&Ms, a blank postcard showing a stereo-pic of Mammoth Mountain on a clear day, or even something as simple as a pink barrette. Nothing that ever had a cost that amounted to anything, but it didn't have to cost. It vicariously let me taste the freedom I might someday again have. At the same time, it forced me to walk the tiles all the faster Thursday nights before falling asleep in exhaustion. But I looked forward to his visits all the same. I always slept best on Thursday nights.

Box brightened my internment, not because he was exceptionally handsome or terribly witty himself. He brought just a piece of the outside with him. Not just in the tiny gifts he always fetched with him, but in his manner. I began to imagine what the news could have been just by looking at his face. A frown meant that Russian Premier Alexivich had been assassinated, a smile showed his Tampa Raiders winning the Super Bowl, or a thoughtful look when the UN declared martial law in the Antarctic. Who knows if I was right? But it was a fun game.

Box always puzzled me. Right up to the very end. He seemed to limit himself to no more than a few words at a time. I never found this trait in him boring when we were together, but I would think about it afterwards and wonder. What goes on behind those placid brown eyes? What did he think when he kept his mouth closed?

We played Uno, with a deck missing a red five and a wild draw four. We also managed dominos, and chess. I found I had to spot him a queen's rook when we played chess, but it didn't seem to bruise his ego that I was better than he was. Most of the women had given up playing against me, but he would keep trying. I wondered at the time if it might have been his male ego that forced him to play me until he eventually won. I admitted to it as an uncharitable thought on my part.

Our conversations, if they could be called that, never focused on any one thing. They always drifted from place to place. One week it would be the inequity of the judging in world class figure-skating championships. The next time he called it would be the viability of setting up a permanent colony on Ganymede like we had on Mars and the Moon. Discussing hydroponic growing techniques to help alleviate the food shortage problem followed. You never knew what kind of twists and turns we would come up with: stock prices, building materials, color effects. The discussions never repeated themselves. As well read as I considered myself, he matched me by being a broad encyclopedia of experience.

Box wasn't a mental giant but he did have two things going for him that very few people around me had. I couldn't have told you at the time what they were, but I know now—compassion and empathy. That doesn't sound like much to someone who has someone, ANYONE, but I had no one. You certainly can't count parents who would just as soon that I had been born to another family. While Box may not have been quick, he did know a little about everything.

I also didn't underrate the incredible experience of sharing an opinion with a hormonally balanced individual—someone who wasn't pregnant. Box gave me a bit of perspective, of the definitely male variety, which I couldn't get anywhere else. The few male Ay-Dees that there were, wouldn't even think of talking to us "clients." Just the appearance of impropriety would have Spouse bouncing them out in the quickest way.

As much as I looked forward to Box's visits, I detested his leaving even more. I knew the freedom he provided I would have to replace with those scarred and cracked linoleum tiles to while away the seconds, minutes and hours. I could almost sense the time when he had to leave. Maybe it was an internal alarm clock, the look of his ebony face, or maybe just his posture and mannerisms. No matter what triggered it, I would become increasingly anxious. I knew those yellowed, twelve-inch squares awaited me, eager to dominate my mind once again.

After his visits became regular, I started making a big hairy thing of myself before he departed. Sometimes I would just cry or sob. Other times I would rant and rave. Even others I would turn away and not speak to him. With a big dose of guilt I admit to the cruelty I inflicted upon Box. I tried to manipulate him. I could claim loneliness, hormonal imbalances or even general fatigue, but in the end I knew better. I knew I tried to change his will. I wanted him there so I would be a little less bored and a little happier. My ways had all the finesse of a four-year-old's temper tantrum. It got me as much attention as a child throwing such a fit should receive. Box usually just turned his back and left. I can only recall one time that Box made any comment about my behavior. Only once. It sank home quite well. Shortly after I became a Five, my moods were swinging like a nymphomaniac in a nudist colony. I screamed at him.

"You fucking nigger. Don't bother to come back!" Tears were rolling down my face in as steady a stream as the abuse I heaped upon him. "I don't need your black ass here to tease me with what I can't have. Just torch out of here and don't bother to send me a postcard!

"And don't bring me no more of your addled little gifts." I reached under my bunk and threw a tiny china teacup at the floor, shattering it not into splinters but into glass powder. "I'm not your woman and I don't want your pity. Why don't you donate your brain to science and save us your drivel." I stood there defiantly, with my hands on my hips and wet red eyes. I wasn't going to wipe them away until he saw how strong I was.

Box spun around with all the fire and change of mood that can strike a pregnant woman and lit into me in a barrage of retribution that I've never forgotten.

"Missy, ya know not'in' 'bout how it is here. Ya t'ink it's easy comin' here t'chat ya? Ya is sometimes stupid as the rest o' t'ese empty-headed bitches. Ya shut ya mouth and Box might jus' tell ya. Instead, ya whine lik'n a shot gang-banger." Box turned his back and stormed away. I thought I wouldn't see him again. I had been certain I had driven away one of my only real friends.

I bawled for hours that night. I cried to myself even when Tina, a Seven in the next cot, whispered for me to clam up. I tried to bury it in a pillow but it wasn't enough. One of the Ay-Dees took it upon herself to keep me from waking the whole room and prodded me with a shock rod, my first time since the brawl some two months earlier. That didn't even stop it, but I was able to bring it under control, dropping it to a mere sob that the pillow smothered.

I kept to myself for nearly a week. I all but ran away from Anita when she came to visit. I even stayed away from the teaching school. I took to one of the tiny hiding places I had found and stashed myself there, desiring nothing more than Box to stride back into my life. I hoped that he would forgive me for being an empty-headed twit. I knew I deserved every hateful word he had whipped at me. I think I would have preferred a whip. It wouldn't have hurt so long.

I sat there, my hands piously folded together, crying and praying to God to send back my friend. The hypocrisy of begging a powerful being I didn't believe in to do something for me wasn't lost on my mind.

My mood worsened a week later when Box didn't return. I knew I had driven him away. My prayers took on a more frenzied desperation. I promised God things I don't even remember now, but I do know they were significant. Box and Anita alone made that place bearable. Each passing day yielded a wine bottle full of tears and an even stronger moral certainty he wouldn't return. Each tear felt like Box dying in my breast.

But Box appeared the very next week. He showed up like nothing had ever happened. I'm sure I wasn't good company. My marginal looks had been damaged. My eyes glowed red with all the crying I'd been doing. I had bitten my nails down to the quick. I must've reeked rather badly as I hadn't even taken a bath in three days.

But Box said absolutely nothing about our harsh words or about my appearance. He never mentioned any of it again. I learned a valuable lesson and I kept my negative feelings to myself after that and our time together. In my own defense, I can say that I never learned how to be a friend. My family wasn't any help, either directly or as a role model. Oh, sure, I was a friend with Anita but that was different. Wasn't it?

At one of Box's visits I got my first idea that everything at the School wasn't on the up and up. Oh, I'd heard the rumors and all the guesswork by some of the new girls. Some thought that our babies were to be part of some modified humanoids that would populate a new colony on Mercury. Still others believed in the grown soldier concept or any of a million other paranoid or hopeful theories. Most of them weren't even worth wasting this green crayon on. As I know none of them came close to the truth, I'm not going to bother. The women who had been there before, and admitted it, wouldn't even entertain the subject. They knew and weren't talking or they didn't know and didn't care. I decided to emulate them until I had the real story. By the time the answer revealed itself, I didn't want to talk either.

Around my third month at the School, and I know it was a Thursday because Box sat across from me playing chess, two Metros, policemen, came in like they owned the place. Box didn't say anything, but as he turned to look at them I could see the muscles on his jaws clenching and unclenching. The cops stopped and flirted with some of the girls, who fell all over themselves to be near their almost shiny black uniforms. They didn't stay long on the floor but went directly up to Spouse's office. They didn't remain there much longer, returning with a leather gym bag. My razor-sharp instincts told me that it didn't contain dirty socks and a sweaty jockstrap.

By the time I learned that their names were Metro Officer Edwin Ramirez and Metro Sergeant Theodore Smith, I knew I didn't like them. I guess they were like any other cops on the take. Later, when it was my job to deal with them, I always felt slimy afterward. Maybe I'm hypocritical because I didn't want to deal with crooks, but bent cops stood at the head of the line, worse than even shower mildew. I never swore to uphold anything but was rather born to the laws of this land. These men agreed to "protect and serve" when instead they just lined their pockets at the price of their integrity.

That visit, and the visit of those same officers at the same time every month, led me to understand that what happened there didn't exactly tick all the legal boxes. Someone was getting paid to clam up. Only someone with something to hide paid people to be quiet. Back then I remembered wondering what the School hid from the world and us girls.

October 24, 2050

Well, another appeal shot. Ten days and counting. I won't trouble you with the details.

I cried last night. I don't know what caused it, but I couldn't sleep and I began feeling sorry for myself. I even got to thinking the way Father wanted me to when he held sway over my brain and emotions. Why bother? Why not just let them do it . . . Kill me? Because that would be quitting, idiot, and I'm not a quitter, I kept saying to myself. People could call me quite a few things, but "quitter" wasn't one of them. I'd like to think I always managed to find a way to move on, crawling or slithering if necessary, but not quitting. Never quitting. Why is it so bloody important that I not be a quitter? But I'm not.

I know this is trivial, considering the seriousness of what I just said, but I just oiled Frances on the basketball court. I don't even think she got three points. It provided a brief and happy moment today—one of very few left. Am I morbid for dwelling on it? Or am I stupid for ignoring it? Time to ignore it for a while.

Father IronSky showed up again today with his lively ponytail dancing behind him. He is such a dark man. He rarely smiles and when he does it is because of some nasty thought like burning alive to fulfill your word to God. I mean, take the conversation today about my impending demise.

"I really hadn't given it much thought, Father." On the chest of his black pantsuit he played with the silver cross of his rosary, twirling it about his fingers.

"You should, my child. I would like you to be saved before your Day of Judgment comes upon you." His wrinkled fingers worked up each bead. I could see him silently mouthing prayers as he did. His lips would move just a fraction. "It would be truly sad if you were to meet your Maker without having absolved yourself of sin."

"So am I to lie to myself and God, Father? You are asking

me to do something I don't believe in. To atone for something I'm not certain was wrong. Let's even assume that you have the honest gospel on who turns the universe. What makes you the bearer of the right word? Where is it written that 'The many shall perish so the few can be unloved?' I don't buy it, Father." The shriveled, puckered lips of the old man continued to slowly move as his fingers squeezed across each bead on the rosary. I realized it must be an unconscious habit formed over his fifty years or so in the priesthood.

"I cannot ask you to betray what you believe. I just think you should consider that you might be wrong, Elizabeth. Murder is wrong. And who was it that said, 'The road to hell is paved with good intentions'?"

"Well, if I can't count on my own good intentions, Father, then I'll be forever a lost sheep. I won't go against what I believe is right for some arbitrary doctrine. And besides, when have I ever had a choice? The closest I could have come is to martyr myself in two places. The best I could have hoped for was to be some welfare-dependent, whining bitch . . ."

"But at least you would be alive . . . I mean . . ." Father IronSky's voice drifted off and he just smiled at me.

"I know what you mean, Father Peter. I guess I'd have to say that if you want to have someone repent, seek out my father. You could probably trace all of my virtues and faults through to him."

"It's not good to lay guilt on another person's head instead of taking responsibility for it yourself."

"I'm sorry, Father, but this discussion is going nowhere. You are telling me that I should ask for forgiveness for something I'm not sure that I did wrong. And you are blaming my lack of virtue on me instead of the man who was supposed to instill it within me. You can't have it both ways, sir.

"I think our conversation for the day is done, Father IronSky." I could see his hand clench hard on the cross of his rosary. He probably dug it painfully into the palm of his hand. He deliberately stood, carefully pushing his chair back against the ceramcrete and brick wall. He dropped the cross so it hung on his black leather belt. Father Peter caught my eye through the cell bars and inquired, "Have you chosen your method of execution, yet?"

Catholic priests weren't supposed to play so dirty. I just glared at him and refused to speak as he turned and walked away.

Per the Judicial Reform Accords, I have the choice of my own method of execution. Bizarre, but true. They range from the standard electrocution, lethal injection and gas chamber to some of the more bizarre, like hanging, firing squad, beheading, drowning, burned at the stake, and being drawn and quartered. The method isn't important as long as the outcome is death. One man, back in '01 decided that he wanted to be dropped from an airplane without a parachute. They planned it so that he would land in water no matter his glide. At terminal velocity, water is just as hard as the ground. He landed in a cove just off the Florida coast. It worked.

I had intentionally put off making any rash decisions. Damn you, Father Peter.

Anita left the School one hot September day. Even with the cooling on high, so the loudspeaker told us, we all sweated off liquids almost faster than we could replace them. I have to assume that Anita felt it long before I saw it, but her complexion turned from her healthy brown to greenish-gray. With the loss of color from her face, she began quaking.

"Are you all right, 'Nita?"

"Sure, I'm fine. Just cold and my belly hurts."

"Cold? You do look like you are shivering. Could it be time?"

"Naw. Not due for another month, girl. Ow!" Anita doubled over and vomited all over the floor.

"Ay-Dee!" Medics showed up before I finished my cry for help. The red-jerseyed men picked up Anita and put her on the stretcher. They whisked her away from the center of a small crowd that gathered. As far as I was concerned, Anita had ceased to exist. Did she live? Did she die? I didn't know. I bowed my head down and watched a single drop of water roll off my nose onto the floor and realized I didn't know if it was a tear or a bead of sweat. As a chill ran over my body, I felt even more lonely than normal in this room full of women.

I lasted almost a week without Anita there. The other girls ignored me as completely as they could and this just added to my depression and boredom. I existed in hell. I spent nearly every waking moment pacing the damned tiles. Eventually, when I thought my legs would fall off from so much walking, I heard something not meant specifically for my ears—Spouse's secretary had been taken for her time.

It crystallized action so spontaneous that I didn't even wait for Box to show up that evening, nor did I continue to stand in the medical queue that I had already invested an hour into. I marched right across the floor to the metal steps leading to Spouse's door. Unfortunately for me, there was an Ay-Dee at the base of the stairs.

"Excuse me," I said as politely as I could, attempting to worm my way around him. It wasn't easy as my belly already marked me firmly a Six and no longer small anymore.

"You're excused, but you aren't going up those stairs," he returned.

"And why not? I wish to speak to Spouse . . . er, I mean Ms. Fox."

"Not one single person who has ever climbed these steps to talk to her has been pleased with the outcome. I'm trying to save you trouble."

"I don't want to be saved, by you or anyone. I can take my own responsibility, sir. So if you would kindly step aside."

"I'll make you a deal," he said thoughtfully. "If you are still all fired up and ready to see Spouse in the morning, even though I might get in trouble for it, I will let you up—but not until tomorrow." I thought about calling him a name, but passed on the option as childish and immature—not to mention that I might not even get my audience the next morning.

I didn't even mention the incident to Box when he arrived. I remember that night because he brought me a postcard from Redondo Beach, showing the sea and a pair of brightly colored sailboats tacking across the water. I have to admit that I wasn't the best company. My mind was on other things that evening. I even lost to Box in a scholar's mate.

"W'at's wrong, Lizzy?"

"Huh? What? Oh, nothing. Let's play again."

"Ya sure?" That's all he managed to get out of me that night. Though I did manage to concentrate for a win. Thinking back, I find it amusing that our normal roles of pryer and pryee were reversed.

The next morning, as soon I'd showered, I made my way back to the stairs. The same Ay-Dee stood there. He got a frown on his face as I came up to him.

"I'm back. I want to see Ms. Fox," I said calmly.

"You really do have a bee in your blouse. But then it's your neck. Remember, proceed at your own risk, woman." I didn't forget. I counted on my audacity as part of my plan. In spite of that, it took every bit of my courage to march up those steps. I paused at the door, staring at it. I knew I had to make my move now or never—I knocked on the door and entered without waiting for Spouse to respond.

"Beth Zimmer reporting," I announced, my heart beating wildly, like that of a rabbit cornered by a coyote. I stood as ramrod straight as my back could manage. It wasn't all that straight, as my hand had found a permanent home by now in the middle of my back to help balance me a bit better. Ms. Fox looked at me with a very neutral look on her face.

"Ms. Zimmer, may I ask what the hell you are doing here? Or would that be a little too presumptuous of me?"

"Ma'am, you need a new secretary. I am it." Spouse leaned back in her chair, crossing her arms. Her face betrayed amusement.

"And what gave you the mettle to butt in here and announce that you are the answer to all my problems?"

"Because I am. I type seventy words a minute. I file, do double entry accounting, and mostly because I was bold enough to barge in on the ogre of the Wayward School." Spouse just looked at me for a moment or two, still with a smile on her face. Our eyes locked. An old Elton John tune in the background broke my concentration and I blinked first.

"Be here tomorrow morning at ten a.m. I want to have you checked out before I put you to work. That is all." She leaned forward to her work. "Don't let the door hit you on the way out, Elizabeth." I kept from cheering as I turned around and strode out. I had my first victory. It hadn't been without cost. Nausea gripped me and every muscle in my body remained knotted in anxiety. I did manage not to throw up, although I didn't eat a single bite of food the entire day. Sleep also chose to elude me. It felt like I had barely a short hour before the morning gong announced the day. I swear the acid in my stomach could've eaten through a battleship's hull before I made it to Spouse's office. She waited for me with a scowl on her face.

"Well, Beth. I hear that you have a brain in that pretty little head of yours." I decided not to dispute the pretty part nor argue the potential slur built into the comment. Thinking back on my other two meetings with her, I realized that this was a pattern with her. Any comment, no matter how flattering, always contained a barb, a sting, a cut. Put bluntly, her caustic nature matched my own.

"Yes, ma'am. I try to use it from time to time."

"I will take you on a trial basis of two weeks. Don't screw up, Ms. Zimmer. I don't suffer fools lightly."

"You obviously checked me out and want me. What's in it for me?" I don't know who used my mouth. My lips and tongue made the words, but they weren't coming from me. I didn't seem to have any control over it.

"Oh, you are a smart one. You get your own quarters here on the second floor, even if they are the size of a postage stamp. You will eat, when you have the time, out of my own personal kitchen. But I'll warn you, now, I'll work you almost constantly." No more tiles were in my future. I could see them shattering before my eyes. My nemesis was destroyed in my mind with one brief flare known as work.

"I'll do it as long as my quarters have carpet on the floor." Spouse gave me a quizzical look.

"What color? Pink or light blue?" she snapped sarcastically.

"Actually, green. Shag," I declared blandly, ignoring her gibe about maternity hues. "And none of that carpet tile, either," I added with as much venom as I could summon.

"It will be done," she said with another odd look. I offered my hand to her to seal the deal but she just waved me away. "Tomorrow morning at wake-up, be here."

I couldn't help thinking of Spouse as a slave driver, but the next two weeks were the most wonderful I could ever imagine at the time. Of course I was so occupied I didn't notice how happy I was. But then again a starving man would say that about the stalest crust of bread.

At wake-up the next morning, I put on my clothes and did my best imitation of the fat hippo fifty-meter dash up the stairs. I arrived to a storm already in violent full rage. "Elizabeth, I told you to be here at wake-up. It is now ten minutes after! If you want to work for me, you WILL be on time!" Spouse had a wonderful way of shrinking people down to midget size. She rarely cursed, but she could get more vinegar out of each of her normal words than most people manage with profanity. She had a gift. I felt the size of, oh, say an earthworm's navel lint. And since worms don't really have navels, that tells you how small I really felt.

True to her word, Spouse managed my life into another sort of ritual. I woke an hour earlier than anyone else to shower, dress and be in the office before even Ms. Fox, who seemed to live by the credo "Early to bed . . ." I can't ever remember getting to bed before anyone else, either. I worked easily seventy hours a week, sneaking in a bite of sandwich and sleep in between the demands Spouse put on me—even though she insisted I get at least seven hours sleep a night and eat properly. The workload kept my mind occupied trying to come up with a new and better way to do things to cut down on the mountain. Efficiency became my watchword. But unlike most nights before, when my head hit the pillow, I dropped asleep almost instantly.

Spouse's organizational skills could be summed up as "Dump everything into a basket. I'll find what I need later." Her previous personal assistants weren't much better. It took me the better part of my first month there to get her files arranged into something that didn't resemble the exit end of a paper shredder.

I did everything. I wrote letters, learning to take dictation in my copious spare time, cut checks, ordered supplies for both the office and the kitchens, conducted inventory (or at least part of it, I learned later), answered phones, and made calls. At one time I thought about phoning my parents, but I couldn't think of what to say.

"Mom, I'm really pregnant now. Round as a house." Or maybe, "Dad. How are you doing? Oh, me? I'm pushing a fifty-inch waistline and my nipples are sore." How about, "Oh, I'll be home as soon as I get this little bastard out of my belly." I just couldn't envision it. I had to wait until it was over and my unwanted baby was a thing of the past.

Just as we were calling it a day at the end of two weeks, Spouse summoned me to sit in the chair in front of her desk. "Ms. Zimmer, I must say that I had my doubts about you, but you've handled everything I've shoved at you. You're faster and more accurate than any other secretary I've ever had. I don't have to explain things to you more than once." I was about to bust with pride at this point, but I had forgotten about the barb. "This doesn't get you a brownie button. I will just expect more from you. You have also been neglecting your health and the health of the baby you carry. Don't ever skip another meal. Dismissed."

"Does that mean I'm fired?" Ms. Fox gave me a stern look before answering. She always seemed to think before she opened her mouth. This trait I consciously cultivated over the years.

"Not at all. Be here at wake-up as usual. Off with you."

Spouse clung to paranoia like a caffeine addict to her morning Starbucks. She read every item I put in front of her for her signature before putting pen to paper. I felt untrusted in most respects but over time I learned that Spouse trusted no one. I mean I hadn't noticed it before. Some things were so incredibly minor. For example, after watching her so closely over days and weeks, I realized she never let anyone behind her. Or at least an unusually small amount of times, and those few times she allowed it, her shoulders tensed and her concentration was nonexistent. Like I said, it took me weeks to discover because the signs didn't jump out at you. I think by the end of my probationary period I had some of her trust. She would occasionally allow my path to wander behind her. By the end of the first month she even forgot to tense when her back was to me.

It took about three weeks of her ranting before I managed to get things down baby-picture perfect. I realized that Ms. Fox wasn't quite the ogre everyone thought. Oh, don't get me wrong, she could teach a royal bitch many cruel tricks. She was fair even if fulfilling her desires approached the level of lifting Mount Shasta. Papers that waited for her signature had to be arranged just so or she would throw a raving snit, but at the same time if they were right she would thank me. Ms. Fox embodied a true manager's manager. She knew the old adage of honey catching more than vinegar, but at the same time she knew that discipline had to be maintained at all levels. She used both the carrot and the stick with equal alacrity.

She proudly displayed a carved wooden plaque behind her desk: "The way to make any organization perfect is to punish stupidity and reward intelligence! —General Theodore Calson." Spouse gave me the impression that she had met Teddy Calson, American hero of the China-Russo War of '25, and had been quite taken by his manner. I also got the idea that the word taken might have another meaning, but I kept that to myself, as I was the perfect secretary, even if that isn't the politically correct way of saying it.

Nowadays, people in my position have titles like business efficiency expert, or junior business partners. Sometime in the past they were administrative assistants. I revel in the ancient title "secretary." Something that some people forget is that secretary has the word secret within it. I kept more secrets than I can remember today. I will even keep some of them to the day I'm executed. Spouse learned over time to trust me with little tidbits of her life. Those rare glimpses into her soul I cherished more than anything. She won me over by her personality and strength of character. I hoped I might one day possess those qualities.

As drawn as I had been to Ms. Fox, I found that it had been mutual. Much later she confided in me that our rapport had been the quickest and easiest of any of her secretaries. It must have been some type of sympathetic bond. Just like any relationship, it took quite some doing to get off the ground, but our friendship spanned a gulf in me that had rarely ever been crossed to that point, and rarely since. I found myself, over time, trusting her. None of these bonds sprang up overnight or even in the few months that I had left to go on my pregnancy. But as it happened, I found that mutual-trust is a very scary term. Despite our rapport, Spouse never really lost her caustic edge.

While my relationship with Spouse had just begun, my relationships with almost everyone else were ending. Anita had been one of the Queens of the Roost. Anita had been one of three women who were, for want of a better term, in charge of the floor. Now that I'd thrown my lot in with Spouse, the few tenuous acquaintances I'd made among the other women of the School disappeared like the morning dew off the cactus flowers in the desert sun.

That loss wasn't necessarily a bad thing for me. I'd never been very social. What little acceptance I did get from my peers, I usually found unnerving and unsettling. When I accepted Spouse's offer everyone assumed that I became the eyes and ears of Her Highness. I became queen snitch overnight with all the baggage that went with it. In reality, I couldn't give a flying damn what the other girls did as long as they kept out of my way. They'd never really accepted me, so now I could return the favor.

No one would talk to me about anything. They would intentionally hide things from me, whether they were against the rules or not. Just like in the villages of medieval times, I almost became a leper among the clean, healthy community, shunned with a vengeance. I could see that these women would just as soon stone me as have me among them. Despite the turning away, the evil looks, the whispers behind my back, the taunts, and even the spiteful pranks, my time as Spouse's secretary with my first pregnancy was probably one of the happiest times of my life. As a result, I feared that the happiness I felt might burst like a soap bubble and I would be totally alone again.

Luckily, I then had my own quarters (with freshly installed, green, deep-pile carpeting) and rarely had to associate with anyone I didn't want to. Remember where I started all this? Yes, now I had obtained some power and it felt good. I could choose to have the people I wanted around me. I didn't think of it this way at the time, but that was how it was. Not only that but it got worse as time went on. "Power corrupts . . ." goes the quote, but perhaps a more appropriate one would be "Humans are the cruelest animal," by Nietzsche.

While I wouldn't call my clout at the time massive or even moderate, it was something. Because of my position I never, ever had to stand in lines. I always sauntered up to the front with as smug a look on my face as I could muster. Doctor, shower, food, bathroom . . . it didn't matter. I had the authority to get to the very front. Someone valued my time and not theirs. I made it a point to take my shower at the height of the morning to show people my new status so they could envy or maybe even fear me for a change. The look of hatred I continued to get amused me as I knew they could do nothing about it. It gave me an adrenaline rush. I made quite an ass out of myself for the first few weeks. The charge it gave me surpassed orgasmic.

On a different level, I was somewhat concerned but too busy to worry about the fact that Box did not visit me at all once I started to work for Spouse. After eighteen faithful weeks, two misses in a row were significant. I knew he was still around and well because I would catch a glimpse of him in Ms. Fox's office or on his way out but I never got a chance to speak to him. He did show up the Thursday after Spouse told me I was staying on.

"Ya like a game o'chess?" Box said from behind me. I was trying to choke down a few calories before trying to resurrect some life in the filing system my predecessor left me.

"And where have you been, you big oaf?" I replied, not turning around to face him. Box sat on the chair next to me so he could see my reactions.

"I'm sorry, Lizzy, but I couldna take t'chance I might get in yer way with Ms. Fox. Ya had t'prove yerself."

"Maybe so, but you could have given me the benefit of the doubt, you clod. Let's play." The files would wait for a couple of hours.

During the game I summoned up the nerve to question my friend on his apparent power in the School hierarchy. "Box, how is it that you can come and go? I mean you're not an Ay-Dee, but Spouse trusts you and calls on your opinion from time to time. Just where do you fit into the big picture? Check." I asked him as I pulled a sweet discovered check and threatened a rook with a pawn.

"I work fer Ms. Fox."

"C'mon. There is more to it than that. She trusts you—and she doesn't trust anyone else that I've seen."

"Well, Lizzy, ya see, she's m'mom, but I donna want t'rest of 'em t'know," he said in a whisper that I barely heard as he didn't lean toward me. I suppose he didn't want anyone to become suspicious that we were being secretive about anything.

"Your mom? But your last name is Boxner," I whispered back as low as I could.

"M'daddy's name. Mom took her own name back when Dad died." The subject faltered and we stopped talking for the night. I was sorry I had brought up the subject.

From then on, Box continued his weekly visits, regular as clockwork. He personified the model of the male-man. Come see me, I am "Man." 7:15 p.m. every Thursday he walked through the doorway into the main room like he had the Greenwich Mean Time ticking in his head.

Box remained an anomaly to me the entire time I knew him. I could look into his brown eyes, past the color of his skin, the nose that went awry, the acne scars on his face, and see a gentleman from times past. As an example, he never allowed us to be totally alone together. Even with my private quarters, he would not go there. He insisted that we were chaperoned at all times.

Part of this evolved from the petty jealousies that some of the other girls fostered toward the friendship Box and I shared. They were not allowed any visitors, and seemed to think that this rule should be applied to everyone. In hindsight they were probably right, but as Spouse's son, Box bent the rules as he saw fit. I mean I wasn't doing anything wrong if the powers that be approved, was I? Later I learned how much exercising the equality of the rules maintained order, but at the time I couldn't see the harm in our visiting, especially under the watchful eyes of the masses.

Most of it came because too many of the girls wanted Box for themselves, I mean as a boyfriend. They thought I staked a claim to the big black man. I had nothing further from my mind. Box was—well, Box. He was a good friend and one of the best listeners I'd ever met. But the thought of him as a romantic interest never really entered my mind. No matter how much I thought on it, it always came up with the same answer—not interested.

Even discounting my father's rhetoric, I guess I carried a predisposition against people with skin not of my color. I tried hard not to prejudge. Hell, my father would have beaten me for hours if he knew I was even TALKING to an oilstain. I always thought my father would have made a powerful Knight of the Ku Klux Klan. Oilstains, grease-spots, frostbacks, ragheads, jaundoids, slakes, kikes and any other non-white were the targets of Father's fury. He always claimed they tore down the Real America. He always grumbled that the government had outlawed the Neo-Nazi Party. "Now there was an organization that had something to give the world: a pure America."

I remember several times when he and the boys were watching the TriVid and he would comment on this actor or that. "Damned slake. Shoulda killed them all in WW II, Korea, Vietnam, an' China." Or another one of my favorites (I tried not to listen to it if I had the chance) was the infamous slave speech. "Boys, them damned grease-spots should still be our slaves. We're better than them. We brought them over and gave them a place to live and food to eat while their whole fucking continent was going to the shit-hole. Then they get that fucking Lincoln to fight his own kind to free 'em. Sneaky and dangerous, so you boys watch 'em close. Never give 'em a chance at your back and take one at theirs if you can. Remember they ain't real people, boys. Just like killin' a rabid dog." Even being around such hatred will rub off on a person.

But no, even if I could set aside my own learned prejudices, I had no romantic interests in Mr. Boxner. He had gentle hands, the few times I was able to get him to touch me. It seemed I had to threaten to scream "Rape" to get him to rub my neck or back—my muscles were so very sore most of the time. Abe Boxner (not Lincoln) had many good features and attributes, but my idea of romance involved a good massage after leaving this hellhole.

Very early in my tenure as Spouse's Girl Friday, I stumbled across something that made me literally stop my work. About five weeks after I took the job. The letter was in Spouse's handwritten scrawl, addressed to one Carl Draper, father of Caroline, that had me shaking. It bothered me so much that I couldn't go on with my work and needed to take another shower. Fortunately Box was due that evening because I had to speak with someone about it. I trusted him to give me the real story.

Dear Mr. Draper,

Our standard reimbursement for your pregnant daughter is as follows: five thousand upon your daughter's arrival at our facilities and an additional twenty thousand at the birth of her child. These are in American Dollars but can be converted into any form of currency at the rate of exchange on the date of payment.

To qualify for this amount, you must sign away all rights to her unborn child before she arrives. If the pregnant woman will be age 18 or older, at any time during the pregnancy, she must also sign away her rights to the fetus.

We will be 100% responsible for the unborn child from that point on. No information will be provided on the whereabouts of the fetus nor of the adopting parents.

Contact us if you should wish to take advantage of this program.

Signed,

Margaret Fox

I showed the finished letter to Box so he would know what I was talking about. He read it so fast that it seemed he had it memorized.

"Lizzy, I told ya t'at ya donna know not'in' 'bout what goes 'round here."

"But Box, this means that my father is being paid for the child in my belly."

"Yeah, and ya aren't. T'is a sad world."

"You can't buy a baby!"

"Not in t'law ya can't. But Lizzy, everyt'in' is fer sale. Everyt'in'."

"But children?"

"Are worse t'ings t'sell, Lizzy." I'd never seen Box so down. His face was as long as his legs. I didn't know what bothered him, that babies were being sold or me being upset by it. "What'n if t'at babe is born ta a family who donna wan' it? Ain't it better t'at 'nother family luvs it? Or maybe it might be better not bein' born at all?" That thought stopped me and made me think. I'm certain my family would rather that I had not been born. I barely got fed and clothed. Was I loved? My mind issued a Bronx cheer at the thought. Maybe my mother might have loved me, on a nice warm, fuzzy day, but not anyone else. Maybe Abe was right. Maybe had I been born and given to some other family, I might have turned out better. Maybe Wayward School was a blessing to these unwanted children after all. I was wrong in just about everything, but I didn't know this for many months.

I returned to my job with some trepidation, but it soon passed. Looking down at the mass of women still on the floor and the babies they all represented. I realized how much unlove it represented. Improving the lives of others I could live with. Better yet, it allowed me to get rid of the bastard in my belly and return home. Eventually I wanted a normal life—the Holy Grail of my existence. Had anyone asked me, I would have told him or her that I would give just about anything for that normal life—but ask me what it was or even is now I couldn't answer. At one time I looked for that blue house in the suburbs with the white picket fence and the neatly mowed yard. I didn't know that it was a myth. At least it was for me.

Days flew by. I found myself an Eight. I would soon justify my part in the baby-for-sale ring that I participated in. It didn't bother me. First because I had never been too terribly fond of children, and second because I wanted to be back to my old self again. Those thoughts never exactly surfaced as it was a time of happy days full of long hours and hard work.

Spouse trusted me and my work more and more, at least as much as she trusted anyone. She also mellowed and warmed to me slowly—ever so slowly, like an iceberg being melted by a 40-watt bulb. Sure, keep the bulb lit and it would eventually melt the whole huge block of ice, but it sure would take a freaking long time. That was our relationship in an ice cube.

That thaw provided me with tiny unimportant little tidbits of her life. She owned a pale cream-colored Siamese named Doris Helvan, after the famous siren of TriVid fame. She bowled every Sunday on a team named the "Fireballs." She shared that she had spent two years at the UCLA Business College under Professor Timothy Galdwhich. Through correspondence I found she also owned a four-bedroom home up near Lake Don Pedro. And although she shared that she was a widow and had one living child, I only learned things about her life outside the School in dibs and dabs. I'll note that she didn't offer that Box was her son. The trust only went so far, I guess.

Spouse also found it personally ironic that she owned a home in such a ritzy area, and with all her illegal activities that it should be so close to the largest penal system in the world, Yosemite Minimum Security Prison. She showed me pictures of it (her house, I mean), on a gentle slope just above a seasonal creek. Her home was an old wooden structure, unlike the fiberglass homes of today, charming in its own right, although the thought of using wood in construction gave me the shivers. Most wood-bearing trees remained firmly implanted on the endangered species list, especially oak and redwood. Pine still had a firm hold on the north, but not for building. To cut down a tree for a house seemed—I don't know—evil. Maybe that's the pot calling the kettle black, but that's my opinion.

Her pictures showed a dark brown, split-level home on a field of wild, natural grass the color of straw. Vegetation wasn't very plentiful as the soil in the entire area consisted of mostly crushed shale, she explained. Some tough bushes or a ubiquitous form of wild, tall grass managed a meager existence. But that had never stopped people before. Most of the nearby homes, she told me, had trucked in tons of topsoil just to give a place to plant other flora. Margaret said that she preferred it the natural way.

She continued showing me pictures of her home. One picture showed huge living-room windows and a three-car garage. Inside the garage I could see a green antique BMW, a bright-red Collector's Edition Z28 and a new model Ford Thunderbird. I tried not to drool. The Thunderbird, in any model year, had always been my favorite car even after the Toyota-Mazda RX11 came out. I understood they had to open a second manufacturing line for the RX11 because they were so popular. I had to admit to jealousy.

Margaret was a cat mother and Doris her second largest source of pride. Doris won medals for best of breed in several cat shows. Margaret even brought Doris into the office a few times. A general unease came over me as the cream- and-smoke-colored cat weaved around my legs. I've never had the opportunity to learn to be a cat person. My family didn't have any pets, other than the gerbil that my brothers regularly tormented with near-starvation and dehydration.

Fortunately, Doris shared manners with the most mellow of felines. It loved people, unlike most of its breed. Doris managed to teach me how it liked to be rubbed and stroked, by sheer persistence. I never knew a cat could be so pushy. Doris stropped my legs repeatedly until I paid it some attention. Once she had me as her pet slave, she wouldn't let me alone after that.

Margaret showed me how to hold Doris in my arms like a little baby, her paws sticking up in the air. Doris purred, and with her eyes firmly closed let me pet her belly. After that I ended up with another growth attached to my body. Doris wouldn't leave and kept coming back to demand attention at the most inopportune times. It was nice to have something so warm and cuddly against me. Doris became something of a regular fixture from then on. You could always find her sleeping on the papers you needed to work on, on the top of the back of my, or should I say, HER chair, or on the computer keyboard.

Doris gave me a glimpse of what normal people share in happiness. I was hooked.

October 25, 2050

The skin is still red and puckered, but the prison Doc says that the stitches should come out later today. I think they should use the biodegradable ones so they won't have to have the violent criminals out of their cells so often. I mean they did do that on my internal stitches, but the ones on the outside are normal surgical silk. Oh, what the hell. I don't know much about real medicine. The doc, an old gray-haired fart that reminds me of a dour Einstein, said that the intestines seem to have closed up well enough.

Part of me wonders why they are bothering. I'm going to be dead in a week anyway, so why all the fuss. Poor way to run a business, is my opinion. I guess it just doesn't need to make sense. First, they pay to put me back together and then they pay to pull me apart. If I ran my business that way, I'd have been bankrupt within a week, for all the good the money did me.

The Judicial Reform Act also forced a salary cap to lawyer's fees. It sounded more like football than legal justice. Hiring your own lawyer to represent you in court is now no longer a viable option. They all work for a fixed pay scale. So most of the best legal minds went elsewhere. You guessed it. They went into politics.

I realize I have been writing for how long? Hold on. Let me check. Gads, has it only been ten days? Well, I've been writing for ten days and I haven't really said word one about my pregnancy. I mean what I felt, how it was. "Every true confession story from a woman has to include her symptoms and the like."—Edna Lewis. For those of you who somehow have fallen into a hole in the last few years, Edna is the woman who killed over twenty-two hundred people on eighteen different airline flights with homemade bombs over a six-year period. Her reason? She wanted to prove that it could be done. She is my cellblock mate. The schedule has her slated for lethal injection in just three days.

Edna is such a sweetheart that if you just look at her you can't believe that she's a deranged psychopath. At thirty, she looks like the seventeen-year-old girl you'd like your son to take to the prom. To say she has long blond hair and a figure that won't quit would probably be understating her physical attributes. She also, obviously, has a brain to have snookered all of FAA and Homeland Security's regulations over twelve years and eighteen fatal flights. It might be a sick and twisted brain, but she has one.

In the end, though, Edna confessed to all eighteen, and three others that she said didn't work. She showed the authorities how it was done and even asked to be put to death so that no one else would get her secrets. She says that she didn't do it just for kicks, but rather to prove that airport security is a joke. She claims that she has proof that it will, in the end, save lives. I wonder if that is the same sort of rationalization that I use.

There are two other cells in our block, but only one occupied. It holds an older Caucasian teacher who, after knocking out her first-graders with sleeping pills in their milk, poured gasoline over thirty-three unconscious children and set them ablaze. Only one lived and he probably wishes that he hadn't. Fortunately for Edna and me, Kathy doesn't say much. About the only thing she does is drool and mumble from time to time. I wonder how she managed to get a teacher's license. Well, it doesn't matter now. Four days until her plug gets pulled.

Back to my true-confession story.

My symptoms, for the most part, could be copied out of any maternity book as typical. I endured nausea, bathroom troubles (both ends), heartburn, leg cramps, and backaches. Multiply my symptoms by the twelve hundred girls in the overcrowded living conditions at the School and you could see, hear and often smell the results at any moment of the day.

In the beginning, the nausea plagued me the worst. Typical morning sickness started back before I even left home. At the School, the aroma of too many people in too small a space exacerbated my tumble tummy. Ben Gay, vomit, urine and feces (from not quite making the bathroom in time), coconut oil, sweat, tears, and overripe bananas were just some of the lovely joyful odors we shared with one another.

Back at home, as with most girls, nausea and very tender breasts tipped me that something wasn't quite right. The sore nipples twigged me first. Just putting on my bra when dressing felt like someone rubbed them with very rough sandpaper. But back then, soothing sore nipples had to wait. I found myself running for the bathroom right after waking and it had nothing to do with a full bladder.

I double-checked it with a home pregnancy test I got from a rather progressive teacher at school. I am intentionally leaving her name out of this because of the trouble she could get in/could have gotten in. She could have not only lost her job for that act of kindness but also been arrested. I now silently thank her and hope her life is so much better than mine turned out. May there be more like her and fewer like me.

I think of all the symptoms, though, I hated the leg cramps the most. A significant number of the girls got them, but usually not until they were at least a solid Five. I started getting them as an early Three. Oh, but talk about praying to whatever power you believe in—I could be awakened from a sound sleep by my thigh or calves tying up into what felt like hang-man's knots. The first time this happened I screamed out in agony at about three in the morning. Not a single woman stayed asleep, I shrieked so loudly. Even the Ay-Dees on watch were awakened (no small feat, that). It took three people on each leg to stretch them out. I couldn't do it myself. I'd never had muscle cramps before so it offered a novel, if undesirable sensation. Anita and another acquaintance named Susan rubbed my legs down until they loosened enough I could go back to sleep. Not a pleasant experience, but one that kept repeating itself. While I never learned to live with it, I did learn not to wake the neighbors with mind-bending shrieks. But . . . "OW!"

If I remember, the cramps showed a potassium deficiency. Bananas were supposed to help, but no matter how many of the mushy, bland things I ate, no matter how many potassium supplements I took, I still got the freaking cramps. I was by far the worst in this respect in the entire School population. I don't particularly recommend it as a distinction.

But something I said earlier about Anita and Susan brings up a very good point. We helped one another at the School. Not just friends, but everyone. I've talked about the petty rivalries, the jealousies, and the mean women, but on the whole, you could count on just about anyone to help you. You never were in the main room without seeing someone rubbing someone else's back, neck or legs. Another normal sight was a woman rubbing baby oil into another's skin to help prevent stretch marks. Oh, times happened when things went quite a bit farther than just some mutual comfort—with a little finger diddle there or a tongue tickle there, but as the exception rather than the rule. Normally, it was just women helping each other with the aches and pains of pregnancy.

You could be standing in line, not really knowing either of the women next to you, and just by asking, one of them would rub the knots out of your neck. It seemed like sisters in misery. Usually you would stand in line next to your friends anyway, but more than once, before becoming Spouse's secretary, a complete stranger kept me out of screaming agony with a rubdown.

Anita, second only to Box, had the most wonderful hands: short, stubby fingers and all. Unlike most of the women she had a very firm touch, which just chased away the tension in my muscles. I came to rely on Anita as a masseuse. Most of the women were too soft and—well—sissy. I guess I'm too butch. I wanted to be feminine but life just kept getting in the way of that. Like my parents, Jimmy, the School and even the bastard in my belly. I never really learned how to be a proper feminine girl.

Back to my original point. Most of the girls just rubbed too softly for my tastes. The tightness in my back and neck took strength to knead away. I could barely feel the fingers of most of the other girls. They must have been afraid of breaking something. So Anita, the brute, was my designated rubber of choice.

We would while away a late evening just taking turns kneading each other with moisturizing lotion and clucking over each other's stretch marks. Yes, I got those, too. Only about forty million of them. Still have them if I lift my prison-issue orange T-shirt. If I had a g'zillion, then Anita's body seemed composed of them. On those evenings, seeing what we could of the stars through the badly scratched Plexiglas windows forty feet above our heads, I would wheedle out of Anita what few details I had of her life.

"Beth, why do you think we're here?" Anita said one late evening, lying on her back as I spread oil into her bare belly. For a change, the entire room seemed muted and the sound level burbled relatively low. The room never fell totally silent, even in the dead of night, but that night there seemed to be a blanket on everyone's mood.

"Here-here or just here."

"Both, really. My man keeps me pregnant and sure it makes us loads o'money, but I never see him." I puzzled over the money part, as I had not yet learned the financial benefits of the School, but didn't say anything about it.

I had forgotten that particular conversation until this very moment. Wow. The signs were all there; I guess I just didn't put them all together. Anyway, I kept soothing the lotion in as I responded.

"Well, if you are asking for marital advice, you've come to the wrong line, 'Nita. Try one of the others. The closest I've even had to a relationship was being pinned to the ground and raped. Try a marriage counselor."

"Ha!" she exclaimed, almost breaking the mood. "Never messed with those half-baked shrinks. Who needs 'em. If two people can't make it work, how can three? I mean I know my man cheats on me. I probably would too, if I could get a real man in here. But when I'm out he is good to me. He don't let me know about them other girls. It seems to work for both of us so I got no beef there." She was quiet for almost a minute. "I mean why am I here? What am I supposed to do? Am I doin' the right thing?"

"Ouch, Anita. Now you're talking religion. You think I got the answers to that one? Definitely next queue, girl."

"Not so rough," she said, wiggling one of her oversized thighs out of my tightening grip. "My mama used to take me to church when I was a young'n, but I ain't been in a heap of years. I remember thinking that God was this jolly ole skinny black man with short white hair and little gold horn-rimmed glasses. Kinda like my favorite uncle, Jon Bemen. I think I'd like a God like that.

"Really, though, what do you believe? I ain't believed in so long—" Now it was my turn to be quiet. When I was younger, just like Anita, my mother dragged me to Sunday school. I remember it well. Blessed Mary's covered most of the block on Third Street right next to the old movie theater, the one that burned down after everyone started going to Holovision. I remembered the Fridays of fish; rubbing burned matches on my forehead once a year; Christmas and Easter Mass; and our priest, Father Benjamin Foster (a jovial, younger man with hair the color of grenadine), but I couldn't remember a single piece of anything that I could call faith or belief.

"I'm not sure, 'Nita. God, if there is such a person, has never looked very kindly upon me. I don't know that I really owe him the honor of believing. But I do think we should do the best that we can and hope that it's the right thing."

"Church seems like a rather rotten way o' instilling virtue in people, don't it."

"Yeah, it does. Now get up off that big black ass of yours. It's my turn."

Anita and I talked about almost as many things as Box and I managed. Of course our discussions were never were far away from movies. She did have a fantasy about Denzel Washington, Jr. She had seen every one of his movies at least a dozen times and had most of the dialogue memorized. Box told me a bit about DWJ (as she called him) that I just had to pass on. The Beverly Hills Police arrested Mr. Washington for lewd acts with a prostitute in a public park. Anita shook her head slowly from side-to-side and looked a bit sad. "Tsk, tsk." Then she brightened up a bit and informed me, "He just needs a real woman, like me."

"Only if I don't get to him first."

"Oh, but I'm more a woman than you are, girl," she said patting her now baby-bulging belly. We liked playing that game. We both knew it was just a game. Neither of us would get the chance to meet Mr. Washington, but we liked to tease one another.

I'd have loved to give heartburn the heave-ho. Of course I could say that about any number of pregnancy woes. Luckily, that didn't come on until I was about a Six but when it did, it came on with a vengeance. Basically, I traded my nausea for heartburn. I'm not sure it was a good trade.

Eating always provided an experience at the School. First of all, our nutrition came in the guise of 32 ozs. of milk, two eggs, three veggie servings, four grains, two protein servings, two vitamin C sources, at least two fruit, half a potato, bright red iron pill, chlorophyll pill, a maternity multivitamin and enough water to float a boat. Now I've told you probably more than you wanted to know. The School made sure that we got everything we needed and then some. I have to admit that they did a darned good job of varying the meals and menus; but when you have to eat that much food every day, it made for some wonderful digestive problems.

When I became a Five I noticed that they began adding an antacid to my tray as standard fare. I didn't understand it right away. I learned. I don't think there is anyone out there who has not experienced the loving joy of heartburn so I won't spend any more time on it. It was just another precious gift from my bastard child.

Like I said before, most of what I experienced was nothing different from any other woman during pregnancy. It was the unusual things that make any pregnancy stand out as unique. Two stand out like no others.

The first was something as simple as it was painful and irritating—hives. Some people get hives as an allergic reaction, but not me. I got them when I got too warm. Throw a blanket on me as I slept, anytime in the last five months of my pregnancies, and I would be covered in hives for days. Even my panties would cause them if the day was too hot. The day the air conditioning went out prompted a week of hair-pulling, screaming hell for me.

Oh, my gawd did they itch. With no willpower, I scratched. I rubbed. I raked. I scratched so hard that I bled. Calamine lotion didn't touch it. Benedryl didn't even come close. Nothing the doctors came up with would keep me from being in agony. Wouldn't you know it, Box came to my rescue. Was it some new and powerful drug? Nope. He brought in mud. There wasn't anything special about it. No medical properties, just black loam moistened with water. Box all but had to kick the idea into the doctors' heads. They laughed at him but they were running out of treatment options. Spouse OK'd it so they went for broke, knowing all the while it wouldn't work.

They laid out a large sheet of plastic and covered me with this black oozing stuff, even between my toes. I giggled at the thought, but I stopped laughing and scratching as soon as the cool gooey muck touched my skin. Someone had turned on the "No Itching" sign. I wallowed in heaven as I realized then how good it was to not feel something. The hives went away within an hour.

From that point on, the doctors kept a big bag of dirt around, just for me. I never again needed a full immersion mud-bath. If I just locally troweled mud onto my trouble-spots, the hives magically disappeared. Anita teased me mercilessly about it, though. I knew it was all in fun but we couldn't help but giggle.

"Girl, you are the only woman I know that needs a landscaping architect." Or how about, "I know those gardeners are cute, girl, but isn't that a bit much?" I also liked, "Planting time again?" She also got me with, "If a man made love to you, would he be a brick layer?" The variations were endless. "I thought I was older than dirt." "Your mother never teach you beyond the mud-pie stage?" 'Nita even took to calling me her "dirty, filthy tramp." Like I said, it was all in fun. It still gives me a smile.

The other unusual symptom by far made the rest seem normal. It first manifested one night that it poured rain. None of us were sleeping all that well because the roof leaked and so provided such a perfectly acoustical media that it sounded like we were in a drum. I woke up at four in the morning with this massive craving to eat a bar of soap. I know what you are thinking: Why in my right mind would I even consider such a thing? You would be quite right. I wasn't sane at that moment, which goes to prove that the body (especially a pregnant body) can affect the mind. I wanted . . . nay, I needed, that creamy texture and bitingly sour taste.

I even went so far as to get up and open my foot locker to dig out my half-used bar of Ivory. I guess it wouldn't have hurt me any, 99 and 44/100 percent pure and all. I mean, the thought of it now is just revolting, but you weren't there. The texture alone appealed to me so much that I almost couldn't resist, kinda like a chocolate bar right out of the refrigerator. I probably would have taken a big bite had not an Ay-Dee come to see why I was out of bed.

"Excuse me?" she asked, swinging her baton in a gentle arc, not menacingly, but making sure I took heed. The Ay-Dee was Caroline. She was one of the only Ay-Dees who I could call a real person. She knew what it was like to be pregnant and alone. She had raised a little girl all by herself, so she knew.

"Just wanted a bite before I doze back off."

"Soap? What brand?" She knew, but I hadn't quite caught on

yet. Hey, it was four thirty in the morning.

"Ivory, of course."

"I was always a Caress girl myself."

"I think that would be a bit spicy."

"Girl, are you even listening to yourself?"

"Huh?" I was always one for a snappy comeback line.

"You are debating the relative tastes of soap bars. Don't you find this a bit odd?"

"The only thing odd about it is that it's four thirty in the morning. I'd already be back to sleep if you hadn't interrupted."

"You aren't quite awake and I'm losing an argument to a sixteen-year-old." She paused for a moment and then said, "Not that I don't lose regularly to my daughter, but this is important. I think it's time to see the doc."

"I don't want to see the doc," I said, raising my voice. Until now we had managed to keep it low enough that the sound of the rain drowned us out past about three feet, but she'd made me angry. I'd darn well have a soap snack if I wanted, and no Ay-Dee was going to tell me different. A flash of lightning lit up the sky and the room around me. As much of a cliché as it was, that moment made me realize just what I was saying. I dropped the bar of Ivory like it was going to bite me. "Yuck!" I exclaimed as it hit the floor with a dull thud, not bouncing at all. Caroline just looked at me. "I'm sorry," I said as contritely as I could manage. "Maybe I'd better see the doc."

A thrown pillow caught me across the face. "Yeah, see the doc and shut up about it," came the comments of one of the nearby girls. It proved to be just a minor vitamin deficiency. I guess my body chews up something when it's pregnant. It has happened every pregnancy. Now at least I know that feeling and what to do about it. Each time I still think that Caress would be too spicy.

Oh, I had other more normal cravings. Ice cream. I remember times when I would have killed for a bowl of even vanilla, but I prefer mint-chocolate chip. Late one night as a Five, I was jostled from a deep sleep. In the minimal light left on at night, I awoke to find Anita kneeling next to my bunk with her index finger across her lips indicating silence. She then motioned for me to follow. I had no idea where we were going. Anita led me silently and quietly passed rows of sleeping women. The low buzz of many snoring individuals covered any little noises we made. One girl, about a Six, was just getting back from the bathroom, walking right by me with her eyes almost closed. She obviously just wanted to get back to sleep and really didn't even see me.

The Ay-Dees also sawed logs. As usual they leaned up against the steel support girders. We walked boldly right by them. None even twitched. We finally made it to the kitchen door. Anita produced a key to open the locked door, motioning me inside.

"What is this all about?" I hissed at her in a whisper as I passed her.

"Shhh!" She closed and locked the door behind us and stood up to her full height. "It's about ice cream. Want some?"

"You're kidding, right?"

"Nope . . . I bribed one of the caterers. He told me that there was nearly a full five-gallon tub of it in the freezer."

"What flavor?"

"I didn't ask. I just gave him a fifty and took the damned key. Ever been in here? Know where the freezer even is?"

"Nope. They keep that door locked tighter than a doxy's corset." Stainless steel pots, pans, worktables, whisks, spoons arranged neatly over every surface. Even in the dim illumination of the tiny nightlights they gleamed and shined so brightly that it seemed like I had fallen into some late night horror movie. I waited for silver-clad, ray-gun-toting aliens to come out at any moment. Fortunately, the feeling disappeared as soon as we found the walk-in freezer. We opened another lock (Boy, but they didn't trust us!) and went inside. Ever been in a freezer with almost nothing on? Trust me, those gowns we wore rated almost nothing! In fifteen seconds my thighs had goose bumps the size of gopher mounds and my nipples stuck out like light-switches.

Worse, there was no ice cream. There was a mostly empty tub of rainbow sherbet. We double-checked before carting the sherbet out into what had to be the caterer's breakroom, giggling at our misfortune.

"I'm going to hang that guy up by his family jewels!" Anita managed to get out between giggles. We then realized another problem.

"Uh, Anita . . . I don't want to seem ungrateful, but how are we going to eat this stuff? I don't see any spoons lying around," I said, turning red and laughing even more. Ever been in a mood where you laughed at everything? Even rabies or the black plague would seem like the punchline to some lengthy joke. Anita made a motion of scooping up sherbet in her hands and putting it to her mouth. We both broke up in hushed laughter, our hands covering our mouths to stifle the noise as best as possible.

"Shhh!" Giggle. "Shhh." Hahahah. "Someone will hear, now shush!" Chortle. The more we tried to keep each other quiet, the worse it got. Once I managed to silence the worst of my snickers, I went into the kitchen. There I found a large stirring spoon and a ladle and brought them back.

Do you have any concept how difficult it is to spoon up sherbet and eat it out of a ladle while someone is trying to spoon out of the same tub as you? Mind you, all this while trying not to laugh your head off? I will tell you that if you wish to try, do not wear anything that will stain.

The giggles slowly wound down while we savored each mouthful. Not as good as ice cream, but an almost acceptable substitute. By the time we had eaten and cleaned up our mess our attack of the giggles dissipated. When we sneaked out of the kitchen and back to our bunks, I realized that every exposed part of my body above my waist was covered in sticky. I decided that I couldn't do anything without a shower and a change of clothes. I got almost no sleep that night, but it was worth every dozing moment during school the next day. I had even sated that ice cream craving. I remember thinking that it would be perfect if I could have only gotten a stack of barbecue pork ribs delivered to my cot.

Oh, fuck! I almost forgot about the mood swings. I think they coined the phrase "Psycho bitch from hell" just for me when I'm pregnant. I mean one minute I can be as warm and squirmy as a newborn puppy, the next I'm scratching your eyes out for mispronouncing ziti. Then I go into a crying fit that lasts three days. What the hell is it? Oh, I've heard all the medical terminology and read all the books, but I hate not being in control. It depressed me and that led to more tiles. I knew it wasn't me, but I couldn't help thinking that if I tried just a little bit harder I would be able to beat it. I never could—not even once. My emotions seemed to have a mind of their own. Am I nothing more than a collection of chemical reactions?

One thing I do want to spend a bit of time on is how I felt about the bastard in my belly. Most of the time I didn't. I treated the entire experience more like a prolonged medical problem than anything to do with reproduction. But later, when it started moving, I couldn't wish it away anymore. I couldn't ignore it. It was—I can't even today quite put into words the total revulsion I felt. I know I'm not supposed to feel that way about a child I'm bearing.

Imagine, if you can possibly, that an insect, say a two-foot-long, horror-picture-sized digger wasp, implanted a larva under your skin and you couldn't remove it. It grows within you, feeding off your blood, your body, squirming around to get the next best bite, ready to burst forth into God only knows what. All of this moving, twitching, and unhealthy jiggling inside me made my skin crawl. I never had the slightest bit of maternal interest in what was within me. Never did I feel like I even wanted to see what Jimmy's seed had produced. But going back, honestly, the larva analogy isn't fair to either the wasp or the child.

One, the digger wasp puts an egg on the surface of its prey and the larva, when it hatches, devours the entire food source before emerging from its cell. Jimmy firmly forced his larva within me with a vengeance. Two, the digger wasp larva is a hunter. The fetus that lives off my body is a true parasite. Merriam Webster defines a parasite: n 1) an organism living in an intimate association of two or more kinds: esp: one in which it benefits from a host which it usually injures 2) something that resembles a biological parasite in dependence on something (one) else for existence or support without making a useful or adequate return.

That was the fetus in my belly. Rather than the wasp, maybe a more appropriate comparison would be a tapeworm or ringworm (so much better). They are at least true parasites. Does this come close to conveying my feeling for the thing I carried within me? Sometimes during that first pregnancy I just wanted a knife to cut it out of myself.

It is almost lights out. Overall, my first pregnancy tortured me because I didn't know what to do or what to think. I was in a place I wasn't comfortable in and all the while wondering what would happen to me. I think if I had one overall comment about my first pregnancy, I would have to say that between the hormonal changes and the aches and pains in my body, I was usually not quite in agony.

October 25, 2050

I'm due for a court appearance in a few hours, so forgive me if I cut off in the middle. While not my last appeal, it's darned close. I've never been hopeful about Lawyer Kafka's chances at getting my sentence overturned, but I'd be willing to sit jaded in court for day after day if it weren't for those damned TriVid lights. Even the boredom of court couldn't touch the dullness of my first time at the School. But by the end of the day under those miniature suns, I'm drenched in sweat. I look and feel like I've just run three marathons.

I guess the highlight of my day was watching the Minnesota Bears wale the tar out of the Washington Redskins. The Packers play tomorrow night against the Cowboys in Dallas. I'm torn. I've always liked Dallas, but the Bears haven't won a division title in my lifetime, and I'm hopeful. Unfortunately, I doubt that I will know who wins the title. It depends on whether or not you believe in an afterlife. I've already said it, but I'm just not sure. I want to believe, especially considering my eminent demise, but I can't summon anything that will logically give me comfort. Instead, I lie awake at night wondering what will happen.

One of the Alcatraz matrons, Peggy, is a good gal. Ugly as an '04 Mustang, but a great gal. I wonder if she would look any better if she got her teeth replaced, put on a dress and some makeup. Naw, probably not. I asked her if she could get me some sleeping pills. Mind you, I've no interest in advancing the day of my departure. Like I said, I've just been having trouble falling off at night. At first Peg was a bit skeptical. She did bring them but one at a time. She would then stand there, making sure that I took it and swallowed.

All I have to say is, "Thank goodness for Peggy and the legalization of drugs." I've been able to get some sleep. When rested, I can put a cheery face on and feel optimistic. Tired, I feel nothing but depression.

Even though I've offered to pay Peggy handsomely (it's

amazing the flexibility with these new Cuban banks), she won't touch my money. She tells me that they didn't cost her much and that I've done her more good than I could possibly know. When I pressed for more information it turns out someone close to her had a transplant from the School. I left it at that. Her pride would not allow her to take my money. I didn't force the issue. She didn't have to bring those eight-hour packages of chemical sleep. The truth of the matter is that she could get into some serious trouble for it. Practically, however, matrons have been smuggling since prisons were first invented. Besides, I have one other possible service I'd like to get Peggy to perform for me—one that is much more important than sleeping.

Anyway, back to my tale of sin and corruption. As I turned Eight, I became more and more into the business end of the School. I had always been good at accounting so I took to doing the books. To my amazement (not) most of the transactions were in cash. Both total revenues and expenses of the business managed to surprise me by their magnitude. The amounts of money that nominally went through the hands of the School reminded me of a large multinational. I say nominally as I never saw a dime but rather huge numbers in a green ledger book. They had very little real meaning to me except what I had seen on some of the TriVid shows ("I want a million dollars or I'll kill your little girl"). Back then, I didn't know how one kept that kind of money or, for that matter, where. I certainly never saw Spouse carrying the kind of money represented by those numbers with all the trailing zeros.

The cost of keeping up the girls in clothes, food, medical attention, and schooling was both larger and smaller than I had thought. It exceeded any amount of money I had ever considered, but then I had never really given it any thought. When I did consider it, I realized that it was smaller than I would have expected. Economies of scale really kicked in when you were providing for over a thousand people.

Consider as a fairly typical dinner: six hundred cans of peaches, three hundred pounds of broccoli, two hundred pounds of cod, one hundred heads of lettuce, eighty-five pounds of carrots, four hundred pounds of potatoes, eighty gallons of milk, forty gallons of orange juice, one hundred twenty loaves of bread, and nine gross iron pills and multivitamins. All of that for just one evening meal! Similarly, breakfast used up sixty gallons of milk, ten cases of pancake mix, two hundred dozen eggs, three hundred pounds of bacon, fifty gallons of orange juice, thirty gallons of grapefruit juice, four hundred cantaloupes, and another one hundred twenty loaves of bread. I won't even touch lunch. You can see how quickly the School went through rations.

When you are buying six thousand dozen eggs (that's seventy-two thousand eggs for those without a calculator handy) every month, you can get them down to a very, very reasonable price. So on the whole, the price per month per person boiled down to about two hundred dollars. Now that didn't cover all the expenses by a long-shot. Laundry, medical attention, electric, gas and water, Ay-Dees, the plumber, and the list went on and on.

Worse, if you could call it that, none of this could be kept a secret. It took trucks to deliver the food and a kitchen staff to prepare it; a laundry service for both bed linen and those ugly white grandma-gowns; electric, gas and water services; a plumber to keep our drains running; and a great number of other normal businessmen roaming around, inside and out of a highly illegal operation. I didn't know quite how illegal, but selling babies isn't thought of very well in any society, except maybe some of the oriental social systems—and we weren't even selling babies, but rather something far worse. Bottom line, we had a number of people being paid off, including the pair of cops I mentioned before.

I'd like to take just a moment to interject. Some might ask why didn't we use these highly bored girls to prepare the food and work the laundry? It would give them something to do and alleviate the tedium of the School and increase the bottom line by lowering expenses. Put bluntly, it wouldn't work. Had I never been pregnant myself, I might have asked the same question. Even pregnant I considered posing it to Spouse at one time, until the primary answer dawned on me—like a heavyweight boxer hitting me in the stomach. I dare you to try and get a typical Three to make supper for herself let alone for over a thousand. The smells would have provoked some interesting reactions, not the least of which would be losing whatever she had to eat the meal before.

The same went for the laundry, which harbored a great number of nasty and odd smells. I mean we can't have some dim bulb puking into sixty gallons of Boston clam chowder or over ten gross clean sheets. It made sense, for both real and financial reasons, to buy these services. The other thought didn't really come to me until later. Women can do a great amount of work while pregnant with little chance of losing their baby through a miscarriage—but there are small percentages of women who can't do much of anything without losing their fetus. We only made money if we delivered a baby. A miscarriage cut into the profits. No, we wouldn't have these women lifting and toting.

Anyway, back to the number crunching. When you summed the total cost and divided it by the average number of girls, the costs were about a thousand dollars a month for each girl, or two and a half million dollars a month for all the girls. When you factored in bribes, payments to the clients themselves, and medical costs charged to the product, not the clients, our costs hovered near thirteen million dollars a month. If you assume that we had one hundred thirty girls delivering each month, that means each baby cost the business around a hundred thousand dollars!

As incredible as that seems, the income side of it was even more astounding. The data I saw then didn't label the source of the money. It always showed as several mysterious lump sums for each child. By then I'd figured out not to ask any questions. If I just did as much as I could, everyone (namely Spouse) was happy. The average revenue for each child was approximately five hundred thousand dollars!

Only a rich family could afford that, so it meant that our babies went to good, loving homes. Even then I thought that was too high a sum for a child; I didn't see the whole picture.

Back to the calculations: each baby netted four hundred thousand in profit to the business or over fifty million a month. I finally saw why the School found it worthwhile to break the laws so egregiously.

I'm not sure exactly where the profits went, but I wired money to at least six different numbered Cuban accounts. The Swiss had become too nosy to make reliable money brokers. If we assume an even split, the take of each of these principal accounts amounted to a bit over eight million dollars a month, or nearly a hundred million a year per person! I had never imagined the School generated such a profit. Someone made a fortune off us girls.

Well, it did make for some interesting late night thoughts. I never brought up what I had learned to anyone, not even Spouse. I had a creeping suspicion that maybe remembering things of this nature didn't promote a long life. You know the old adage, "Dead men tell no tales." I think that quote can easily be applied to women-folk as well. Or maybe the powers-that-be assumed a normal person saw only large numbers in separate ledgers. Or maybe I guess that everyone assumed that a women's natural curiosity took a vacation while pregnant. Bottom line, I kept my own counsel.

October 27, 2050

The tour groups are the lowest part of any week. They bring them in and show them the old Alcatraz. For the "tourons" they keep some parts of The Rock in its original state and then they're shown the new shiny inescapable version with Kevlar impregnated ceramic cells. As an added bonus they get to look in at the most heinous female criminals of any jail in the world.

Even worse, I don't think that there is anyone who hasn't seen my trial coverage. I mean who could have missed it? The governor ensured it showed on every TriVid set in the country and was spoken on the lips of every group of people who met each other. I made OJ Simpson look like a figure cloaked in obscurity. Every Saturday at least three tours came through as the prison guards give them the standard spiel in a tired voice. "And here in cell 14-D, the D meaning death row, you will see the infamous Elizabeth 'Baby Butcher' Zimmer, arrested for over five thousand counts of—" It is always the same. I wonder what they expect to see? The mothers pull their children close to them, as protective as a lioness guarding her cubs. The childless women all touch their own bellies and shiver in horror.

The men at the same time are the least and most honest. They look at me intently with a certain sexual appetite. I know I look much better now than I did as a child or during my first pregnancies. I've slimmed down and, with a large chunk of money in reconstructive surgery, I now look, if I do say so myself, somewhat appealing—even if the orange jumpsuits they give me to wear don't do anything for my figure. I learned and took my cue from all the girls from my youth and got pretty. It's amazing where a bit of money will get you. I wanted to be the one picking the teams and I got it, even if it was for just a short while.

Yes, I draw quite a crowd here. I can see them trying to get into my head. Wondering what could have possessed me. I wish they could see the truth. My life's role has been Fate's archery target.

Here are more of the "slings and arrows of outrageous fortune,"
only I was not quite as susceptible to melancholy as poor Hamlet,
nor, it seems, as cunning. An interesting parallel, Hamlet's life and
my own.

Ten days after I turned into an Eight, it was my standard
time to visit the on-staff physician. I went into the infirmary,
cutting to the head of the line as always. I moved more and more
like a pregnant woman—a bloated, waddling figure. I never got
anywhere quickly. Inside the doctor's exam room, I got out of
my chic white gown, and into the split-tailed version of the same
thing. I had a theory that the split-tailed pullovers were once our
normal dresses and they were converted with a pair of scissors
when they no longer serviced as regular wear.

With a great deal of trouble and much physical effort, I got
up onto the cold examination table. Why is it a requirement that a
doctor's office has to be ten degrees colder than any other room? I
had shiver bumps all over my body, and the hard frozen peas, my
nipples, ached. I must have gotten spoiled over the last few weeks
as Spouse's assistant because the wait for Herr Doctor drove me
crazy. I had work that needed to get done so as not to get a nasty
lecture from Margaret.

Just when I'd about had enough, the doctor came in and gave
me an injection. "Just a vitamin supplement. Now lie back and
relax." He began his exam in his usual cool and efficient manner.
I remember feeling just a bit light-headed. The business problem I
worked in my head became more and more difficult.

"Doctor, what was in that—" I never finished.

I woke in a hospital bed, groggy, a bare lightbulb from an
archaic looking lamp shining in my face. I don't know why I knew
it had to be a hospital bed. I think it was because they never feel
like any other bed. Even the cot I slept on for months in the School
offered more comfort. This bed could have been used as a torture
device all on its own merit. I lay flat on my back but instead of the
bed cushioning, it felt like it was made of a mixture of granite and
sharp limestone gravel, in the most uncomfortable combination.
The remarkably white room glared under the incandescent lights
in the ceiling. It had to be a recovery room or a ward. Nothing
looks like it and nothing smells like it. I'd been in the hospital

twice before. Once for three days to put a tube in my ear, for chronic ear infections, and once for two weeks when I was eight to have pins and screws put into a badly broken foot. My father had dropped his hundred-pound toolbox on it. I'm not entirely certain that it had been an accident. He had been angry with me for not being able to tell an open-end wrench from a crescent wrench or some such silliness.

It must have been the night shift as I could barely hear anything until a muted "Doctor Golds, call hospital security," came over the loudspeakers. A large off-green sheet hung from the ceiling surrounding my bed and another was flung over my body. I still didn't have any curiosity other than trying to decide why everything looked so far away. For what felt like nearly three hours a single thread blowing in a tiny breeze mesmerized me. The way it fluttered back and forth in the tiniest of gusts of air fascinated me. I could even make it go crazy by blowing hard in that direction. I don't like the way I am on drugs.

I finally began to notice me. My back still ached but in an entirely different way than I remembered from before. The second that my brain cleared enough to accept self-awareness, I realized my belly was empty. I rattled some thoughts around in my head and searched, but I didn't remember delivering the baby. My flat abdomen spoke for itself. I felt a bit tender around the middle, but someone had strapped my hands to the bed at my side, so I couldn't explore.

A cheery blond nurse, about forty pounds overweight of being overweight, pulled aside the curtains enough to enter, but not enough for me to look out. Her white outfit left no question that she was a nurse or a woman.

"And how are we this morning?"

With a mouth that felt like the floor in a glue factory, I managed to croak out a response. "Fine, I guess. I don't think I need these straps anymore."

"We'll just have to wait for the doctor to decide that, Lizzy." I gritted my teeth through the nickname and her smugness. The nurse, whose nametag announced that she was Hera, checked some yellow fluids in a clear plastic bag attached to a catheter inside me. She jotted information from my vital statistics monitor into my chart, just like nurses have been doing for centuries and probably will do for centuries more. Only the technology around it will change.

"OK, then. How did my delivery go? I don't remember anything about it." The cauc nurse beamed at me and we both said at the same time, "We'll just have to wait for the doctor to decide that." The nurse added "Lizzy" to the end. I just lay there in a huff. I couldn't really do anything else.

My middle definitely ached, but in a far away and not of immediate concern way. I figured the IV dripped some kind of painkiller into my arm, or maybe the buzz in my ears had another cause. But time slipped away quickly as the drugs drifted me back off to sleep. A voice woke me several minutes or hours later.

"Good morning, Elizabeth." I silently thanked an attractive looking doctor in his late thirties for his use of my proper name. With his wavy black hair, his over-six-foot, tennis-player build and his olive skin, he might have been a subject of my early teen fantasies, but I doubted it now. This doubt troubled me as I didn't know where it came from. "I am Doctor Rob. How are you feeling?"

"Ready to rip these restraining straps out of their sockets if I don't get let up soon."

"Oh, very good. Nice and feisty." The doctor ignored me as he furiously scribbled on my record. He put me in that space where doctors ignore their patients. Which of the Inalienable Rights covers patients being disregarded and annoyed by their physicians? "Life, liberty, the pursuit of happiness, and the neglect of medical professionals." He miffed me the longer he made me wait. He looked at the monitor strategically positioned above my head and quite unreadable to anyone in the bed. I guess that the medical profession thinks it's better that we laymen don't know anything about ourselves. He finally put down my chart and pulled back the bed sheet. I got my first good look at what had happened to me. "Do you feel any pain?" he asked, probing the stitches over a long, thin, angry-red incision horizontally placed across my midsection.

"Just a dull ache. OUCH!"

"Sorry. Just have to make sure these stitches don't come out before their time." I glared at him. He put me back into the ignore box and went back to his indecipherable scratching in my chart. "You gave us quite a scare, young lady."

"Oh?"

"Yes, there were some complications. Suffice it to say that your surgeon was quite skilled. He probably saved your life." He continued to make more notes. For all I knew he could be writing a love letter to his mistress.

"And the baby?"

"Not good news, I'm afraid," the doctor said as he looked up with what passed for his compassionate face. I wondered if they practiced it out of a textbook somewhere. It seemed cold to me. He did take the time to unstrap me while he talked. My arms, while tingling with disuse, hadn't been hurt by the soft bonds. "We had to go in C-section after the baby. It was born dead."

That point changed my life. Don't ask me "Why?" or "How?" I still don't know the answer. If I had to pick a moment that my life turned to what it is now, that would be it. The baby's demise lifted a burden off my soul. I never wanted that child. I still think of my pregnancy as It. By the same token, something inside me said that if I knew that It lived somewhere else, with someone else—I just think it would have been too much for my mind to handle. I had always felt this weird revulsion for what grew inside my body. It had been grown by me, but planted by people so low as to be less than reprehensible. It was dead, and I think that was the best possible outcome as far as my mind was concerned.

The doctor watched my reaction closely and quite intently. He was clearly ready to call the Cossacks if I freaked out, but it wasn't necessary—not in the least. It took me all of three heartbeats to realize my good fortune.

"Thank you, Doctor," I said with the brightest smile I could manage. Dr. Rob didn't seem fully convinced, but let it slide. I really didn't care what he thought, as long as he didn't try to keep me there. I wanted to go home and have life get back to normal. I was free.

"You will have two more days of bed rest and one full week here before I will release you." OK, I was almost free. "The stitches in your abdomen will dissolve when they are no longer needed. Is there anything else, Elizabeth?" I thought for a moment.

"No, thank you, Dr. Rob."

"You have a visitor but for no more than fifteen minutes. You need your rest." The doctor disappeared, being replaced almost instantly with Hera.

I lay there wondering if my family had come out to take me home. Intellectually I dismissed the possibility, but emotionally I couldn't. I needed to think they would. They were my family. But when Hera left, I couldn't help feeling apprehensive.

The huge, square shape of Box entered and I felt something akin to relief play over my body. I didn't know why my anxiety spiked but the black man made me feel better than any alternative I could imagine.

"How is m'Lizzy girl?"

"Well, I don't think I should do any slam dancing, but I'll be all right." Box gave a tiny chuckle—the largest show of emotion I think I'd seen from him.

"Whatcha gonna do naw, girly?"

"Go home. Maybe I can live this down. Go back to school. Let everything go back to normal."

"Never easy, goin' home."

"I know, Box, but I don't have anything else. They may not be great but they are my family." Box looked away and was quiet for a long time. He wouldn't look me in the eye for some reason.

"I won't keep ya. Doc said ya should rest. But if'n ya don't find home t'yer likin', come see me. I'll help ya get yer feet under ya." He then walked out through the curtain. I must have been stupid back then. No, that's not honestly fair to myself. Inexperienced is a better word, or maybe naive. Tears welled up in the corners of my eyes. I rolled to my side and cried myself back to sleep.

The next few days were very hard. I rested until I my ass became numb no matter how many times I shifted in bed. I spent most of my time thinking about Box. He didn't come back to visit as I convalesced. I thought I might have hurt him—but now, years later, I'm quite sure I did. Smart about things didn't include smart about people or even about myself. I know it is no excuse but it was a reason.

I learned that I hated bedrest worse than I hated tiles. Whoever said "Patience is a virtue" had no idea how to make things happen and had absolutely nothing better to do. I raised such a fit with the nurses that they called Doctor Rob and he allowed me up half a day early. It may have been a Pyrrhic victory as it really hurt to stand and walk. My back ached and my stitches pinched.

While Box didn't come and visit me again, Spouse shocked me by her arrival. She showed up on the day after Doc Rob and his merry nurses allowed me up and around. I was walking with my legs apart and with all the speed of a terminal invalid, pushing my IV stand in front of me, when she suddenly appeared at my side.

"Ms. Fox!"

"Hello, Elizabeth. How are you?"

"Quite fine, ma'am," I said with a wince as one of the stitches pulled.

"You never could lie well." I blushed, or at least I thought I did. My cheeks felt like they had taken too much of a summer sun.

"I'll live. Nothing a little time won't heal."

"I hope so," she muttered under her breath so softly I almost didn't hear.

"Excuse me, ma'am?"

"Oh, nothing, dear. Have you contacted your parents yet?"

"I didn't know I was allowed."

"Quite. There is a phone in your room. You may use it at your will. I suggest you look toward your future."

"I will, ma'am. And thank you." Ms. Fox turned and looked at me like I had suddenly grown another head. She delivered a long, measured stare before shaking her head and turning away.

"I do believe you mean it. You're quite a piece of work, Ms. Zimmer."

As soon as she was out of sight, I put my body into overdrive. Phone home! It excited me and terrified me all at the same time. I ignored the twinges of pain from the incision and raced back to my room at the speed of a herd of wild snails. I got back to my room only to find my roommate, Simone, on the one phone in our room. I sat patiently on the bed waiting, trying not to look obvious.

"Yes, Danny, I'll be out in just a day or two. Yes, only one more of these things and we can retire." As one of the mercenary girls, Simone bore babies for money—a baby factory. "Yes, I'm looking forward to that as well. I so hate this place—I will. Love you, too. 'Bye."

"May I, Simone?" I asked as my hand all but beat the receiver to the cradle. Simone delighted in tormenting the other girls. I tried not to sound too eager, but wasn't all that successful. I hoped she might take pity on me.

"Sure. First time in, isn't it?"

"Yes."

"Family?"

"Yes. I have to find out when I can go home." I heard Simone stifle a snicker. "What are you laughing about!" I all but shouted, stopping my dial.

"You are naive. There is no going home." The phone's earpiece made a wavering sound and a voice announced that I had surpassed my allotted time to dial.

"Why?"

"You'll see, sweetie. Go ahead and dial." Simone shut up and just sat there watching me as I called. The phone rang twice before my mother answered.

"Hello."

"Momma? It's Elizabeth. I'm sorry. I lost my baby."

In the background I heard my father bellow, "Who the hell is it?" My mother covered the phone with her hand. I could still hear her talking, but not my father's responses.

"It's Liz. You should talk to her—No, I won't. Now come here and deal with this." There were some even more muffled sounds as the phone changed hands. I could hear each of my heartbeats, each like a gunshot in an enclosed basement. Time dilated until my father came on the line.

"Hi, Papa. I'm ready to come home."

His voice was dripping with anger. "You listen to me, you little bitch. Don't you ever call here again. You're not my daughter. You're nothing but a whore. Go live like one, you ungrateful cunt. I won't have a slut in my house." A loud slamming sound punctuated the conversation before the line went dead. My face must have spoken volumes because before I even took the phone from my ear, my roommate commented.

"I told you so, girl. There's no going back." All I could do is sit almost catatonic and make believe that it had never happened. Simone took the receiver from my hand after it had begun to wail.

I was oblivious. "Girl, it's life. You have to make your own way. Do you hear me? Well, the hell with you then." Simone turned her back and pulled out a magazine.

Why is it that I can remember ever minor little detail about crises in my life? I remember that Simone read Cosmo, which proclaimed "Sixty-Three Ways to Improve Your Sexual Stamina." The cover had Diana Adams wearing red, white and blue body paint in a surreal American flag where a blue star covered each of her nipples. Simone wore Ravish perfume, by Pamela Anderson. The hospital speakers played a Muzak version of "Rock and Roll Ain't Noise Pollution." The hospital cleaning solution bottle on the sill proclaimed itself Mr. Clean, New Improved Cosmic Strength.

I sat there for several hours. My eyes dried and my vision blurred from not blinking. The ugliness of the world that showed when I'd been raped opened up its maw and swallowed me whole. I thought families protected children from the harsh realities of life, but instead my family fostered those real world pains. I couldn't believe my father could have been that cruel. I had no one and no one had me. I didn't know which thought was sadder.

A nurse came in, adjusted my IV drip, charted my vitals and left. I eventually teetered over onto my pillow. I don't know what specific thought started it, but I began to sob and cry. I kept it as quiet as I could. I don't know why I cared. I guess because for so long I'd been crowded into too small a space where I didn't want to bother anyone. I cried for several more hours, filling my pillow with snot and salty tears, not to mention the occasional scream of despair.

October 28, 2050

Well, that's it. The only thing left between me and my final reward is the governor of Southern California, and that is about as likely as a cheetah in downtown San Francisco. I can't say that this is unexpected; it still is rather a cold feeling when you are no longer among the living and not yet quite among the dead. Brrr.

The State of Southern California gave Edna her injection today while I was away. I'll miss her warm wit. Despite being a hopeless nut case about some things, her pleasant manner made me want her around more. We talked about life, our impending deaths and the society that bore us. It's hard to look at her empty cell without wondering. I think I am glad I wasn't here when she left. Rest in peace, Edna Lewis. I will miss you even if I think justice is served and mankind is safer with your death.

I do hope that wherever she went that I can go as well. It would be comforting to talk to her sympathetic soul. She truly believed in what she was doing, just as I did and I think I still do. Does that make me as sick and twisted as she was? How rationalizing we can become. That is what worries me. Have I rationalized away my guilt so far that I don't feel it anymore?

Well, I guess it doesn't matter what I feel or think anymore. I'm going to be put down like a rabid dog. I'm not quite a failure in the scheme of life. Many, many people are alive because of me. For that little bit I am thankful.

I think I need a chance to think about this for a bit. Or maybe I don't. I happen to know the Gov and while it is extreme, I do have something on him. His wife was once a baby-maker for the School. I wonder what the press will do with such a tidbit? It will be a feeding frenzy. Even more direct is the fact that his Royal Highness, the governor, is one of the partners in the School. He's also the one who had it raided to further his grab for power. I may already be dead, but he will be going down as well. Maybe not all the way, but he'll not hold any other public office. I don't know that it will help in the grand scheme of things, but I will have my revenge this time. Vengeance is better than just waiting here until I'm terminated. Is it vengeance or karma?

Interesting. I've always felt euthanasia, either by the request of a terminally ill patient or by the order of the court, was right. I never considered it otherwise. Even now, when I'm on the brink of being put to death myself, I still feel there is nothing intrinsically wrong with the death penalty. Do I still think so in my specific case? I wasn't sure before, as I think my conscience nagged me just a bit, but I am certain now. The answer is no. I could give you an eighty-page master's thesis on why, but the bottom line comes down to the fact that I have given more far more lives to this world than I have taken, even if those lives I took were worthwhile.

I personally don't feel that those fetuses had any real meaning, but society does. I also know that a vast majority of the world is going to cheer when the State of California pulls the trigger, drops the gas pellets or whatever. I can't get the thought of those poor patients who will suffer because I am not able to run my business. Well, there I go, getting ahead of myself. I'm trying to keep a cohesive account but instead I'm rambling on.

It's already late and lights out will be very soon so I'm going to stop here and think about a few things.

October 29, 2050

Matron Peggy is doing an exceptional job as my "gopher." She has already copied my diary to this point. She is stashing it in a safe place for the final delivery she is going to make for me. Funny how hard Father Peter had to push to get me to write it and now it's probably more important to me that this gets delivered than anything else I have ever done in my life. I only fear that it might not make it to its intended audience.

Speaking of fear. They took Kathy Klips out of here today. It took eight guards. The first one they sent in ended up with a broken wrist. She kicked, punched, bit and screamed until they subdued her with a tranquilizer gun. The rifle reports of the firing squad sent chills up my back. The world is better without you, Kathy. I'm not sorry you had to go. I am sorry you reminded me of how little time remains in my own hourglass. Maybe the Wicked Witch of the West will let me turn it over.

I think it's time to continue the real story.

The medical profession released me from the hospital, oh, what, three days after my cesarean? Yeah, something like that. I cried myself out over those three days. My pillows soaked up my grief that came in the form of an ocean of saltwater drops. I could hardly look at anyone without my eyes tearing up. The nurses kept threatening to have the doctor back to prescribe Xerium. I didn't need antidepressants. I needed a real family. I begged off each time by putting on a bold face until they had retreated. It took only moments for the veneer to melt away like a sandcastle in a hurricane.

After the first night of catharsis, I started to feel each tiny drop turn inward and cold. Each of the drops molded itself like cooling lead, weight and all, over my soul. I blamed God. I blamed my mother. I blamed Jimmy and his goons. I blamed myself, but mostly I blamed my father. He sold me. He got paid for the agony of my rape. He almost got paid for the disgusting parasite that grew within me. And then he repaid me by abandoning me. It hurt. You can't even imagine the hurt unless everyone has abandoned you.

It hurt so badly that for almost three years I plotted the worst kind of revenge on my father. Jimmy I could excuse, like one could forgive a stray dog who had bitten and drawn blood. To pardon my father would be like allowing the family dog that had attacked your seven-year-old, to babysit your infant. No, I couldn't forgive but as the years rolled on, I realized the man wasn't worth my time. I could have had either my father or Jimmy killed, maimed, or abused in a number of cruel ways. I had the means. It just mattered less and less. I learned to live in the present and future until one day I realized I had no more tears for either of them.

Doctor Rob did come and visit me on the last day, examining my belly for the record and the discharge papers. The nurses must have confided in him about my lamentation as he questioned me about my emotional state as he probed my abdomen. The once angry red wound was now just a scarlet line. It would still be many weeks before it completely healed, but the stitches were properly dissolving. They would hold for another two days.

"I'm fine, Doctor Rob." I gave him my cheeriest smile just to allay any of his fears—but winced as his fingers probed a tender spot.

"Are you certain? I know how traumatic these experiences can be. Does that hurt?"

"Just a little tender. And no, Doctor, really, I'm fine."

"Well, losing a baby is one of the hardest things a young woman can go through. I'd be happy to have you stay an extra few days, or even have a colleague visit with you about it. Your insurance would certainly pay for any additional costs." It had never occurred to me that this hospital wasn't just an extension of the School, a private hospital run by Spouse's fingertips, books and money. I wondered how much the good doc knew of the School.

At the same time I realized that my medical friend implied that my grieving had been for the lost child. Good, I thought silently. Let him keep thinking that. I knew what kind of colleague he was talking about. The last thing I wanted was another prolonged stay at the behest of a social worker of some kind. As little respect as I have for doctors, I have none for psychs, and much less at the thought of being penned up while having my brain harvested like an orchard.

"No, quite certain, Doctor Rob. I'm fine and will be quite happy after you let me out of here." I lied with all the skill I could muster about my mental state, but it wasn't fabricating my desire to be released. I'd spent seven months all but jailed and I wanted my freedom.

"Hmm. No blood in your stool or urine?"

"No, sir." For a brief juvenile moment, I had thoughts of a conspiracy as he seemed determined to find a way to keep me. He looked down at his chart.

"I see you're barely eating, however."

"Just haven't really developed an appetite. My belly's been too big as it is. Small portions." He paused as he wrote on my chart. Again my imagination was getting the best of me, but I managed to sit still, as dignified as the hospital gown would allow me.

"I can't see any reason to keep you here any longer then, Ms. Zimmer." I nearly fainted with relief. I was going to have my freedom. I wanted to jump up and down and scream for joy. "If the incision gets any more tender, there is any weeping, gets split or drastically changes color, please comes back. In addition, please note any blood in your urine or stool. If it continues for more than a day, please contact us or your own doctor."

"Thank you, Doctor Rob."

Herr Doctor released me at 9:36 in the morning, by my watch. By the time all the papers had been signed, the paperwork had been processed, I had my clothes, had my maintenance dose of erythromycin, and was ready to walk out the door, it was almost three in the afternoon. I wondered if someone was going to tell me I couldn't check out because the damned hospital bill wasn't yet prepared and it was after business hours.

Which reminds me. I did get a hospital bill, with a balance due of $0.00. All the rest of the cost was paid care of Lillian Estate Management. LEM was one of the dummy corporations I managed for the School. I should have remembered that, but so many of those fictitious agencies paid so many different bills that I would be hard-pressed to remember even one now.

Is it written in some book that a patient must be delivered to the curb in a wheelchair? I dressed to leave in exactly the same clothes I had come to the School in. I slipped into the white man's

T-shirt and a faded, flannel, long-sleeve shirt. I didn't quite fit into the jeans so I had to keep the top button open but I wasn't going to let that stand in my way. I started to walk for an exit and I thought that one of the nurses was going to fall over from a coronary. The Nurse's Bible must state, "It is a sin to allow a patient to walk out unassisted." She busted her bustle to get me a wheelchair and escort me to the curb.

Once she had me to the street corner, I sat there looking out at the opening of my freedom. Even in Pasadena the morning air carried a chill on this early February morning. It must have been an omen.

Other than on TriVid, I'd never even seen such horrible conditions. Fast food wrappers, used condoms, and movie fliers littered the streets. I could even see a dead kitten in the near gutter. Through many cans of vivid paint, a thoroughly tagged sign still managed to proclaim, "Ronald Regan Memorial Retreat." Five elm trees managed to eke out some form of living within a greenspace, however sickly. They stretched their arms to the sky, covering me with cold shade from their leafed branches. The sun occasionally peeked through the gentle breeze that rolled the verdant foliage from side to side. I closed my eyes and could almost envision myself in Halcomb Park back home next to the river in the middle of summer. When I opened my eyes, all I could see was the ugliness of the city.

Weathered "Out of Business" or "For Lease" signs covered up most of the buildings. Warped, torn, and sometimes broken boards over windows sported more bullet holes than a police shooting-range backstop. One building even had a bloodstain splattered across its front. Rusted out heaps that had been automobiles studded the street. Graffiti lay across every surface that could hold paint. Two hookers, their business licenses prominently displayed over more of their skin than the clothes they wore, took the corner across the street. By their yawns and the bare attention they did give the few cars that passed by, they just started their day. Two living-quarters-challenged people took turns drinking Lysol from a gold plastic bottle.

The reality struck me like a hammer blow. I sat there rigidly and did not know what to do. I had almost no money, no home, no family and no friends. As stupid as it sounded, my father's idea of becoming a whore even raced through my mind. That didn't really apply. I didn't have the body, the face, the vocation nor the money to get a license—and I've heard horror stories about what happens to unlicensed girls. The nurse looked at me as I sat there in the wheelchair.

"Are you all right? Someone is coming to pick you up, aren't they?" I thought briefly that I might step in front of one of the fast moving delivery trucks that dotted the six lanes of Fair Oaks, but I'd never considered suicide exactly right, somehow.

"Ah, my boyfriend is coming. He'll be here any minute." Cover up. Hide. I didn't know what to do, who to trust. I shook as I panicked. I hated to lose control. *NOOOOOOOOO*, my mind screamed like a jet engine in a sealed cave. One part of me yearned for the freedom before me and it warred with the knowledge that there was nothing out there for me. I gripped the armrests of the wheelchair tightly.

"You want me to wait?" I didn't know what I wanted. My fingernails bit deeply into the vinyl.

"No, that's quite all right. He won't be a minute." No home, no one to help me. Where would I sleep? What would I eat?

"Well, this isn't exactly the greatest neighborhood for anyone. You sure you don't want me to wait?" My mind finally locked up. I couldn't think. I couldn't even make my mouth spew more brave lies. I don't know how long I sat. My palms and fingers began to cramp as they locked around my last semblance of safety.

Time stretched out to infinity as it seemed to take hours for the streetwalker across the street to light her cigarette. Each spark from the butane lighter sailed out like golden stars filling the sky. The plume of diesel smoke from the truck directly in front of me floated up in a mushroom shape, slowly expanding like a lopsided ball over several hundreds of minutes. In truth it couldn't have been too long because the nurse said nothing more before a beaten-up Ford Aerostar pulled up along the curb. My knight in shining armor on his great white steed had arrived.

Box got out of the car and around to my side. "Lizzy girl, ya ben sittin' there fer' most of fifteen minutes." I chose that time to break down and cry again. After nine months of mood swings and several days of sobbing I had thought that my reservoir of tears empty. I threw myself against his charcoal colored chest and covered it wetly in my joy and pain. I couldn't seem to get my breath. Every time I did, I broke down again. I couldn't tell if I suffered from happiness, relief, or anguish. I just let it seep out of me onto my savior. After minutes of my crying jag, I felt Box pick me up and put me in the passenger seat. I clung to his arm, but Box firmly removed my hands so he could get into the driver's seat.

I don't remember much of the drive. I held my friend's one free hand, wrapping my fingers within his. As my life raft in the ocean of sewage I wouldn't release him. The urban setting slowly changed into smaller buildings, in much better state of repair. That evolved into occasional foliage between one- and two-story houses, and eventually melted entirely to scrub grass and green, healthy trees on one side of a canyon. By now it had started getting dark and streetlights popped on, making their own little lighted domains. We slipped through the borders of each, the light growing bright in defiance of our entrance and then becoming dim as we left.

Box stopped at the apex of a long horseshoe gravel driveway in front of a ranch-style home. He coaxed me through the doubled off-white doors, each seemingly four or five inches thick. You could feel the air pressure change when he closed them so they must have been tighter than an airlock door. As strange as the thought was, I wondered if a police assault car could break down that portal. Radiant panels in the wall only dimly lighted the house, so I didn't notice much at first. Box led me to a room and put me into a soft comfortable single bed. He didn't bother with my clothes. He just pulled the covers over me, like a parent covering a child who had been out too late.

"Don't leave me!" I cried out as he turned. "I can't be alone anymore." Box didn't say a word. Instead he climbed onto the bed beside me, on top of the covers, and wrapped one of his arms around me. I felt safe, like I had been all the time at the School. I'd been bored and wanted to get my freedom, but I had been safe.

My mind crystalized to the craziest solution I'd ever considered. I turned to face Box.

"Please give me a baby. I want to go back. I want to go back to the School."

"Lizzy-girl, ya don't know what t'ey do."

"I don't care, Box. I'll be safe and I'll have my own money. My father won't get a dime. It's the perfect solution."

"Ya sleep on it, girl. T'en we talk more."

I stewed but decided that he was right. I couldn't stop thinking about it, though. It seemed the perfect solution to my problems. I would work for nine months (all expenses paid) and receive twenty-five thousand dollars for my trouble. This time it would be for me. I could wait out nine months. Then, when I got out, I'd have enough money for my own new beginning. Maybe I could have that real life and find a husband I could love?

I don't know when I went from thinking to dreaming. I can't say, but my dreams drifted off onto that perfect life—a loving husband and a little beige house in the suburbs of Minneapolis with friends to gossip and share recipes with. I went to dinner parties with my husband to extol his virtues and fend off passes by slightly over-liquored men. Hubby brought me roses, daisies, and even some star-gazer lilies. On the weekend I watched him ride the lawnmower to cut the Kentucky blue-grass. I couldn't have painted a whiter picket fence.

But my dream held out on me. My husband's face dashed away just when I thought I would see it. Even when we made love, my hair obscured it, and no matter how much I raked it out of the way, my vision never cleared. Who was this man? Despite the mystery he kept me safe and warm.

Also the children were gone. There were two picture-perfect children's bedrooms. One had walls covered in pastels, with ceramic dolls taking their place in neat rows on the window. A satin spread covered a white-lace-canopy, four-poster bed with a big brown bear sitting patiently in the center. Books waited, neatly arranged in a mahogany bookcase. A pink lace dress with petticoats hung neatly on a hanger from a crystal knob on the matching dark wood armoire. Space ships dominated the decor in the other room. A rug showed the lift-off of the Apollo moon launch. On both the top and bottom bunks the bedspread sported spacemen on a black star-field. A glass aquarium, containing a slowly moving box turtle occupied the top of a slightly banged up desk with schoolbooks and folders strewn all over it. A mobile of the solar system hung from the light fixture in the center of the room. A pair of boy's shorts lay askew in the middle of the room.

But those two rooms held no children. My husband and I ate supper and went to bed. I couldn't even remember having children. Where were they? I brought the subject up to my faceless husband.

"Don't worry, honey. Enjoy the time off," said the anonymous stranger I seemed to be married to. I panicked. I called all my friends, but no one would answer. When I finally got someone it was my father. He screamed and yelled and called me all types of names. His voice drifted off finally, fading into other sounds . . .

Crickets chirped outside the window, the grunts of passion from the next home, and the screech of an owl broke the brittle stillness of the dark night air. It woke me because it had been so long since I'd heard them. Box's arm still rested across my body. He slept peacefully, barely perched on the edge of the tiny bed. His face looked the same asleep as it did awake—serene and calm. I carefully climbed out from within Box's hold and got up.

I remember my dream clearly and vividly to this day. The smells had even been real with the earthy smell of freshly cut grass, the faint whiff of little-girl perfume, and even the slightly sick smell of a dead frog in a denim pant pocket. That dream held as much reality as those next few months slipped into the surreal.

Back then I put the disturbing images to the back of my mind and looked around. Box had decorated his guestroom in a turn-of-the-century motif with a great deal of leather and chrome. On the wall hung a Melissa Etheridge "Bright Light" tour poster and a mint condition Elton John "Farewell Yellow Brick Road" CD. Excepting Sir Elton John, there was nothing I would have chosen, but it was a very serviceable guestroom, with little maintenance required. The three-inch-thick window, open just wide enough for a gentle night breeze, beckoned me. I sat on a barstool next to it, looking out.

Box's home perched high on a hill overlooking Greater Los Angeles. The always bright city lights and darkness of water drew a clear outline of the shoreline. The permanently choked highway, some ways off in the distance and down in a little valley, presented as a clear bright line of ground vehicles' lights. The beacons of near-ground vehicles cluttered the air above those same roadways.

I remembered cool nights like that back at home in Bear Creek—or should I have said what used to be home. I just sat by a window and looked out. One of my fondest desires at that time was to have a home in the country away from even the tiny Bear Creek—a white clapboard two-story house with a porch swing. Very retro or even ancient of me, but I liked being a part of the night. Night never demanded attention like the day and lay peaceful over everything. It took what you gave and remained happy. There was nowhere better to appreciate the night than on a porch swing. My grandmother had one on her house in town. I remember sitting there and just listening to the quiet. On those evenings I felt I lived in another world, in another more peaceful age.

I heard Box stir behind me. I turned to look but he just changed position on the one-person bed. Gratitude for my friend and savior overflowed my thoughts. And if he granted me the boon, I would have something more to be thankful for soon—once I had another baby in my belly and could go back to where I would be safe. I hadn't changed my mind. The School had been the only place I'd been loved for what I was. Box, Anita, and Spouse provided a safe haven and a warmth, of sorts, that I needed. I was going to go back. I might not ever see Anita again, but I would still have that little place called home.

A low bass rumble brought my attention back to the window. I saw a Low Orbit Craft launch on a tail of brilliant red, yellow, and piercing white from what could only have been LAX. I was close enough to even see the secondary plume of crimson reach out over the sea in a fiery false sunset. That meant I must be up near Mulholland Drive, and the highway below me must be the San Diego Freeway. I looked back at the rapidly dwindling LOC and could only guess at its destination; Green Station One, Tyco City, or maybe even rendezvous with the generation ship, Garden of Eden. My mind wandered at the thought of being on that ship as an explorer to another world, a colonist of new lands. How much better than stuck on this sad globe.

Breaking my woolgathering, Box spoke up from behind me, softly and with a trace of compassion. "Ya know what t'ay do with those babes ya make? All of 'em?" I hadn't even hear him wake. I didn't turn around. I didn't want him to see my face.

"Yes, Box, they sell them. It is a blessing to the baby. They go to a better place. They go where they are wanted and needed. To a family that wants a baby, not to someone who would disown them or hurt them." My eyes leaked at the thought like a silly fem. How could I have been so unemotional and still feel the world being pulled out from under me at the same time? It didn't make sense. I could almost hear Box hesitate.

"Yes, t'ay sell 'em al'right, Lizzy. But ya gotta know, girl. T'ay sells 'em as parts, Lizzy. Not whole babies." I turned to look at him.

"What? I don't understand."

"A heart here, a liver t'ere, a leg, an arm, skin grafts. Sainthoods have been giv'n to men fer less'n we make t'em babes live and die through."

I mentally froze with the thought of parts cut a piece at a time away from a child. Box's words might as well have been in Greek for all the initial impact they had. My brain swallowed up and caged the thoughts so that they wouldn't rape my consciousness.

"Ya babe din't die, Lizzy. I sold it, a piece at a time. I done it."

A part of me screamed at the outrage, cruelty, and horror. What bestial mentality could do such a thing? At the same time another part was telling me that it didn't matter. It wasn't real. What had grown inside me hadn't been human. It was a Jimmy larva.

But Box selling pieces of a child seemed barbaric.

"But that's illegal .. it's immoral .. it's .. impossible."

"Yes Ma'am, it is, everyt'in' 'ceptin' t'impossible part. And it's callous, heartless and a great number o'other t'ings t'at I've told m'self all m'life, Lizzy. But it pays good and gives t'ose girlies a place ta quietly git ridda bastards. Not only t'at, but t'em babes save lives. Alota lives. Each part saves a life and what kinda life t'em babes gonna haf if'n t'eir momma's and poppa's don't want 'em?"

My stomach flipped in a queasy, much worse than any morning sickness I had endured, way. "Maybe I don't want to do this after all."

"Don't judge before ya know. In the mornin' I wanna take ya somewhere. T'en ya judge, girl. I believe in what I do. It may be illegal, but it helps people even if'n it hurts t'ose not quite babes." I looked long and hard at Box. Of all the men I'd met in my life, he stood at the head as a good man—the best, I decided. If he wanted me to wait, I'd wait. He couldn't make up my mind for me, but I could trust in him enough until I had his insight.

"I'll hold my thoughts until I've seen, Box."

"The shower is in t'ere. Towels in the cabinet. Or ya can sleep s'more."

My leaking nipples had soaked through my shirt and my hair felt greasy. At that moment my mind felt even dirtier. "I'm slept out, Box."

"Good."

I couldn't stop my mind from thinking about it. I never promised I was able to do the impossible. The concept of baby parts had been too morbid not to think about. The vivid flashes and grim mental pictures reminded me of the anti-abortion ads I'd seen in textbooks about the nineties, all red and gross. I even had visions of a butcher's carving diagram. I can't say the pictures appealed. What kind of people would do those kinds of things? It seemed . . . I couldn't come up with an appropriately odious adjective. But I needed to hold off making mental decisions before Box presented all the facts. I had to wait until he showed me more. I forcefully shoved the bloody images from my mind.

The hot water of the shower ran over my body for several minutes before I realized that it melted a tension that had grown in my shoulders. The gruesome images must have gone with the tension down the drain because I stopped thinking of them and began thinking more of me. My position in this lovely home rode entirely on Box's goodwill. I knew he was a friend, but friendship could only be tread upon so far before it turned to something worse. I remember something my mother said after a relative, my Aunt Bernice, if I recall, had stayed with us for a week: "Elizabeth, guests are like fish dinners. They are great the first night and even pretty good the next, but after the third day they begin to smell something awful."

As the only friend I had, I didn't want to abuse Box's kindness.

I would find out what he needed to share with me. Then, one way or the other, I would make sure I didn't turn into a burden to anyone.

I wished I had Anita to talk to. She always seemed to help me solve problems. That black bitch rarely had the answer herself, but she always helped me organize things so I saw the right answer for myself.

Anita, where are you? I could have used you then, and I can certainly use you now.

October 31, 2050

I look out my little two-by-three bullet-proof window, and I see the almost featureless steel-gray sky of San Francisco. No blue shines down. Only a general lightening heralds the day. Depressing, even if it lets me know that morning has arrived. Not that this is unusual for this time of year. At least San Fran isn't quite as bad as Seattle or some odd towns in Alaska that have over two hundred fifty days of full overcast. Here it is a bit less than two hundred. That is disheartening enough. After several years in LA, the gunmetal color of the sky is unnatural and cold.

Four days left until my fateful and fatal appointment with the hooded rider. My execution is scheduled for 10 a.m. If we assume it is 10 a.m. now, that's four days at twenty-four hours per day or ninety-six hours. Sixty minutes per hour, that's five thousand, seven hundred sixty minutes. Sixty seconds per minute yields three hundred forty-five thousand, six hundred seconds. It sounds longer that way. Yes, I'm deluding myself, but sometimes self-delusion is necessary. We can so rarely deal with the true view of the world.

I remember walking those tiles at the School and how each of them was half a second less of my imprisonment. I guess the same is true now; the difference is that the cells here are one-piece molded ceramic and Kevlar. There are no tiles to walk, no tiles to hate, no tiles to push my emotions upon. At least when I left the School I thought I could have a future. Here . . .

I did have the barest of Catholic upbringing. I guess I wonder what I believe in. Do I believe in an all-knowing, all-seeing, benevolent God as preached by the Christians? No. No equivocation. I found the concept repellent. To quote one of my favorite author's character, "Religion is a crutch for those who can't stand up to the unknown without help."

One of the few boons I've had in this place is access to the prison library. I've made some studies of the religions. The Christian religions are polyglots of pagan religions, so to believe in that would be to believe in the more pagan gods. This leaves out almost all the commonly thought of religions, Catholicism, Mormonism, Islam (they even believe that Jesus was a prophet), even most of Judaism. If you remove those, that only leaves the older more bizarre religions like Norse, Greek/Roman, Buddhism. I can't buy most of those either. Yes I know it is a built-in prejudice, but there is nothing I can do about that without proof. And don't even get me started on Scientology.

But most of all, I just can't believe in an omniscient, omnipotent, omnibenevolent God after what I've been through. At one time I had been innocent and good. Now I'm neither. Why would a God put someone in such a position? To have no viable choice but to do something that, while for the greatest good, was against the very precepts of the people it helped. No, there is no Christian God. It is a mass neurosis.

That doesn't mean I don't believe in something. I really do think that there is something (someone) cranking the universe, because the Hallowed Scientific Theory doesn't hold water either. Everything just is. Please, let me get on my hip waders because it's getting deep here.

This whole subject has been on my mind over the last few weeks. Father IronSky certainly implanted a seed of doubt in my mind. I assume that means he's been effective at his job. I just don't know what to believe. Is there life after death? I don't know now, but give me a few days and I'll send you a postcard.

As the future won't be of any help to me, let me go back to the past.

Box, wearing a three-piece pinstripe suit, took me to a nearby hospital. It wasn't the same one I had just left, but rather JFK Surgical Hospital. We rode the elevator in silence until we got off on the third floor. I've never liked hospitals, even though I'd not been in one often. The pervasive stench of disinfectants and the unmistakable aroma of sickness probably had much to do with it. Several of the floor nurses nodded in acknowledgment toward Box as he walked through a pair of ward doors. The sign on the door proclaimed that visiting hours were 9 a.m.—3 p.m. We were considerably earlier than 9 a.m. He was obviously known and accepted there. And that made obvious sense, I thought to myself.

The hall behind the doors continued further than I expected. At each door, Box stopped and looked into the room. The first room held a small boy, about fourteen. His face was almost bloated with a yellow, jaundiced appearance. About eighty different machines snaked out and coupled intimately with the boy in ways that should be left without description for the boy's dignity and everyone else's stomach.

"This is Carl. He is sixteen years old. Carl has a congenital liver disease. He needs a new liver or he will die within the week." Box's voice had changed and now held an Oxford tinge and no trace of his previous speech patterns. It was so incongruous that I shook off the pathetic view of the boy. Box took my hand and pulled me away to the next door. "This is Gwen." A thirty-something brunette lay motionlessly in the bed. Casts and bandages covered her body. A cervical collar encased her neck like a constricting python. "She was in a serious automobile accident last month. She is paralyzed from the neck down. Gwen has a husband and three small children. If she doesn't receive a spinal graft in the next few days she will remain paralyzed and unable to care for her family."

Box tore me away again. "This is Terry, thirty-nine. He is a lawyer and father of four. He is about to be appointed Judge Advocate General of Tycho Base. His heart gave out and he must have one soon. His body rejected each of the four mechanical replacements." I looked in horror as the man's blood came from a tube in his chest, through a big mechanical pump and then back in through another tube. Box began to walk faster, not stopping at the rooms, just pointing left and right as he rushed us by each door. "Cancerous kidneys . . . Defective heart valve . . . Emphysema . . . Damaged retinas . . . Lymphatic cancer . . . Heart failure . . . Damaged liver . . . Prostate cancer . . . Spinal meningitis . . ."

Box was almost out of breath; I knew I was and we had barely made the halfway point down the length of the ward. Box pointed at the uncompleted length and said, "The list goes on. I know each of the people here. At least unless someone new has been brought here." Box turned to his right. Our expedition thus far had stopped us right in front of the nurse's station. "Sandy, have there been any new cases since yesterday morning?" I learned my big black friend knew every nurse on the ward by name, marital status and capabilities.

"Two, Box. An eyeball replacement and a burn victim," a pert brunette said, barely looking up from her charts.

"This is the largest transplant ward in the world. Each of these people needs what Margaret makes available. Each donor can supply the needs of five or six people." I noted Box didn't say baby or fetus. Donor contained no emotion—sterile and distant. "But even more importantly—" Box took my hand and led me to a door that proclaimed, "STERILE ENVIRONMENT."

"Here, put this on." Box handed me a pink vinyl, full-body suit that looked more appropriate for a moonwalk. I slipped into the loose garment until I came to fastening it. I couldn't reach the zipper. Box zipped me up from the back and requested I do the same for him. He then handed me what looked like a stiff plastic bag with a white cottony patch in it. Box slipped his over his head. I followed his example. The white area nestled right in over my mouth and nose.

"Ready?" he asked, his voice muffled by the multiple layers of plastic and cloth. Without waiting for my response, he went through the door. I followed close behind. He went through three widely spaced layers of plastic hanging from the ceiling. Between each layer we were misted with some chemical or other. I had begun to think I had been the filth of the earth before I made it through to the clean-room. I had heard of germ-free environments but had never been in one. Inside I saw four other pink-suited individuals sitting at the edge of a bed where lay the most sickening sight I'd ever seen.

The remnants of what had once been human, now a blackened, charred hunk of meat, lay spread-eagled on the bed. Clear liquid and blood oozed out of angry red cracks in the black-seared flesh and intermittently a nozzle above the bed would spray water in a mist over the lying form. I had no clue as to the sex or age of the person in the bed, but from the small size I assumed that it was a younger child. I was very glad I couldn't smell anything through my suit because the stench of burnt flesh would have sent me reeling. All things being equal I was happy I hadn't eaten anything yet today.

The four others must have been family. There was a father

type, solid and trying to be strong (but failing, to anyone who took the time to look), a much older woman and another younger lady whom I assumed, from the tears, to be the mother. A teenage boy looked on with disbelief on his face. He obviously didn't know what to do, for to cry would not be manly, and to have no expression would be unfeeling. He looked a lot like I probably did the previous day in front of the hospital—in emotional trauma. Box motioned for me to stay put as he went over to the family. He looked at the father and reached a hand up to tap his own white filter. Just then I noted that their filters were a forest green color. The filters must have been chemically treated to show when a certain time limit or bacterial count has been reached. The man spoke to the rest of the family and they departed, with Box and me on their heels.

As soon as I stepped out of the room I tore off the helmet and sucked in some relatively clean hospital air. I was proud of myself for not getting sick. Box stripped out of his clean-room garb and tossed it into a hamper next to the door. I quietly listened as I also removed my own protective garment.

"That little girl is eight years old. Her name is Susan Miller. Yesterday the father of Susan's close friend, Debby, was taking the girls to a birthday party when a natural gas tanker hit his Jeep. The tanker exploded. The rest of the car's occupants were lucky. They died almost instantly in the fireball. Susan was partially protected and was blown clear. Her internal organs are almost completely destroyed. She no longer possesses any skin or hair. She managed to keep one eye, although God alone knows how.

"It took a great deal of luck to get her this far, but her heart and liver are both about done for. Only the use of Thetren has kept her alive." Thetren was a new drug that kept damaged tissues functioning, but only by consuming themselves. They literally used themselves up to continue. I had heard about this questionable drug before I had gone to the School, but its use was considered last resort and of no specific long-term benefit. My involuntary gasp must have been what Box was waiting for. "She has only five or six more hours. I understand they are prepping O.R. at this moment. They are going to remove most of her organs and all of her charred skin. This girl will be receiving many different parts and grafts to sustain her and bring her back from death's grasp.

Many of those parts came from your baby, Lizzy. But ultimately that is not the point. Note the family? Susan's individual life is only one direct link.

"Think about what the family would have to suffer should she die. How many years would they live seeing only the burnt corpse of their daughter lying in that bed? What is the chance that the husband and wife would be able to weather that kind of disaster and be any kind of parents, much less a family, to their son?

"Before you judge what Margaret and I do, think of all the people it benefits. One tiny unwanted, not-quite life to spare five or ten lives. And don't ever forget the families—daughters, sons, mothers, fathers, brothers, grandparents, sisters. Each baby we sacrifice salves the pain of hundreds of living, breathing people."

I wasn't quite willing to concede the point yet. "What about accident victims? Donors? Cloning?"

"Cloning is prohibitively expensive and must be done well in advance of any possible accident. The rich can afford it but no one else. Even with that, don't you remember the near revolution in '27? Maybe you were too young. 'People come before Xerox copies,' the chant went. Those that do cloning, even for scientific research, keep it very quiet.

"As you know, stem cell printing causes rampant cancer. And accidents—not enough. Not nearly enough and even fewer of them are donors. Even with the School, and the three others like it in the world, that I know about, we fall behind a little further each year." It was clear from his emphasis that there probably were other such institutions that he did not know about. It was still too much for me to absorb in one sitting.

"But how do you fit such tiny organs into an adult recipient?" Too many questions were swirling all around me and that was the only one that popped out, as incongruous as it was.

"Actually, Lizzy, I don't know all the details. I do know that in most organs size is of a minor consideration—the kidneys, the liver and such. Even the heart can be much smaller than one would think. They've been doing heart reductions for many years where they actually go in and remove a large part of the damaged heart muscle. The smaller heart often functions better than a full-sized and undamaged one does. I do know that there are ways to stimulate growth in most organs by repeatedly injecting hormones, steroids and then electrically stimulating them. I mean don't get a cartoon idea that it balloons up in seconds, but we can easily double the size of any organ in a matter of two weeks. We can triple it in three. It never takes more than that."

"That sounds almost too incredible to be true."

"Not science fiction, Lizzy—science fact. I mean I can show you the culturing tanks where it is done, but it would mean very little to you."

"I don't know, Box. I have to think about this."

"I want you to, Lizzy. I want you to know exactly what you are doing and why. I have thought about it all my life and I still feel uncomfortable some of the time. I don't want you to have second thoughts . . . or if you do, I want you to have them before you commit yourself."

I stood quietly for a minute. All sorts of things spun in my head and I didn't know how to stop them to make sense of it all. I knew I had to have more time.

"Box," I said slowly and softly. "Could you come back for me later? I want to look around and ask some questions."

"Sure, Elizabeth." Box reached inside his suitcoat pocket and handed me a card. The card announced, in a fancy green pseudo-engraving, "Abe Boxner, Medical Procurement and Facilitator." Below was his phone and pager numbers. "Call me, Elizabeth, and I will come back here for you."

"Thanks, Box."

"You are more than welcome."

Box went over to the nurse's station and talked in low tones to a different young brunette. She looked up at me with a scowl before jotting a note and posted it to a corkboard over her head. Box waved at me as he left through the swinging double-doors. I didn't know exactly what I wanted to do, so I sat down on a nearby chair. How many other loved ones had sat in that chair and wondered if their relative, friend, spouse, child would get the transplant they needed? It took me a few minutes to mull over my decision but I finally made it.

I walked directly up to the dark-haired nurse, Jasmine according to her nametag. "Where is the Delivery Ward in this hospital?" She gave me a puzzled look.

"First floor, West wing." As she spoke I looked over her shoulder to read the note she had posted. OK, I'm paranoid. "Brunette Caucasian girl, twentyish, to have run of Ward per Boxner. Name: Elizabeth Zimmer."

"Thank you," I offered in as sunny a voice as I could muster.

It didn't take me but a few moments to find the viewing room for the newborns. The room held very few infants as JFK Surgical was not a general practice or an OB hospital. I must have stood there at the window for hours. Ten infants, six girls and two boys, filled the room with a variety of vocal and flailing antics. All of them wrinkled balls of love, need and hope. One of them, a Hispanic girl, with just the beginnings of brown curly hair, proved to be the loudest infant it's ever been my pleasure to meet. She screamed her head off no matter what the nurses did. They picked her up, fed her, changed her diaper, and rocked her, all to no avail. The other five remained quiet most of the time.

The two boys both had a thing for trying to suck their hand as it waved aimlessly in front of them. One of the girls slept the entire time I stood there all curled up in her pink blanket, not moving save for the occasional start when the Hispanic girl provided an exceptionally raucous noise.

My mind rebelled. What right did we have to steal their futures? Why did we have the right to take away their chance at life? I saw one mother walk in, bowlegged and sway-backed. Oh, could I empathize. I still wasn't upright yet and my back ached in a new and unpleasant way. It was almost as much fun, sarcasm intended, as being pregnant itself. The lady staggered into the room and picked up her sleeping baby girl. She sat gingerly into an oak rocking chair and loosened the top of her gray-green hospital gown. She pressed the tiny, helpless girl against her breast.

"That's my baby girl," said a giddy father, proudly, as he eased up to the window. It was obviously his first as he still hadn't figured it out completely and it certainly hadn't sunk in.

"Congratulations, sir. Take care of her." My parents didn't, I intentionally didn't add. It was tempting, but it would have only been self-serving.

"We will."

But this blond father, his hair greasy and slicked back with lack of sleep, gave me one part of the answer. He cared about his child. This one wouldn't have her foot crushed or be abandoned. She would be one of the kids that were picked by teams at school. If she came home crying and said that she had been raped she would be believed.

I left the happy family and headed back to the transplant ward. I spent at least fifteen minutes with each patient. Some of them had been in for weeks or months waiting for the right donor to come along or to die. While I kept my disposition sunny when I talked to each, I had to dry my tears between rooms.

These were real people with real lives. The future of his three teenage daughters worried one man. He offered me a picture showing a trio of beautiful, smiling girls with long, shiny brown hair. They were all very close to college age and if he died they wouldn't be able to "attain higher schooling without a miracle." His words, not mine. He had a very eastern pronunciation and diction. He waited for a new liver. Cancer had chewed his up and spit it out so quickly that he was in the hospital before he really knew he had a problem. A routine exam had caught the ailment.

One, an infant in an incubator, had been born with spina bifida, and seeing the bone stick through the skin of its back almost caused me to sob in front of her parents. Fortunately for the baby, it was not an extreme case as just a spinal and skin graft would solve the problem. The parents sat twisting their hands. They never even acknowledged my presence. They just hugged and held each other, speaking in tones too low to hear and with tears that needed no sounds.

The rest of the day blurred from one patient to another. All the needs I saw were pathetic in some way or another. Tubes violating the utmost privacy of their bodies. Men, women, and children all with severe medical problems or trauma, and all with people who cared standing by the bed with tears in their eyes or a brave face for the patient or to the outside world.

I ended up back into a pink space suit and in the room with young Susan, her skin so blackened and brittle that it broke if touched. I stood there watching the machines breathe and pump blood for her. I don't know how long I stared, but it must have been quite a while. A nurse touched my shoulder and pointed to my greening breathing filter. I went out and sat in the chair outside the room, still in the pink plastic.

No matter what I thought or did, I kept getting one single vision. I kept seeing a human equation with ten people and each extended family on one side and one carved, butchered baby on the other. Several hours passed as I thought it through. I don't know that I found I didn't care about the "not quite children," but I did know what the greater good was. To that add that the babies from the School weren't wanted in most of the cases anyway, I rationalized. I know what it felt like to be unwanted with a family that threw me away. I had turned cold and callous and very self-centered through that last nine months. I was a different person. I hardened on the inside. I can't say I liked it, but you can't deny yourself and remain sane.

The gruesome picture of a flayed baby came back to mind and I compared it with the horror of the patients I had just visited. A vision of human body parts on a giant balance scale and the grim reaper stood on the other.

A decision formed in my head. I knew the answer. I knew what the answer had to be for me, no matter how horrible it was.

Maybe my decision had been selfish. Maybe I could have been able to get somewhere with my seventeen-year-old self with the help of some charity organization or social program. But I really didn't feel safe. If even one mishap came my way, I would flounder and fall amongst the lost souls of this world. I'd become a homeless wretch, doomed to die alone. It frightened me too much to even give it adequate consideration, especially as it seemed as if I was going to do the right thing anyway.

"Box," I said, once I'd found a phone, "I'm ready to come back. I don't care, Box. It's wrong, but so is the alternative. So I'll do the least wrong and do something for me at the same time. Everyone has always taken what they want from me. I want for me for a change. I want a baby to sell."

"I'll be t'ere as soon as I can."

I had taken the next step toward the monster I am now. Was it the wrong thing to do? What was right? Was it even possible to do right at that moment? I still don't know, but I do know that I'm going to die for that and one other decision.

November 1, 2050

I don't know who is more nervous, me or those around me. Even the guards are quiet when they walk near my cell—especially Peggy. No one speaks and if they are talking, they stop. It's like a fucking tomb. I mean I'm not dead yet. I feel like some unclean, diseased thing. I seem to keep covering the same ground over and over again—life, death, God, religion. If I weren't so depressed I'd make some wisecrack about being overly superfluously redundant.

"Tell me about Box, Elizabeth," Father Peter asked this morning as he rubbed the center of his cross like he was trying to take something sticky off of it by friction alone.

"Box was a wonderful man. I don't think I ever heard him say a bad word. Of course that's not hard when you say as few things as Box did."

"Did he ever tell you that he loved you?"

"That's a funny question, Father."

"Why is it so funny?"

"Well it just seems that way. But thinking back, I can't ever remembering him saying those words but he showed love in his actions."

"Like what?"

"All of the things he did for me."

"I think you are missing my point," Father IronSky said, readjusting himself in his chair. "Let's try something a bit more basic. What is love?" I tried to answer until I realized I didn't know how to answer something that I could only feel. It was so seemingly simple. I sat with my mouth opened to say something but nothing came out. "I thought that might stump you. I think I can put into words what you are having such difficulty with, Elizabeth. Love is the ability to put aside your own needs for the needs of someone else."

"Well, then Box definitely loved me. He gave his life to save mine."

"The ultimate love. Now, did you love him, Elizabeth?"

Father IronSky could really get to you. He asked simple questions that haunt you for hours. He didn't often get an answer to his query before he had to leave. I think I'm closer to crying now than I've been in years. I need Box to tell me what to do. He always could cut through the crap and see what really mattered, just like Anita. I hope that someone is taking care of you, Box. You are a good man. Oh, fuck . . .

Sorry for the tear stains. That felt good. Everyone needs a self-pity jag from time to time; it helps make things clear. Anyway, back to it. I don't have much time to finish this story and this is one thing I want to complete.

Box took me back to his home. In the daylight I could see that his ranch house sat on a large plot of land, maybe an acre or so. For LA, that is huge. They pack houses in there like sardines. If you have a two-foot grass strip around your house, you have a grand yard. With elm, oak and black pine trees set up strategically so that you couldn't even see the neighbors, the open glade-like atmosphere of Box's estate reminded me of the country. The land alone must have been worth a fortune.

He took me directly inside to a chef-quality kitchen, with copper-bottom pans and cooking utensils hanging neatly from the ceiling. I sat in a little breakfast nook just on the other side of a long, butcher-block counter from the kitchen.

"What ya want fer food. Bet ya din't even eat yesterday," Box said as he planted a chilled glass of tomato juice in front of me. My stomach chose that moment to let out a rumble loud enough that even Box heard it. "I guess t'at answered t'at question," he said with a smile. I managed a little giggle.

"I guess I'll eat anything that doesn't eat me first. By the way, what is with your voice? I mean one minute I would take you for an Oxford graduate and the next you sound like a hick out of the Deep South." Box moved busily in the kitchen, but the lighting, almost directly in my face, kept me from making out the exact details.

"T'is is how I talk normal-like. I grew up wit' it, girly. My pappy talked like t'is and now I do, too. It be comfortable wit' no strain." His voice abruptly changed both in tone and timbre. "I have to concentrate to keep up this facade in my voice, but when I do business, I can't very well sound like an uneducated ne'r-do-well from the southern extremities of our fair nation, now can I?" I giggled again. He did have a point. Box smiled at me. His white teeth sparkled brightly against his black face.

"I guess not."

"Ya do light up when ya smile, Lizzy," Box said as he rummaged in the kitchen for this or that. I'm sure I blushed at least pink and maybe even into a deep mauve. Box stood up from behind the counter wearing a full-length chef's apron. I laughed again. My large benefactor showed me his white teeth. "What? Ya never seen real cookin', girl?"

"I guess not," I said with a grin of my own. Box turned away to the stove.

"I can get ya doctors to impregnate ya, girly." It took me by surprise. I wasn't ready for it. Box was never one to let something important slide by in a change of topic.

"No, Box. I don't like doctors and I don't like hospitals. Scratch that, I hate doctors and I loathe hospitals, but I do like you. Would you please do it?" Box did what he normally does. He kept his use of words to an absolute minimum. He didn't directly answer my question.

"Ya gonna need yer strength, girl. Doct'rs say it'll take a minim o't'ree months fer ya t'get yer body back. Start now. One mushroom'n Swiss omelet," he said putting a green stoneware plate bearing a beautiful, fluffy omelet garnished with two quarters of a navel orange. How did he do that so fast?

"So ya gonna stay in m'guest room, right?" I must have been hungrier than I thought as I already had a full mouth. The omelet should have been in the Getty Museum as a work of art. Box was more than a cook; he was a master chef.

"Uhhhhh," I mumbled intelligently around my food.

"I might be able t'get ya an advance from Spouse if'n ya gonna get knocked up, but even wit' t'at yer gonna stay here." I reluctantly swallowed what was in my mouth so I could talk.

"I couldn't, Box. This is your home and I'd just be in the way."

"Alligator feat'ers. I got more room here'n I knows what t'do wit'."

"Well, if Margaret will give me an advance then I can get my own place for three months and I won't be in your way at all." I sneaked in another bite. How can someone make such a simple food so delectable?

"Well, I know yer stay'n here, but I know ya are a stubborn bitch. Here's the paper," Box said, tossing Thursday's two-pound *LA Times* onto the counter next to me. As the sharp cheddar cheese, mild mushrooms and fluffy egg whites created a symphony across my taste buds, I turned to the "For Rent" section of the paper. I nearly dropped my fork. I did have to swallow very carefully to prevent myself from choking. The cheapest place I found was a studio apartment in Watts at $700 a month, or $400 a month as a roommate in a one bedroom apartment; both were way beyond my means.

"Uh, Box. I've reconsidered." He didn't even look up from his own omelet.

"I knew ya would."

Box was very businesslike about the whole arrangement. He would charge me $300 a month, payment due when I delivered. I didn't hesitate. I later found out that he had "performed this service" for several of the mercenary girls in the past, but that was his business—and just business (although it dredged up an uncomfortable feeling within me nonetheless).

Later in the day he managed to wheedle Spouse into letting me have an advance on the money I would get for showing up at the door pregnant. This allowed me to pay the rest of my own way and not feel like a fifth wheel or a mooch.

Box even went so far as to offer me the use of one of his cars. The green '97 Taurus was a classic, but I'd never buy one—yuck. It didn't matter to me other than as a gesture. I politely declined. Hell, I didn't even have a license. Box took me down and corrected that lack a few weeks later, but I still didn't take him up on his offer. In fact, I stayed at home unless Box took me somewhere. I never asked but he did it for me anyway. I still thought of it as our friendship. What Anita and the other women believed hadn't stuck or sunk in to me.

We went out to various restaurants most evenings. Box showed me the nightlife in LA. I must say that I found most of it totally boring. Flashing lights, deafeningly loud, depressing music, bungee dancing, and multiple-partner sex on the floor wasn't my bag. From the look Box wore, it wasn't his either. After I confessed to him, one evening before I went off to my room, that I didn't want to go out the next evening, he took the hint. That's all it usually took with Box, a hint. He read my moods like a book. After that we found more sedate entertainment.

We went to an incredible acoustical guitar concert in Highland Park. Box found a chess exhibition by Daniel Fischer at the Museum of Natural History. Fischer played one hundred and fourteen matches simultaneously. He beat me in forty-seven moves. He beat Box in thirty-five. A classical symphony, a quiet walk in LA National Forest, La Brea Tar Pits, Universal Studios, The Museum of Tolerance (rebuilt after being firebombed in '22), the West Coast Smithsonian, Huntington Library. These were amusements I enjoyed.

I took most of the money from Spouse and started my own savings account at Far West Savings. The greenbacks that I didn't use for nights and days out, I used to buy some things for me— my own clothes. I burned out even Box's tolerance on the first shopping trip. I think it was when I spent four hours trying to decide between a royal-blue, knee-length lace dress and a powder-blue pantsuit. I ended up buying both. That Box didn't like my shopping worked for both of us. Box still indulged my newfound fetish by dropping me at some mall or other and heading off to conduct business, while I tried hard not to think about what he did. He would pick me up in the evening after his rounds. I found being alone with all the unworn clothes in that mall titillating. By the end of the second day I was glad that I had already deposited that money and it was safely where I couldn't get at it. I was hooked. One of the only drugs I've ever succumbed to was the need for new, fresh clothes.

It must have been because my parents deprived me as a child, or maybe men are right that women just have a shopping gene. The reasons didn't matter because I loved all the different fabrics, colors and styles. I was giddy and dizzy, out looking for just the right thing. I did learn that clothes could make the woman. I found myself just a bit less dumpy when I had just the right outfit on. Shoes! Oh grief, but I could have spent my entire advance just on shoes! A pair of azure blue ankle-strap pumps I just had to have. Just getting the right shade was a glorious experience. Ahhh. By the end of my first night of shopping I think I was sexually aroused. By the end of the second night I was sure of it. My Gawd!

After my second splurge, I decided that I'd better be a bit more practical with my purchases. I talked to Box about the things allowed and disallowed at the School. It was an enlightening list:

- Any clothing (except platform or high-heeled shoes) was allowed but discouraged (!)
- No automobiles (as if I could afford one!)
- No animals/pets of any kind
- No cameras
- No boom-boxes, TriVid sets (could be distracting to neighbors, both in and out of the School)
- No single item valued at over $100
- Books and games were highly encouraged
- Pictures, allowed
- No weapons of any kind (yeah, right)
- No drugs (medication must be re-prescribed by the School's physician)
- No phones, pagers or computers
- Diaries and letter-writing materials were encouraged
- Makeup was allowed but not encouraged
- Craft items encouraged
- No "sexual materials" (Spouse was something of a prude so no magazines, toys or the like. This included MEN. Now how in the heck am I going to smuggle one of THOSE into the School, huh?)
- Bedding materials allowed but discouraged
- Pillow (allowed)
- No food of any kind (!)

To play it safe, I decided that I would stay away from anything that was discouraged and make sure I had anything that was encouraged. Other things, I would make up my mind for myself. I decided to make a list of things to buy that I would take with. I knew I wouldn't NEED anything, but I wanted to be more comfortable.

Encouraged List

- Books and games
- Monopoly
- Scrabble and dictionary (the School didn't have this game and it had driven me to distraction as I loved to play)
- Several decks of cards (found I could buy cases of card seconds from the LA casinos at a fraction of retail)
- Diary and letter-writing materials
- Reams of paper and dozens of pens
- Lockable diary?
- Feather pillow (The rocks wrapped with cloth that the School hands out are only good for weapons. You end up chasing lumps around in them all night)

Items I Want to Take

- Makeup (!)
- Two "changeable combination" locks (for my footlocker)
- Robe
- Chewing gum (marginal item per the list)
- Flashlight
- Watch (with alarm)

I wanted to experiment with makeup. I really didn't have a clue, but maybe one of the other girls at the School would help me. I was learning the importance of fitting in. Properly attired people no longer looked at me as if I belonged in a petting zoo. I found that most of my dumpiness could be traced back to my own lack of caring rather than innate ugliness. Oh, I still wasn't beautiful, but when I was happy and dressed well, I didn't make dogs howl.

When my spending spree ended, I was surprised how far I did manage to stretch my dollars. Well, it seemed quite a lot at the time, but this was from a girl who didn't have anything. I had managed to spend less than half of the $1200 Spouse had advanced me. I was ready to return to the School. I was now armed against the potent adversary—boredom.

Getting back in shape was no picnic. My first post-delivery period had me nearly bedridden for three days with a brick red discharge thick with large mucus clots. The period cramps themselves dwarfed any pain of being pregnant. The agony had tears dribbling from my eyes despite popping ibuprofen like a chocoholic eating M&Ms. My back ached constantly. I moaned like a ninety-year-old woman on her deathbed. My requests for back rubs went through the roof. Not that Box would have complained, but he later handed me a certificate for three massages by Rudolph Heddi, "Masseur to the Stars." Box did a better job.

Even no longer pregnant I still got those bloody leg cramps. I regularly downed potassium supplements prescribed from Doctor Rob. Not to put too fine a point on it, the cramps weren't pleasant, especially as they habitually arrived while I slept. They weren't quite enough to make me wake up screaming, but they did coincide with The Nightmare, making it all the more real.

Not a night went by since Box had told me about what happened to each fetus without me living this same specific horrific dream. I had quit calling them babies because it was easier to lie to myself. "Fetus" carried a much softer connotation and lighter emotional baggage. I know that my conscience punished me with The Nightmare.

The Nightmare always started the same. I was a peasant farmer girl sent by my father, who looked like my real father, to harvest the crop. When I got to the field I saw nothing but tiny arms, legs, hearts, livers, kidneys and other body parts growing surreally out of the ground. I knew it was a dream, but no matter how hard I pinched myself in the legs to wake myself up, my father would call me a whore and a slut. He would throw a wrench, a pair of pliers, or a screwdriver at me—whatever happened to be handy within his large, shiny red toolbox. If I persisted trying to wake up, he continued to fling heavier items at me. I could even feel the pain of the cold metal tools bouncing off my flesh.

Eventually I would relent and wade into the field. A scythe would appear in my hand and I would begin swinging it in a gruesome arc. A wail of anguish perceptible only through the soles of my feet became the only thing I could hear. Hands, eyeballs, spinal columns and more fell with sweep after sweep of my great blade. Gouts of blood fountained at every swing of my hands and soon my dress dripped in red. As the pseudo-day ended, I looked back at the bloody path I had cut only to see Father laughing, with his arm around Jimmy. They took turns bowling with the head of a baby and drinking beer.

The dream has never completely gone away. It comes less frequently over the years, but it never goes away, as much as I'd like it to.

All in all, the three months I spent with Box after my first bastard, in spite of the dreams, was probably the happiest time I'd had in my life. Box proved to be a wonderful cook, companion and advisor. By the time the thirteenth week of rehabilitation rolled around, the lotus eating had palled. I was ready and wanting to return to the School. It was another extension of a family I was replacing. One minor problem was that I just wasn't qualified yet. I wasn't pregnant.

On that particular day, Box mentioned that I had an appointment with a doctor in town at 10 a.m. I looked at him with some suspicion on my face. He knew I didn't like doctors. For Box, he was wordy with his response.

"Girly, I ain't gonna hurt ya'n any way. Doc's gonna tell us if'n yer body's ready to take another babe." I guess I couldn't argue with that kind of logic. Three months wasn't enough to make it sink in that someone else really might care about me on a gut level.

"OK. In and out. That's all. I don't want to stay any longer than I have to." Box laughed. I then realized just what kind of accidental joke I'd made. I giggled, too.

A stereo-typically pretty nurse/receptionist weighed me and led me to one of the three-meter-by-three-meter exam rooms—with the standard swivel surgical light, tray (with speculum, KY jelly, swabs, and gloves) and the dreaded bed with stirrups. I took my turn waiting in the treatment room, wearing the same paper/cloth vest I had worn numerous times before, when a familiar wavy black-haired head came into the room. Any familiar face seemed good to me at the time. Oddly it relaxed me or maybe it was also just a bit of my self-esteem building up, but I wasn't self-conscious in the slightest.

"Dr. Rob!"

"Well, if it isn't Miss Zimmer. How are you today?" he asked as he stuck my arm with a needle the size of a harpoon for blood. "Bend your elbow over this and keep it elevated. Have you stopped lactating?"

"I'm fine, Doctor. That shot you gave me before I left the hospital dried me up in a week. Nice to see you again."

"I do much of the outside work for Ms. Fox and her school. Feet in the stirrups." As I lay down, I realized that Dr. Rob knew more than I had originally given him credit for. I hated these damned exams but I was going to get through it best as possible. The fluorescent lights in the ceiling were the same shade as always and one lightly flickered just enough to be annoying.

"You know about the School then?"

"Yes. I was just out of medical school when Margaret started it. Slide all the way down. I was one of the first doctors she approached. Now she relies mostly on doctors who have lost their license for one reason or another. Knees all the way apart. It was hectic and dangerous back in the bad old days. Of course danger breeds excitement. This is going to feel a bit cold." It was. "Now it's just another day at the office. Almost makes me long for the bad ole days. But the School needs someone who is registered to work with the women coming out of delivery."

"So what was . . . ungggh . . ."

"Sorry."

"Just a cramp. Forgot to tell you that I always get them. So what was the danger?"

"You have to be kidding, right? Everything looks fine here, no abnormalities. You are a very healthy young woman. I know you were Spouse's secretary for your last few months and I know Abe has told you the whole setup. You do know everything."

"Well, I think I know almost everything," I said, my breathing increasing with my nervousness. I hated the exams, and they were worse than the ones in the School. "This is going to pinch just a little bit." It did. "Back in those days we were dreadfully afraid of being caught by the police. The best we could hope for was mind-wipe. I won't even talk about the worst that could happen. We didn't have the entire establishment in our pocket then. This is going to hurt just a tad." It didn't—it hurt a lot. I didn't emotionally know if something that big should be inside me.

"I don't like corrupt cops, but I really don't feel that we are doing anything wrong. If I did then I wouldn't be here."

"Ow!"

"Sorry. I should have known you would be a bit tender there. I don't think you are doing a wrong thing either, Ms. Zimmer. We need spare parts to keep the sick people of the world healthy. Well, young woman, you seem insufferably healthy. I'll have the lab work by this afternoon and call you. If everything is in order, then you may do what you will. You left your number with the nurse? Good." He snapped his gloves off and tossed them into the trash with, "Have a nice day now."

Dr. Rob exemplified professional. He was that way the entire time I knew him. He was always something of a puzzle I never solved.

A thought came over me. Someone had to prepare the fetus for sale. I wondered about the surgeon who performed the removals. Was he a fanatic to our cause? Was he being paid such a ludicrous sum that he didn't care? Or was he just crazy? Was it even a "he"? Can you imagine the doctor going home after a day of work?

"Hi, dear. How was your day?"

"Rough. Fourteen procedures on one product alone today, and that was in the morning. Eight skin grafts, a spinal column, heart, liver, both lungs and the brain. I didn't even get in a round of golf in the afternoon because there was an emergency C-section needed by the School."

"Poor darling. How about I get you a nice martini?"

No, I didn't envy the doctors, defrocked or not. If I had a moral mountain of my own to surmount, then they climbed Kilimanjaro.

Box and I waited that evening in a deadening silence. Anxiousness seemed to weigh the room down. We tried to play chess but I beat Box so badly that after three games he gave up in disgust. The phone finally rang and Box jumped for it.

"Hello? Yes, she's here."

"Yes?"

"Miss Zimmer, could you confirm your date of birth?" It was a computer-generated response system.

"April 13, 2020."

"Thank you. I can give you the results in scientific format if you like, but the results are that the blood and samples you submitted are all within normal limits for a woman of your age, weight, height, race and social class. Do you have any questions?"

"No."

"Thank you and good day."

"They say I'm fine, Box." Those five words seemed to create an awkward silence.

What followed in my bed managed to be clean, almost sterile, and very mechanical. Box left almost immediately. I can't say that it did anything for me at all, but after what Jimmy Hendsen had done to me, I was sure it wouldn't be excessively enjoyable. It wasn't unenjoyable, though. It seemed nothing more than getting lunch at a fast food counter—not bad, but definitely not good. The "Me First" plan required it as a necessary evil.

November 2, 2050

Death Eve. Rather morbid of me, isn't it. Like some great countdown clock, but it's not the witching hour that will be reached, nor cuckoo's croak, but rather the drop of the headman's ax. Almost sounds like a poem. I'm sorry if I run away with myself or omit things. My time is getting short and I have to finish this for me, if no one else.

I caught the pregnancy bug almost immediately. Over the following years, my womb proved to be a fertile little furrow. One plowing anywhere at approximately the right time and I grew a crop that took me almost nine months to fruit. The next six years were a happy time full of adventure. My belly waxed for nine months with three months or so of waning to break the monotony.

Yes, I went back to the School many times. At several points I had enough money to consider other options but why would I? I was better prepared mentally, physically and emotionally. The women on the floor accepted me. "Faced the devil, haven't you, girl," as one girl put it. I had. I hadn't reached my full confidence yet, but I no longer proved an easy mark for my fears. The fire of experience had burned away my naiveté. Not only wasn't it nearly as bad the second time, but I belonged.

The sounds and smells of the School, once frightening and almost repulsive, now felt like those of home. My new family was just packed a bit too tight. We rubbed together with some friction but there was warmth behind even harsh words. At the School I felt wanted and loved if even only a little bit. When you'd grown up with none or even negative love, a little bit filled your soul with joy. Life provided the briefest glimmer of why women stay in abusive relationships. I started to understand my mother in a twisted way. She had a sad life but one she couldn't give up any more than I could now give up the School, Spouse or Box. So, if you will pardon the pun, I slept like a baby, even on the cot on the main floor.

Yes, I went back the second time with my eyes open. This

time it was for me. My second and later pregnancies never caused the same angst or problems my first did. I have a theory that might explain that odd phenomenon. I think my family, the rape, and unwanted fetus so wound me up that I might have made something relatively normal, like pregnancy, into my own private nightmare. Oh, I still suffered symptoms but they seemed remarkably minor in comparison to what I suffered through with that first bastard. Also, after my first, I didn't feel like my fetus waited to devour me from the inside out like some malignant thing. I have never felt close to the merchandise I created, but I never again felt as if I needed to claw it from my belly in self-defense.

That first time I went back, Spouse immediately picked me to move back into my old job. However, she couldn't just toss my replacement out on her ear, so Margaret left me on the floor with the other women until her secretary's time came.

It took Spouse's assistant about three months to produce. Margaret waited nary a second afterward before calling me in to take up my old position. I squeezed a few more minor concessions out of her. I had learned to take care of myself.

It took me nearly a month to defunk all the things that my replacement had funked up. Worse (or better), as soon as Spouse learned I knew the whole story, I became even busier, dealing with more unsavory correspondence, sales, contacts and phone calls from the supplier side of the business. I treated me like part of the family and that had me up to my neck in work. It was fantastic!

Now that I knew where our gross came from, Spouse gave me more detailed data. I learned why a fetus was worth $500,000.

Let's take some average numbers, as things can and do fluctuate:

Liver	$100K	$100K
Kidney	$180K@	$360K
Skin	$1@cm2	$3K
(yes, over 3000 square cm of skin on each baby)		
Eyes	$300	$0.6K
Intestine	$1K	$1K
Bone Marrow	$50K	$50K
Other organs	$2K	$2K
		=======
TOTAL		**$515.6K**

I guess the human body resembled what happened with a new automobile. The parts were worth more than the whole.

For six years I alternated busier than a one-armed mother of triplets for nine months and being a lady of leisure for three more. With my expanded responsibilities and because of my broad knowledge, I soon had my hand in every nook and cranny of the School's organization.

One day Margaret (I had begun thinking of her as Spouse only when I was mad at her) and I went over the exorbitant expenses for catering.

"Those bastards are stealing me blind," Ms. Fox said with the catering check beneath her hand. "I think they cart out over half of the produce they bring in."

"Entirely possible but you'd need to pay more in guards checking what comes in and goes out from those trucks than they are taking from you."

"I guess what can't be cured must be endured," Margret said, reaching for her pen to sign the check.

I'd been thinking about this problem for a week. My thoughts just burst out of my mouth before I could censor them. "Why not buy individual meals prepared offsite?"

"Huh?" Margaret retorted. "That would cost more per meal per person."

In for a penny, in for a pound, I thought as I continued. "But lower labor costs. No cooks or servers, or at least many fewer. Thus lower bribes needed to keep people quiet. The lowered cost would offset the increased expenditure.

"Also you could also reclaim the kitchen space for more cot space, increasing the gross. Not that you care so much but food lines would move faster. Fewer messes from smell induced vomiting and thus lesser need for replacement snacks."

Margaret just looked at me with pursed lips and a wrinkled brow. Without another word she signed her check. I briefly worried I'd so overstepped my bounds that she would fire me. Instead, one week later the girls were given meals prepared offsite. They were much better quality and tastier. A construction crew began removing the majority of our kitchen space. On the same day Margaret handed me an envelope with a gruff, "Good job."

She walked away and never mentioned it again. The envelope contained a check for twenty thousand dollars. The memo line stated "profit sharing." I almost fell over.

Margaret really knew how to run a business even if she grudgingly gave verbal praise. That one little boost gave me all the incentive I needed to take initiative in other things.

I stopped holding back and offered suggestions from time to time. Most of these were simple suggestions like screening girls for known congenital diseases, high risk to miscarriages, or paying a higher bonus for rare blood or marrow types. Margaret's trust and occasional bonus gave me an even warmer feeling of belonging, like a little girl who'd done the dishes for my mother without being asked.

I suggested to Box (and got my way, after a rather heated argument) that we expand into other markets. A great number of cybernetic machines, like LO Craft, manufacturing assembly lines, space station control, and many other too numerous to mention, required actual brains, human brains, to function properly. Until my brainstorm (pun intended) they had to wait on accidental deaths in children who were killed at or near birth. Now we could supply that need at will. This alone boosted our net by nearly twelve percent.

This latest new market put to bed most of what little guilt I still carried for killing the fetuses. Now a great number of them were going to have a life after all. It might not be the one that God (whoever that might be) had predetermined for them, but it was a life and probably a much better life than they would have had otherwise. As a result, I rarely thought of the "children" that we were condemning to death or other worse fates. Instead they became simply a product to sell—a product we, by necessity, had to sell quietly lest the Secret Service decide that we all needed mind wipes.

Oh, yes, Box regularly came to visit me on business, so we weren't technically breaking any School rules; however, we did bend them a great deal. In addition we would sit and talk for an hour or two over a chessboard at least twice a week or so. By that point, I could have broken pretty much any of the rules, but I wanted the girls to have a good example. Girls? Listen to me.

Women, and many of them were considerably older than I was. But Margaret held me up as the shining totem that they were measured against.

When you think of twelve hundred women from different backgrounds, cultures, and in some cases nations, and all of them hormonally challenged, you have an extremely volatile mix. Realistically though, for a community of our size, we had very few problems with discipline. I wish I could claim the credit for it, but Margaret set up the system long ago and had refined it until it worked. Her true genius is what we rode.

"Elizabeth, come into my office," Ms. Fox said one evening after hours, far into my third time at the School. I grabbed my dictation tablet and sat across from her. Her wrinkled brown and pursed lips foretold her doing some serious thinking. I wondered if I'd done something wrong. I couldn't have been further from the truth.

"Elizabeth, you have become more than indispensable in running the School. You've done more to increase my wealth than . . . well, anyone but me. The other owners of the School have also noticed their increased cuts and have been asking questions."

Being the object of attention among those odd rich but faceless people I knew only as bank accounts made my gut squirm.

"When I explain you to them and how you've increased our gross and profits both by forty-six percent they ask what I've done to make sure you stick around and continue to make them richer. So we've decided to give you a very small share of our profits."

"Excuse me?"

"I guess I'd call you a junior partner. You are to get one percent of my cut as long as you are involved."

At first I thought she was pulling my leg . . . hard. I laughed, until Margaret's face got a puzzled look on it. I choked on my mirth. "You aren't kidding?"

"Elizabeth, you should know by now that I never, ever kid about money. You deserve that money for all you have done for the School."

"Er—" I eloquently retorted.

One percent doesn't sound like much until you look at it from the earlier numbers I computed. Ms. Fox brought in over

100M USD per year. That means my own cut would be almost a million. The twenty-five thousand I got per baby had been a large sum of money to me. I felt comfortable with twenty-five thousand. Someone had turned that easy number into merely a single drop in an ocean. It seemed too big to wrap my head around.

My mind didn't work right for several days as I tried to gestalt this change to my fortune. I couldn't even fathom all of its implications. I stumbled around in a daze. More than once Spouse had to pull me up short because I just stopped doing anything.

I will admit during that time I had several fantasies. Most people think of money in terms of luxuries and good living. My first thoughts ran to revenge. How like the Count of Monte Cristo. I already knew money carried its own power. I just never thought I would have more than enough for just my survival. Now I found that I might have a glut of it.

I figured being on the inside of a criminal organization it wouldn't be hard for me to find someone to hurt Jimmy . . . oh, and my father . . . and anyone else that had wronged me.

It made for some very lovely dreams. One that played over and over had Jimmy being framed for child molestation followed by the gang rapes he endured in prison. I also envisioned my father's work forcing him to take a job building the new Vatican on Titan. He was indentured to sixteen hours a day in brutal conditions, losing many fingers and toes to frostbite.

But they were childish fantasies although they did give me some peace. By the time I actually banked enough cash to put anything into action, my bloodlust had faded. I'd firmly slammed the door on my past. But let me mention what I chose instead, out of order.

I could have had Jimmy Hendsen and his "helpers" eliminated in a most horrible way. I could have had my father reduced to blubbering jelly or an incoherent mass of meat if I had but spoken the word. Instead, I had them watched so that if they even twitched the wrong way, the law would come down on them.

The bribe hadn't cost me much and its source provided a fine sense of irony. George Bunn, the sheriff in my old town, proved rather inexpensive to own and was as corrupt as a high school drug dealer. The honorable Henry Tate, the local magistrate, cost a bit more. I kept him on staff to throw the book at any of my family or the Jimmy Hendsen crew if any of them came to his bench.

Every year I got a report from a private investigator I kept on retainer. Eventually Jimmy went to jail for tax evasion. My father got thrown in the clink for spousal abuse. I have to make it clear I didn't exercise vengeance. In each case those men made their own choices having nothing to do with me. I just gave the local authorities an incentive to keep a special eye on them.

Back to the massive raise, I guess you would call it. It wasn't real. It didn't become real until our business deposited $US 94,834.14 into my virgin Cuban numbered bank account (it had been a low grossing month). Even then it seemed just like digits on a screen. I actually withdrew ten grand and had it wired to me. I kept that bundle of hundred dollar bills in my bedroom. I touched it. I smelled it. It was real.

And while the aphorism "you can't buy happiness with money" is quite true, I learned over the following years that you can certainly find happiness easier with cash than without it.

Families, especially the pseudo family I had at the School, have interesting dynamics. During my third pregnancy I got my own nickname. I overheard it the first time when I passed behind two unaware girls at a lunch table. When they realized I'd overheard them, they were all but struck dumb.

"What was it that you called me?" I could see the terror in their faces. They knew I was Spouse's girl. While I'd never abused my familiarity with the queen bee, they knew I had it.

"Uh, Refer, Miss," stammered out one of the two.

"Refer? Why? I don't do weed."

"Oh, we know that, Miss. It is because you are cold like an icebox." The girl actually used the old term for a refrigerator. Refer and Box. I liked it. I nodded to the girls and walked away. I'm sure they expected me to try to exact retribution, but instead I gave them each a pleasant friendship gift, a new feather pillow, to show my pleasure. They didn't know the why of it as I didn't explain. I don't think anyone understood. They didn't realize they had validated my life and my desire to be envied, feared, and looked up to.

The respect—and I'll be honest, fear—from the women on the floor continued and grew as I handled more of the day-today aspects of the School, including discipline. Somewhere during my repeated trips to the School it became clear to everyone else that I was the obvious and logical replacement to Ms. Fox when she retired. I, in my usual well-defined self-examination (sarcasm definitely intended), didn't notice the creeping change. It took being slapped in the face with a dead fish to make me aware.

Late in the afternoon Box came running into Spouse's office (she had been absent most of the day) out of breath.

"C'mon, girl. We gotta git ya ready."

"For what?" I replied testily. As a bulging Eight in my sixth pregnancy, my back ached, I felt I needed to pee constantly and I leaned backward to balance my latest product. I couldn't wait for the doc to harvest my field so I could have a three- or four-month breather again. It put me in no mood for games, but it wasn't like Box to hurry for anyone. He always moved at a stately pace so I wondered.

"The ot'er partners are here. T'ey wanna meet ya."

"Partners, what are you talking about, Box?"

"T'e partners in ta School. T'ey wanna talk ta ya."

I still didn't understand the implications of those nameless accounts and the billions that they represented wanting to talk to me. "Like this?" I said, pointing at the mustard stain on my gown from the pastrami on rye I'd had at lunch and the slippers on my swollen feet. "You're out of your mind, Box."

"No. We gotta get ya some fancy duds. T'ey meet'n us at Morton's."

Eeek. Morton's restaurant was THE landmark in LA. Everyone who was anyone went there. I did need something fabulous. "No time, Box. There isn't enough time. It's already four. Even if we are going to have dinner at seven or eight we don't have a chance." Box was tired of arguing with me. He grabbed me by the arm and dragged me off behind him.

"We gotta make time, girly." Box took me to Rodeo Drive in Beverly Hills. *Yeah*, I thought, *Lotsa maternity shops on Rodeo Drive.*

From the snide looks, I'm certain the sales staff drew lots. The loser had to invite the frumpy pregnant woman and her black escort to leave.

"Excuse me, Miss, but this is . . ."

Box used his salesman voice. "Miss, but we are in a hurry. Do you have a staff hair=dresser?"

"Why of course, but the costs of our boutique are not insignif—" The snooty bitch almost swallowed her tongue when Box dropped a small duffle on the floor. Only four, of many more, bundles of hundreds spilled out, still with their Bank of America bands on them. "I see. Priscilla, could you come help us."

The women at the shop fell all over themselves to help from that point forward.

I received several pleasant surprises. Atia de La Renta had a line of maternity wear that set my mouth to watering. I did manage not to drool but only barely.

I ended up in a long, wrapped burgundy lamé dress that left no imagination as to my pregnancy status. In fact, it emphasized it. It accentuated my swollen breasts by being quite low-cut.

"Isn't this a bit too . . . provocative?"

"Madame is proportioned perfectly to—"

"Lizzy, ya look great no matter whatcha wear. But t'is is ta right t'ing. Most important t'at ya look rich, not ifn ya look sexy 'r not."

Do men normally just buy whatever the salesmen throw at them? That Box, the man that shied away from any clothing store, would offer *any* advice on fashion gave me the confidence to wear that dress proudly.

I got a matching pair of burgundy flats, which had a built in illusion that they were high heels. I didn't know how it was done, but I was walking flat and it looked like I was teetering on five-inch spikes.

The house stylist, Toni, ELLE-certified of course, did a quick wash and cut for my hair. I ended up with a smashing, short, split-level pageboy cut reminiscent of Katherine Flynn-Seymour in last year's *Three Nights of Autumn*. While Toni performed his magic, a nail artist squeezed in and started on my hands. After placing my arm through a protective screen (so my hair wouldn't ruin her work), she managed to set some medium-length acrylic nails in a French manicure—clear nails with white tips. Just for style, I had her add a small diamond into the center of each. By then, money didn't impress me as I was a millionaire in my own name.

Box kept rushing everyone to get done faster and threw money around like he had invented it. He snapped and shouted at the top of his lungs like a jovial tyrant. And all the while he fitted his big black body into a powder white suit—an event not to be missed.

A blood-red, stretch limousine met us at the door of the salon and then deposited us at Morton's. The maître d' ushered Box and me into a private back room, where I found Margaret and met three well-dressed men without female escorts but each with a pair of bodyguards. A tiny Asian man introduced himself as Mr. Nguyen. The other two were Anglos, one with naturally red hair and the other blond. The blond, Mr. Smith, wore a solid, muscular look beneath his tailored suit. If he couldn't have lifted me easily, pregnant as I was, I would have eaten my dress. When I shook his hand it still carried the calluses from real work.

I watched the redhead, Mr. John Doe, use his pinky to lift a stray hair back into place. His tiny, gold-rimmed glasses perched on his freckled nose. By the way he offered his hand, I wondered if he expected me to kiss it.

I won't mention their real names here. They had provided pseudonyms but it didn't take a private eye to determine who they really were. You could visualize past gangster types, right out of a Hollywood or Tokyo production at the table with me. They existed as cutout men for one of the big corps. Even on death row it probably wouldn't be healthy to name them.

That night the conversation remained quiet and reserved even if it didn't set any records for congeniality. I smiled at the right places, laughed at their jokes, and tried not to show my real feelings for them. I doubt they would have minded, but just the same, if there was a possibility that I would have to associate with them, I didn't want to have to worry about my car blowing up or arsenic in my food. Let them be whomever they wanted as long as they held up their end of the partnership—muscle of both the political and physical kind.

Like I said earlier, sometimes I just have to be slapped in the face with a dead fish. Each of them sized me up. Once I admitted that to myself, I expected to be grilled on a number of topics but it never happened. These men prided themselves on being able to smell a person's worth. Instead, we shared dishes of escargot (I never did care for snails), broiled Maine lobsters, and Siberian prime rib. I wisely begged out of the alcohol due to my pregnancy.

After three hours I felt that the two Anglo men approved of me—I could read it in their faces. The tiny Asian man's feelings I couldn't grasp despite my extensive reading on the Asian cultures of late. I figured I had two cultural biases working against me—the first was the overall Japanese bias against showing emotion and the second was the regional prejudice against women. I think I made a slight impression but couldn't be sure. The evening stuck in my memory as a fascinating look into the underworld—not as outwardly slimy as you might expect.

I didn't get the after-action report until the next day. "I want to congratulate you. You made quite an impression last night," Spouse remarked after she asked me into her office.

"Really? I couldn't tell with Mr. Nguyen."

"Oddly enough Mr. Nguyen is your strongest supporter."

"Really? I think I'm speechless."

"Yes. He said, 'Elizabeth is an attractive, insightful and brilliantly well-mannered woman. She will be exceptional as your replacement.'"

"So if I translate that correctly, I didn't dress like a whore, I could discuss business, and I didn't speak while the menfolk were talking." I had learned how much I could get away with in Margaret's presence.

"Elizabeth, that is a very biased attitude."

"Not at all. Truth is truth. I'd never admit this to Mr. Nguyen, but I found him stuck-up and overbearing for a tiny little shit." What I didn't share even to Margaret was that I also found him charming and attractive. He probably would land in my masturbatory fantasies. "This does not take away from the fact that I am doing business with him, so I adapt." Ms. Fox didn't answer but gave me a charring look that told me I might have crossed that invisible line.

"You know there is one other partner that must agree to vet you?"

"No, I thought I had met them all last night."

"Not at all, Elizabeth. The last one is the governor of Southern California."

"Edwin Cuan," I mouthed quietly. I'd never met him but everything I'd seen on the news and blogs led me to believe that slime would come off his hand if I shook it. Apparently Mr. Cuan, who I never ever met (past, present, or future), passed on me sight unseen.

Despite my overwhelming approval, a year later I decided that I'd had enough. As a solid Eight in my seventh pregnancy, a little more than eight years after a rape that had changed my life dramatically, it was time to fly the nest. Not a three-month hiatus like before, but something much more drastic. At twenty-five I needed to take life in my own hands and live it. Ms. Fox wore more gray in her hair than any other color, but I didn't know when or if she would ever leave her work, so I had to begin to make plans for myself.

Over the years my confidence had grown. I no longer needed anyone's help or love to stand on my own. I didn't need the School to be a surrogate family for me. I decided that once I delivered my seventh product, I would quit the business and find a nice, quiet place to retire and do what I wanted for a change. I have to emphasize that I wasn't unhappy at the School, quite the contrary, but I was tired of having my belly covered in oil and stretch marks. I wanted a shower to myself. I had suffered through too many aches. And, well, it was just time I grew up.

I had spent the last eight years with my uterus waxing and waning. I had accumulated, with my percentage and my fetus fees, US $6,934,443.12. I could have a life anywhere in the world for that kind of money. I could live comfortably on the interest on that money alone. If I wanted to live lavishly I could easily move to a depressed region (Canada, Spain, or anywhere in southern Asia) and lived like a queen. I hadn't quite yet decided exactly what I was going to do, or where I was going to go, but I was going to do it and I was going to go.

Australia had always intrigued me, or perhaps England. The good old U.S. of A. had lost its appeal. Here there seemed to be too many laws with not enough teeth. It made for a bad mix. I wanted to sit on the laurels that I had so patiently earned with my belly. Then, later, if someone wanted to pull me out of retirement to run the School, I would, as an obligation I felt I had to repay.

I hadn't shared my plans with anyone, not even Box. I'd surfed on my computer a bit to find likely locations. I thought maybe I'd start with a world cruise. The thought appealed to me to be carefree and not beholden to anyone.

Well, I should say that those were my plans. Like all things in life, plans have a way of getting changed by things outside your control, or as Margret had told me repeatedly O.B.E—overtaken by events. I was ready to get rid of my last product and get on with my life when fate kicked me in the teeth.

Margaret and I sat in the office sharing our lunch (Chinese, of course). We had passed beyond boss and underling to friends over the years (but never in all those years had she told me that Box was her son).

"Were you ever married, Ms. Fox?" I asked between bites of sweet and sour pork.

In her chopsticks she waved a wonton at me. "My husband was a good man, Elizabeth. I fell in love with him at first sight. We got married within the month."

"That's a rather dry account, Ms. Fox."

She laughed around her food. "I was on a high school science trip to the bayou and Louis was our guide. What else is there to tell?"

"Ms. Fox, you don't just fall in love with someone because he guides you through the swamp. Tell me the whole story." Margaret blushed. I knew I was pushing the boundaries of our friendship as she had never, ever, in the eight years I had known her, blushed in my presence. She leaned forward over the desk like some schoolgirl and started talking in a way I never expected from the crusty old matron.

"He was blacker than a boysenberry and built like an iron girder. He didn't wear a shirt and his chest gleamed with sweat." I giggled conspiratorially with her. "All I could think about was to rub my hands across him and . . . Well, you know." Margaret could get rather shy at times and definitely was a prude about anything sexual. It was something that so few knew about her; I mean the shy part. Everyone knew about her three-generations-ago morals on sex.

"So what did you do?" I asked. Margaret turned three other

different shades of pink.

"Well, what could I do? I found a moment away from the group and told him that it wasn't fair that he got to take off his shirt in the heat and I couldn't. I insisted that he let me take mine off in the interest of fairness. It didn't take much after that." To say that my mouth dropped open at this unabashed look at Margaret's life would have been a gross understatement. "I quit school and married Louis. Everything was right with the world, despite the royal fit my parents were throwing. I learned something back then. Distance and time both have ways of mitigating many things. Mother and Father's tantrums in New York didn't carry much weight in Louisiana, and even less in the deep bayous, where there is no formal law and no way to enforce it.

"Louis turned out to be a good man for me. He provided, although in a way I wasn't used to. I learned quickly how to skin and cook a 'gator, make possum stew and crawdad gumbo, and a great number of other things I never knew existed. The way of life hasn't changed in the bayous of Louisiana for hundreds of years even if the bayous themselves keep getting smaller. They do it the way their granddads and grandmas did it. But somehow I fit in. Somehow I was instantly accepted. It amazed me at how willing the local women were to help me. Louis and I had a good life."

"Must have been a good time."

"It was until shortly after you were born. 2027 was the year of changes. You must have been what . . . six or seven? A huge government project planned on building right over the swamp. I never really did find out what it was all about. Probably some senator's idea of getting more jobs for the state. Louis and some of the other locals tried to stop it. They were murdered.

"Oh, we could never prove anything, but one of the companies involved must have had a huge stake in it. They hired a small army of thugs to make sure there wasn't trouble. Louis got in between an anvil and a smith's hammer, with the predictable results." She was silent for only a moment in respect to her dead husband. "This left me in a bad way with no money, my home being destroyed, a young son, and another baby in my belly. I had little in the way of skills. Father and Mother didn't want to have anything to do with me, so I was on my own."

I hung my head. It was all too familiar. Different, but the same. Does everyone have her own trials that are almost insurmountable?

"I remember how it happened. I was sitting in the hospital when I heard some people talking about how much a liver transplant was going to cost, and that was if they were lucky enough to find a donor. It all fell into place. It took most of the rest of my pregnancy to find a doctor I could trust. We went into business."

"Did you ever think it was wrong, Margaret?" She gave me an odd look.

"Yes, but at the time I didn't think I really had any choice. I now know better. I could have stopped any time I wanted over the last ten years, but all I have to do is visit a transplant ward in any hospital and my guilties go away." Margaret looked just a bit pale. I could see that she was now having difficulty talking. It seemed like indigestion or the like because she grabbed one hand to her middle.

"I guess I'm the same. It is sad." What color Margaret had suddenly drained from her face. I was looking at the moon losing its silver during an eclipse. She elicited only one sound, a low moan, as she rolled off her chair onto the floor. By the time I got around the desk, she wasn't conscious. I didn't know what to do. I knew I couldn't call 911, so I called Box. He told me not to worry and that he would be there in a few seconds. I tried to rouse her by slapping her face but it had no effect.

I guess I'm not much in a crisis. Belatedly I remembered we keep our own ambulances parked outside the School to transport those who have reached their time. Not only that but we have at least one doctor on staff. I picked up the phone and started making phone calls. Box beat the doctor and his staff up the stairs by mere heartbeats.

In typical Box fashion, he didn't say much. "Keep t'ings movin' here. I will call ya." He gathered his mother up in his arms and took her down the stairs. The medic called out orders to his staff and scurried around the big black man. I never realized how frail Margaret looked until Box's powerful arms framed her.

November 2, 2050 (P.M.)

A small delegation of Women for Morality and Purity visited today. Three of them came, each wearing a silk suit with a long, nineties-style skirt, and designer high-heels. Three witches over a great, bubbling cauldron came to mind—harridans wearing the guise of the three fates. Peggy, who was trying her damnedest to be polite, gave straight-backed chairs to the trio. The socialites unsuccessfully hid their distaste at where they were and their accommodations.

"Ms. Zimmer," a brunette with a conservative flat-top said haughtily. I stopped her peremptorily.

"That is Mrs. Boxner, ma'am."

"I'm sorry, but your marriage isn't recognized by the state or the church, therefore I will have to go on the premise that you are Miss Zimmer." I could see that this was going nowhere. Anyone willing to be rude to your face must think they hold all the cards. "But, I will accede to your wishes. Mrs. Boxner, we have come here with a proposition to you from the Women for Morality and Purity." I just sat on my bunk looking blankly at them. Who hadn't heard of the Holy Roller Bitch Queens from Heaven? But I couldn't fathom what they wanted with me. "We'll get right to the point. WM&P doesn't believe in capital punishment and we would like to help you." Immediate skepticism.

"I don't get it. First of all, what are you going to do for me? Second, what do you want out of it?"

"A rather calculated way of looking at things, don't you think, Miss . . . er Mrs. Boxner?"

"I've had to be calculating through my life just to get by. No one gave me the luxury to get out of it. And I'm certain that I won't get that opportunity now. Besides, I don't think there is an altruistic bone in your collective bodies." They stiffened. The WM&P stood high among the powers of special interest groups. They hired enough lobbyists to pave the streets of metro

Washington in human bodies.

"Well, we propose to put our political power behind getting your punishment commuted from execution to life in prison."

"Oh, how nice," I said with as much sarcasm as I could muster. "Here I thought you were going to bring in another bit of evidence that would reopen my case and get me acquitted."

"Flippery will get you nowhere, my dear." Her voice sounded like she would just as soon kill me as look at me. "You are guilty, and we all know it. Please don't insult our intelligence."

"Well, again, I ask, 'What do you want?'"

"In return we would ask that you repent your crimes. You would become our model spokesperson, teaching other young people what to do, or more specifically what not to do."

"Yeah, don't get saddled with an abusive family and get raped," I muttered under my breath.

"Excuse me?"

"Sorry, gas. The food in here is terrible." The three moralistic Hellfire and Damnation fems sat smugly. I'll admit I felt tempted.

I looked into my crystal ball (that gray matter I call my brain) and saw the WM&P pounding their breasts proclaiming how they had the right answer to all the problems in the world. "Here was the proof," they would say, parading me on stage and touting me as an example. I would then stand there, my head hung low, hat in hand, and renounce everything I'd done in my life. Everything I believed in. Whether it was wrong or right didn't matter. My life thus far would be a farce. I would betray what Box and Margaret had stood for—and for what? It would earn me the chance to inhabit these white ceramic cells for the next, what, seventy years? No. I think at one time I might have been able to swallow what was left of my pride, but now a lifetime of hypocrisy I could not stand. I had an epiphany. My entire worrisome existence flashed in my brain like a bolt of lightning.

In their own sick and twisted way, these women, these moral women, gave me the answer—the answer I had been looking for and avoiding from the day Box told me we were making parts. No, use the real words, "killing" and "murdering." We were killing children to save other lives. I had been unsuccessful in trying to pigeon-hole my choice into some cosmic Black and White, Right or Wrong, Moral or Immoral category. There was no ultimate "right" or "wrong." The universe held no cosmic switch that was either on or off. It was making the best of choices somewhere in our lives that defined us. I wouldn't second guess myself now. I had to believe I had made the right choices in life at those times. Nothing else made even the slightest sense.

What I had done was as right as I could make it and no one, especially these overdressed, money-for-morals tramps were going to make me feel otherwise. I smiled like a female lioness. I now knew I had no reason to fear meeting whatever maker I would soon stand before.

"Ladies, how many people have you saved?"

"Excuse me?"

"How many people have you saved from death?" The flat-topped bitch smiled as if she were proudly telling her mommy that she went in the potty and had not wet her panties.

"We at the WM&P have saved one hundred and sixteen lives."

"Very impressive. Similar deals as I'm getting, no doubt."

"Certainly."

"I have saved eighty-one thousand lives, directly or indirectly, thirty-five from my uterus alone. We won't mention the almost two hundred thousand or more I saved from permanent disfigurement, lengthy suffering or illnesses. All because of my so-called failings. Even if you count the eight thousand who gave up their lives before I changed the practice of killing a live brain, I saved a net of over seventy-three thousand lives."

"You murdered them!" screamed a blond socialite who had been silent up until this point.

"Yes. And to a certain extent I'm proud of what I've done. Those were lives that didn't mean anything to anyone, even themselves. They were unwanted and unloved. I know what it means to be hated by those closest to you, to be spurned by everyone around, and to be thought of as a burden. No, those children missed nothing in such a life.

"So when you *ladies* have saved as many lives as I have, then you can judge me."

"Genocidal cunt!" the third woman said, lurching for the cell bars. I was well beyond her reach and knew it. I didn't bother to move. I hope I didn't flinch as she threw herself against the ceramic/Kevlar bars. It just went to show that even the most "altruistic" individuals have a caged animal beneath their surface.

"Temper, temper, ladies. Pursuant to these civil and criminal contractual negotiations engaged in good faith, I respectfully demand that you mutilate and manipulate it in such a manner as to make as many very tiny, acute solid angles as possible and establish forthwith within the petitioners' most excessively impermeable aperture." At least one of them knew what I suggested they collectively do, but it was obvious from my tone what I was implying. They fumed as a group.

"Miss Zimmer, this offer will not be repeated." I'd lived a life. I had fun. Now it was someone else's turn because quite frankly there was no real way to get out of my death. Fear no longer held my heart in its grip. I blew them a nice wet raspberry. Glowering, they got up and left in a huff. I got a wink and a high-sign from Peggy, who had been watching to "protect the ladies from the hardened criminal." I think Peg would have done them in, given the chance.

I repeated to myself, "I'm no longer afraid."

Back to the story. Yes, Box and I married, but that's for later in the story. I don't know when I started loving him as more than a friend, but it happened. I was proud, in more ways than one, to be his wife.

After Margaret's collapse, Box didn't call for three days. I handled all the work at the School, from discipline to new suppliers to accounts receivable. I did everything, forging Margaret's sloppy signature better than she could have signed it herself. I'd had much practice over the five years I was handling the bulk of the paperwork.

When Box finally showed up on the fourth day, I was just about dizzy with relief. I wanted to throw my arms around his neck and hug the stuffing out of him, but two other girls and two Ay-Dees in the office made that impossible. He waited patiently until I had handled the business at hand: two girls caught "pleasuring each other" in the bathroom. I provided a quick decision and sent them on their way without the typical Spouse lecture.

I did manage that bear-hug after the Ay-Dees had taken the young women from the office. I think that was one of the few times I've ever seen a look of surprise on Box's face. He carefully detached me from his neck and told me that Margaret was in the JFK Surgical Hospital, in the Transplant Ward—karma, or maybe poetic justice.

Margaret had liver cancer—a rather virulent strain that destroyed the liver and the kidneys within a handful of years. She had received numerous transplants over the last ten years. I wondered how I hadn't noticed her times away.

I briefly mulled over the concept that her story of how she started the business might not have been entirely true, but who was I to judge. *He that is without sin among you, let him first cast a stone at her*, I thought.

I had no proof anyway, so I put it out of my mind. Margaret's cancer was re-occurring, meaning that any liver or kidney that she could accept as a donor would eventually succumb to the same disease. She was dying now and needed a new liver. Box wanted me to visit her.

"Bitch won't listen t'me. Ya need t'talk some sense int' her t'ick head." Box refused to tell me what she wasn't listening about. I had to find out for myself.

I did manage to squeeze a few hours out of the next day. Because my Thunderbird was in the shop, Box drove me down to the hospital in his old beaten-up white van. He refused to go in until I had talked to her.

A machine wrapped its wires, plumbing and monitors around Margaret like some mechanical parasite—attempting to steal her life-force away. A grade B science fiction movie of the fifties couldn't have done it better. With the exception of her breasts, she had always been thin and scrawny. She used to hide within her wool and satin dresses, but now she looked like a holocaust survivor. Her skin had the consistency of yellowed rice paper. The jaundicing came from the impurities in her system that the dialysis machine would not be able to rid her of.

"Hello, Margaret," I said, pulling back the curtain.

"That son of mine is an asshole. I told him I didn't want visitors. Why did he bring you here?" Her voice didn't carry its usual authority but sounded rather like the chirp of a cricket in a subway.

"To get you to change your mind," I fished. I needed to know more and for once Box's reluctance to share more than necessary aggravated me. My cajoling in the car had produced not a single scrap of information.

"I won't take another transplant. I've lived my life. I'd rather let someone else live theirs." A tiny clearing opened in the dense fog of my ignorance.

"Well, I don't see why you'd stop now. How many have you had so far? Ten?"

"Try twelve, girl. I'm not as young as you think. I'm the product of great plastic surgeons."

"You were always a good one to change the subject."

"No, I'm not trying this time, Elizabeth. I'm tired. I don't want death to follow me anymore. Maybe you'll feel the same way when you are my age, girl.

"I won't say that you were like a daughter to me, Elizabeth. That would be much too trite. I did enjoy your company. I wish you would have gotten a better break in life." She seemed to sink even farther into her pillows. "One more thing, girl. Be good to my son or I'll come back and haunt your ugly hide." As usual she took the last word or should I say, tried to take the last word. She closed her eyes and lay there like that for several minutes. Her breathing was shallow but very regular. If she wasn't sleeping then she faked it well. This was someone who loved me. It was love I could return. I thought of my own mother. I wonder if she had gotten a better break in life, instead of my father, would she have been a better person?

"I love you, Margaret," I managed to choke out around several tears and a throat clogged with sadness. At that point in my life, she was one of only two people I had loved. I wished with all my heart that it were me there in that bed and not her.

Margaret died three days later after a brief time in a coma. As soon as she lapsed into unconsciousness, the doctors pleaded with Abe to sign the papers to give her a new set of organs. Even Doctor Rob got into the act. It didn't sway Box in the least.

"She says she wants t'die. I gonna let her. It's her life, not mine." Margaret Fox didn't suffer long. Abe called me at the School when the end came. I blubbered on the desk. I don't know how long I cried, but it was long enough for Box to make his way from the hospital. True to form, he comforted me, when it should have been me comforting him. As the morning turned into afternoon, I finally let my tears dry and put on my "strong person" front. Practical Liz came out to play.

"I guessin' t'at it be time t'close t'is place," Box said as I decided to face the world. I was flabbergasted. I didn't even know where to begin.

"Box, I don't know what gave you any idea like that, but you couldn't be further from the truth."

"But she ain't here t'run it." I think, for the only time in his life, a tear fell from his eye.

"Box, she left you all the money you could possibly spend. Margaret left you a life. She obviously raised you right and left you with good memories. But she left me this," I said slamming my hand down on the desk. "The School is mine. I've nurtured it and cared for it. I love her and it as much as you do. I have to keep her dream alive. She may not be with us anymore but her legacy will live on. There are people who need our help and if you won't do it, I will."

Box sat there looking at me before wiping at his barely wet cheek. "Yer place, her dream. I'll help."

"Box, will you marry me?" While this might seem like a snap decision, I had been thinking about it long before Margaret took ill and a great deal since. I tried to deny it but Abe Boxner was right for me and I was right for him. Box didn't seem surprised. He just talked quieter than normal.

"If'n t'ats what ya want, Lizzy girl, I'd be proud t'be yer husband." I walked over and placed myself on his lap with as much restraint and dignity that I could. I kissed him thoroughly.

"I think you are the only man I have ever loved, Mr. Abe Boxner. I will be proud to wear your name." I think it was the only time Box has ever blushed.

"I luv ya, too, Lizzy-girl."

I made an announcement to the School's floor and the general populous that day.

"Ms. Margaret 'Spouse' Fox died from liver failure this morning. I will now run the business as it stands. There will be no changes to any standing contract, nor any other aspect for some time. Please say a prayer for her. She will need all that we can give her.

"That is all."

I could see that several of the populous held back cheers, but some of the younger girls didn't rejoice because they hadn't had a chance yet to hate Spouse the Ogre. Margaret had been our overbearing mother. Like that strict and domineering parent, most of the girls didn't realize she did it for love—love of all of those people who would die if the School never existed.

I all but shut down the School as everyone attended Margaret's services later that week. I even went so far as to obtain black shifts for all the girls. Our paid police kept the strangers away. Oh, those nominally civil service employees balked at first, but when I showed them the green, they came through.

Because of some scheduling conflicts, we laid Margaret to rest at noon. The summer sun scorched so hotly that even the mosquitoes took a siesta. A pair of green canvas awnings stretched over our entire School group channeling a tiny breeze, but it wasn't nearly enough for me or anyone else. I was still pregnant and I knew I would be covered in hives by the time we returned. I'd need a full immersion mud-bath. None of the girls sang hosannas in the heat. Being hot, even without the hives, is no fun when you are pregnant—an all-over miserable.

Mr. Nguyen, alone among the other owners, stood with us wearing a black Kao Brothers suit sporting a black armband. His presence pleased me as much as the other owners snubbing Margaret angered me. Nguyen shed not one tear nor did his stony face show the slightest emotion. He bowed to the casket. As he left he offered a tiny jewelry flower to Box, the gift being a Japanese custom.

I thought Box would deliver a eulogy, but he only stoically walked up and gently placed a single Bird of Paradise flower on her casket. When he sat back down next to me, he urged me to say a few words.

For the three days before we laid her to rest, I had kept "Practical Liz" on duty. "Practical Liz" remained firm and strong with a "get-it-done attitude." Too many arrangements needed to be made and Hobson had made his choice—namely me. Now grief welled up and spilled down my face in a steady stream, ruining the makeup I had thrown on that morning. I stood up at the head of Margaret's casket, snuffling and my voice foggy.

"Margaret was no saint. But Margaret did something so few people in this life ever get a chance to do. She devoted her life to delivering hope. She made it possible for many people to go home and live when the doctors told them they faced only death. Many people, anonymously, owe Margaret their lives.

"But closer to home, many of us here owe our lives and futures to this woman. How many of us would be dead or worse right now if Margaret hadn't taken us into her School? Too many for comfort. And those of us who didn't die, how many would have a road full of hardships and misery?" I sniffed hard and dabbed at the Niagara Falls that ran over my cheeks, with about as much effectiveness.

"You might not have agreed with her, but you had to know she cared. May she rest quietly. May the School stand long in tribute to her strength and values." I sat down and remembered Margaret with all of her virtues and faults. No one else said a word.

I managed to maintain a semblance of composure, despite the tears, until I got everyone back to the School. Once I had locked myself into Margaret's office, Practical Liz fled and Emotional Lizzy arrived with a vengeance.

Just like the day Box told me that Margaret had died, I put my head on her desk and bawled. I ignored several knocks on the door, and innumerable phone calls just went to voicemail. As night arrived the office got dark and I didn't bother with a light as I continued to sob.

I felt the contractions even through my grief, but as a veteran of false labor, I dismissed it. Sometime shortly after, my water broke all down the chair and onto the floor. This I couldn't ignore. Gritting my teeth through another set of contractions, I picked up the phone.

"What," came Dr. Rob's barely awake voice on the other end of the line.

"Doc, my water just broke and I'm having contractions."

"It figures. Deliveries always come at inconvenient times. I'll be up right away," the voice said much more clearly.

Hanging up with my finger, I dialed Box's mobile.

"Boxner here," he answered, his voice still gruff from his own grief.

"I need you to cover the office for a couple of days. I'm going into labor."

"All right, Lizzy. I'll be t'ere in t'a morn. Ya be safe."

"It's just a baby, Box, and not my first. I'll be fine."

Just as another set of contractions gripped me, Dr. Rob came into the room with two burly Ay-Dees to help me down the stairs.

"How far apart?" Dr. Rob asked.

"Less than five minutes."

"Then let's not dawdle, shall we," Doc offered in mock helpfulness.

I looked at the two Ay-Dees, "After you help me down, get someone from custodial to clean up the mess I made."

"Yes, ma'am."

After they helped me waddle bowlegged down to the bottom of the stairs and into a wheelchair, the Ay-Dees went off to their tasks.

"Dr. Rob," I said, as he wheeled me out to the ambulance.

"Yes, Elizabeth."

"I have a special request." I outlined what I had in mind in between trying to manage the pain of contractions.

"As you will, Elizabeth."

I wasn't one of those natural birth mothers. I had them put me out. I woke up twelve hours later in a private room.

Normally I couldn't wait to get out of the hospital. That time I relished the solitude. I needed to nurse not only the empty feeling in my middle but the emptiness in my soul with the loss of my mother, Margaret. No, she didn't give me birth but she did give me love and friendship. One could make an argument that my biological mother had more to do with how I turned out than a woman I worked for eight years. One *could* make that argument but I'd scoff. Oh, Mrs. Zimmer set my DNA but Margaret Fox helped set my soul.

By the time Box came to see me the next evening, I'd pulled

myself together and pretty much stopped feeling sorry for myself. Besides, he looked so harried I couldn't help but focus on him. His dishevelment wasn't entirely grief.

"What's wrong, Box?"

"I donna know how ya does it, Lizzy."

"What do you mean?"

"How does ya keep t'ings movin' in ta office? I spent jus' one day t'ere. Vendors comin' in. Girls and product goin' out. Payment requests. Bills. Phone. Doctor. Ay-Dees. Punis'ments. It be crazy. I be t'inkin' that sellin' and deliverin' was the hard part."

I chuckled and got a pain in my middle for my trouble. "I would say that delivering is harder, but my kind, not yours. Box, running the office is just long practice and organization."

"Gracious but it ain't easy."

I patted Box's big hands as I held them. "Don't worry. I'll be back tomorrow."

"Assuming Doc gonna let you go."

"Do you think I give one good goddamn if Dr. Rob gives his OK or not?"

"Maybe not, Lizzy, but I does. Ya ain't gonna leave 'til he say so. I done lost my mammy but I ain't gonna lose you, too." He emphasized his statement with a squeeze of my hand.

So I shut up and was a good girl. Dr. Rob let me out the next day. I didn't even twist his arm.

"You are fine to go again, Elizabeth. Don't get pregnant for at least three months. Take your supplements. You know the drill."

"Yes, I do, Doc Rob. But there is one thing I don't know, and I need you to help me with it before I can take over the School."

Rob eyed me warily over my chart. "Yes?"

I took a deep breath. I'd avoided this my entire tenure at the school, but I needed to see it all before I could continue—all of it. "I need to see the 'production floor.'" What a euphemism. Why not call it by its true name—abattoir, or even slaughterhouse. I needed to witness the killing and butchery of the fetuses.

Dr. Rob whispered low. "We don't do that here and I don't have much to do with that side of the operation."

"Then get me in touch with someone that does. I *need* to do this."

"Yes, ma'am," he replied as he pivoted and exited with more abruptness than normal.

Late that evening a broad man with bushy eyebrows that feathered in the corners came into my room. His balding dome reminded me of an older Gorbachev minus the birthmark. In very Russian-accented English he introduced himself. "Ms. Zimmer, my name is Gospodin Lyakh. I represent the production line you wanted a tour of."

I recognized the odd name from the payroll. "Yes, Gospodin. Very nice of you to come."

"My pleasure, Miss. Will you need assistance?"

While still in my hospital bed, I wore street clothes. "No, thank you. Where are we going?"

He gallantly offered me his arm and led us down the hall. "We have a small facility not too far from here. It is disguised as a clinic for incontinence."

I chuckled but not enough to hurt my stitches. "Not a place most folks would choose to enter willingly."

His dimples showed as he responded. "No, Miss Zimmer. And those few who do come in are directed elsewhere as we have too many patients on the books."

"Sound planning."

A nondescript Toyota Highlander waited for us at the door. He opened the door, handed me in, and closed my door before going to the driver's position. A man of old world manners. As he closed his door he turned to me. "Miss Zimmer, I have to ask a serious question. The production floor is not for the faint of heart. And while I know you to be a person of robust personality, I question the necessity. Do you really feel you need to see this? Couldn't you be more effective if you didn't?"

I remained silent long enough for politeness, letting him think I'd rethought the matter. "Gospodin Lyakh, I feel that I would be the worst kind of hypocrite if I didn't acknowledge the less savory side of our business. As they used to say, the person eating steak is on the same moral level as the butcher. And I assure you that my oft-bloated belly will withstand anything you put before me."

"Very well, Miss Zimmer. I had to ask. I don't know that Ms. Fox ever even came to view our side of the business."

We drove in silence a whole three minutes, most of that waiting at a traffic light, to an unassuming medical building with the sign Incontinence Specialties brightly displayed on the outside. He drove around back and let us in a back door. "The front is only for show. There is a receptionist, a full waiting room, and a single examination room tended by a fake nurse and a fake doctor. Our operations are completely sealed off from there except for a single door locked on our side."

The very dimly lit hall didn't completely hide some active defenses, themselves worthy of a lengthy prison term. Bio locks on two coffer-dammed doors followed up by four guards, each holding Mac12 submachineguns indicated a level of protection nowhere else in our organization.

"Impressive, isn't it, Miss Zimmer?"

"Is all this necessary?"

"In the last ten years we have twice had security breaches. Neither got beyond the active defenses in the entry hall. We did have a scare last year, however. A delivery truck crashed into the building knocking a hole in the back wall. It wasn't something we ever considered. We now have our operations behind a double wall. If someone breaks the first there is ten feet before they reach the second. Both are bank-vault rated at thirty minutes."

I nodded as this man and his colleagues knew their business. Now I walked down another hall with a shining operating room on either side behind wire-mesh encased glass. It could have been any operating room in any modern hospital. Nary a spot blotted the gleaming stainless steel. Instrument trays were covered carefully with pristine white cloth. Surgical lights hung from the ceiling ready to pour illumination wherever needed. Just my stepping into the room would have contaminated it.

I must have gawked because Lyakh said, "Weren't what you expected?"

"No, not at all," I said, without stopping to think. His low chuckle broke me out of my spell. "I'm sorry."

"Don't, Miss Zimmer. Did you expect a filthy basement splattered with blood and gore? Maybe with filth encrusted instruments lying on the floor next to a washbasin of blood and entrails?"

"Yes, to some extent. And don't forget the wood saw to cut them into little pieces."

Lyakh smiled at me, showing his dimples again. "That's not an uncommon misconception, Miss Zimmer. But the reality is that we provide transplants for surgeries sometimes where the slightest infection or bacteria can cause the death of the patient. We have to be immaculately clean.

"If you will follow me, I'll show you the more impressive portion of our shop."

Passing two more surgical theatres he came to the end of the hall and yet another door with bio-locks. Three heavy coats hung on hooks outside the door. "Here, put this on," he said lifting one down for me. It hung on me like a tent but I wasn't trying to be a fashion plate. He opened the door letting out a wave of frigid air. "This is where we keep what we have harvested."

The ginormous two-story room beyond held bakers' racks that stretched to the ceiling. Each shelf held six frost-coated bins with bar codes on the front. I couldn't estimate to the nearest thousand how many bins there were in the room. Even in the coat I shivered, and not entirely from the temperature.

How many fetuses did it take to fill the room? How many lives had been snuffed out? But instead of seeing the death, I saw the life. Skin grafts filled one entire bank of racks. I saw rows and rows of Susans, burn victims, returning to nearly normal lives. One stack held nothing but hearts. Each smallish frost covered box equaled a life and the joy of their loved ones.

"We keep this room at four degrees Celsius. It is the lowest temperature without temperature-induced protein denaturing. If we store them in an oxygenated, metabolism-inhibiting solution, they can be kept for up to seven weeks without loss."

"Sir, I think I've seen enough. Would you please escort me back to the hospital?"

"Absolutely."

"Lyakh, what did you do before you ran this facility?" I asked on the short drive back.

With a grimace he responded, "I was a very prosperous undertaker."

"What made you change jobs?"

He remained silent for a few moments. "They found out I was having extracurricular activities with the . . . ah . . . my clients."

I suppressed a grimace of disgust. I'd heard of such things but thought they were rumors or myths. Defrocked doctors and apparently morticians as well. It fit into the grand scheme of things. "Thank you for your candor, sir. I'll keep it to myself. One question, you never—I mean with our product . . ."

"No, Miss Zimmer. They are much too new for my particular tastes."

The man dropped me at the hospital. After he drove away, I shuddered.

So I took over the School and ran things the way I saw fit for more than five years. I never really felt that I had replaced Margaret because even after death the School did still seem to be an extension of her. Oh, don't get me wrong. I made changes to make it more in my image. My first task eliminated some of the boredom of the girls. We had movies every night and a "company store" to buy comfort-type items. I organized group outings (carefully chaperoned and surreptitiously guarded) and other fun things. I even liberalized the sexual conduct rules (that helped quite a bit). I figured anything to make the "producers" happier benefitted us all.

The changes initially cut our profits by a point and a half, or three parts in twenty thousand, an amount not even worth mentioning. All of the partners excepting Mr. Nguyen screamed until I threatened to quit. They stopped haranguing me but didn't completely stop showing concern. That is until even that minor budget impact disappeared and their profits started to grow. The gross and the net both soared as many more of the girls returned as mercenaries, reducing the significant cost of finding new girls. As long as things weren't boring, more of them saw this as a way to make a buck and live comfortably for nine months as a no-lose situation. I even made noise about expanding as my number of producers had risen from the fifteen hundred that Margaret had averaged to nearly twenty-two hundred. The girls were happy, my partners were happy. I was happier than I could ever say but not just because of the School.

Box and I married in short order after Margaret's funeral. I put Donna Henandez (the civics teacher Ay-Dee) in charge of the business during my absence. She didn't brook any lip from the girls. They respected her as she knew what it was like to be one of them. It worked. Donna became my vacation and one-day-off-a-week replacement.

Margaret had worked herself to death. She spent nearly 7/24 at the School. I learned from her mistakes. I wanted a life outside those drab white walls and off of those cold heartless linoleum tiles.

Arranging a wedding is not all the fuss people make it out to be. Some women take a year to get everything done. I mean I could have, but one question kept coming to mind, "Why?" I finished everything in the week after I proposed.

I know brides sometimes have odd requests, but I guess the only odd thing that I did was to send an invitation to my father and mother. It happened to be the only invitation. I didn't expect a reply. I wrote a short little note on the back, letting them know that I would pay for their way if they would just come. The only response I got was in the form of a tiny package with no return address or name. Inside was a bone white, lace garter. It wasn't new. It was many years old but still in its original package. A scrawled note, in a very shaky handwriting that I didn't quite recognize, left the only clue. After some thought, it could have only been my mother's writing. It said simply, "Something old." It had to have been hers. No one else knew the PO Box that I had used as a return address.

I guess those women from the WM&P were probably right in that it wasn't a properly sanctioned marriage. Box and I flew to Louisiana to be married on a skiff in the bayou by a Southern Baptist minister—call me a romantic. The place happened to be near where my husband had been born (apparently the government never completed the project that cost a young Box his father). The Baptist minister wasn't ordained and we never did get a marriage certificate, but I was married where it counted—in my heart. Neither papers, gods, nor governments can keep a marriage together nor tear one apart. Only what the couple believes down in their souls matters. Box and I started our happy life as husband and wife. We were a team; we were a family. I had found my heart's home with him.

He wore a bone white linen tuxedo with ivory satin lapels

and a black Mississippi string tie. His black shoes shone so brightly they could have almost been mistaken for white. A red rose boutonniere gave just the right splash of color.

My wedding gown wasn't quite pink. It was white with just a hint of rose colored swirls. The pure white of Box's tux made the pink in my dress writhe like a living creature. I guess the term "gown" would apply to it, but it was split so far up the front that it was more like a mini tube-dress with an exceedingly long train. It was patterned after a twenties wedding dress designed by Reem Acra—satin and spandex and showing as much leg as the police would allow. That gown hugged me like Box did afterward. I could have had a designer wedding dress, but when I saw this one it reminded me of my mother's wedding pictures. She had been such a beautiful bride. Even Father had looked handsome in that pic. I guess I am somewhat sentimental especially after the garter arrived. My simple bouquet consisted of three roses—one white, one yellow and one red.

I wore my mother's garter as my something old. My something new was the ruby necklace Box had just bought for me. He said it set off the red in my hair (the sappy dope—I loved it). I borrowed Margaret's "first dollar" from the wall at the School. The something blue was a blue butterfly I had tattooed to my left thigh the week before.

We had no witnesses other than the minister, a solemn older black man with white wisps of hair and a gentle great-grandfatherly way about him. I'll say this for the man. He knows how to pick the spots.

The flat-bottomed wetland craft had a tawny wooden trellis over the pair of us with bright purple and green bougainvillea laced up both sides. The amethyst leaves even carpeted the bottom of the boat and slightly clashed with the red and white rose bushes growing up seven evenly placed stakes on either side of our conveyance. The bright colors sharply contrasted with the rather dim swamp country into which we had motored. The lacey white flowers of the plant "lizard's tail" shot up everywhere on one side of the boat and the brown and green of cattail hemmed us in on the other. Sun shined down through cypress trees to play the scene with dancing lights.

As the minister turned off the electric trolling motor, a disturbed pair of bats hanging from a nearby pine provided the only sound. A bright yellow carpet of horn-shaped honeysuckle on a nearby clump of land provided a heavenly smell. This was God's country, I thought to myself. I understood why Margaret remembered this place with such fondness.

"In the eyes of our God, ya two have consented to be wed. I won't waste the Almighty's time or our'n by preaching at'cha. Only ya'll kin decide if ya have ta mettle ta git through life as Mister and Missus. Marriage takes a conviction o'the heart and the soul to git through the good an' livin' through the bad; ta make it through when yer broke 'r flush; ta be t'gether when yer sicking and when yer top o'form.

"T'is is lifelong bond ya be making. It ain't something t'toss aside if it pinches or don't fit right. Ya can't take this'n back t'the store fer yor money back. Naw that I done made the speech I said I wasn't gonna make.

"Does ya, Elizabeth Sherry Zimmer, wanna have this man as yorn, ta love, ta bed only him, 'n ta mind him, in ta eyes o' God Almighty 'til death strike's one o'ya?"

I had happy tears in my eyes. "I do."

"Does ya, Abe Richard Boxner, wanna have this woman as yorn, ta love, ta bed only her, 'n ta care fer her, in ta eyes o' God Almighty 'til death strike's one o'ya?"

"Ya, I does."

"T'en put ta ring on her finger 'n kiss her. Y'all'r hi'ched." Abe slipped a diamond and ruby wedding ring, which matched my necklace, on my ring finger. We then melted together in a kiss that I swore scorched the plants around us.

There was no cake. There was no reception. The closest we came to either was a quaint bayou custom of toasting the couple with moonshine.

"May ya be blessed by the Lord with love as long as ya live," the old black man said before the three of us raised metal cups together. I took a cautious sip to the toast. It burned all the way down. I felt like it had sucked all the wind out of me. Abe tossed his down neatly but didn't ask for another. The minister drained the rest of mine as he motored us back out of the bayou.

Abe and I sat together on the front of the skiff and held each other's hands. Despite the jetlag I still felt getting here, I think that was the most perfect moment in the world.

We didn't stay in Louisiana except for that night. I'm not going to go into the honeymoon night. Some things are meant to be private and personal. The only thing I will say is that when Box had impregnated me in the past so that I could pay my bills, it was NOTHING like what happened that night. I smiled for a week. That is the way I'll leave it.

Oh, it occurs to me that I never mentioned it, but Box was the only one who ever made me viable to return to the School. Listen to me . . . "made me viable." Sounds like he gave me a certificate or a passing grade rather than gave me his seed to create a fetus.

Back to the honeymoon. I had always wanted to go to the Bahamas. I have heard it is a beautiful grouping of islands. Box wasn't against the idea. He had never been, either. We decided to fly to Fort Lauderdale and then take a cruise ship over to Freeport and tour from there. Mistake. We should have flown directly into Freeport. I'm sure Fort Lauderdale didn't own the title of Dirtiest Tourist Trap but it sure gave every other place a good run for their money (in a later vacation I learned that Orlando was worse).

The ship that took us, the *Princess Grace*, I couldn't recommend, either. No, that's not right. The ship had an old world charm but the weather made the trip a royal pain. A storm front had just blown through the night before. Neither Box nor I had thought anything about weather, the sky being clear and late summer blue. The *Grace* sailed, for the four hours it took to get to Freeport, in eight-foot, quarter-beam seas. I had to ask what that meant. The practical application had everyone on the ship, excepting the crew, dead-dog sick. I managed not to throw up (only through familiar acquaintance with nausea), but Box spent the entire trip in the head relieving his stomach into a stainless steel toilet. I even had to get his passport stamped.

I don't think either of us ate anything for the rest of that day, even after we got off the boat. In fact we went directly to our hotel, the Xanadu Resort, and barely moved. I guess we are both natural landlubbers. We didn't even sleep holding each other, we were so miserable. Our fun didn't start until the next day.

OK, the first thing you have to learn when you go to the Bahama Islands is to say "No!" And you have to say it with authority or you are a sucker for every amateur capitalist that comes along. "No, I don't want my hair braided." "No, I don't want a conch shell." "No, I don't want a T-shirt." Perish even the thought of squeezing my broad frame into one of those.

Conch shells I'd seen, but never had a name associated with them. Conch turned out to be quite a wonderful food. A bit tough, but cheap as hell and tasted like a strongly flavored crab—delicious. The Bahamian's use it in just about everything: chowder, fried, baked, steamed, and the list goes on. I didn't get sick of it the entire time I was there. Good thing because I don't think we had a meal without it.

Box and I spent three days just sunning ourselves and playing in the water of Xanadu Beach. My new husband turned out to be playful in the water, splashing me and swimming around me as I tried to just float and enjoy the rays. He seemed to take to the ocean like a porpoise. We took a snorkeling cruise out to Adam's Reef, where Abe and I saw a five-foot-long nursemaid shark. I nearly swallowed the sea around me. How was I to know that nurse sharks are relatively inoffensive and have never attacked people? Abe swam closer and actually touched it with his hand. The shark ignored him and swam calmly away. I guess we were lucky to even see one. Not many sharks or dolphins come close to any beach anymore.

How come it is that you can know a man for seven years and not really know him? I knew Box bowled, but I didn't know he had an aberrant fetish for the game of golf. The island of Grand Bahama has five golf courses: Fortune Hills, Ruby, Emerald, Freetown Public and Lucayan. My husband politely asked if he would get to play them. I didn't hesitate. "Sure!" I didn't know he meant all five of them. I tried to golf with him on the first one, Ruby. I learned I have absolutely no talent for golf. I gave up after the first six holes. Unfortunately, my better half didn't have any talent either. If I remember correctly, he never got the ball in the hole in less than six shots. Most of the time he swung at least eight. I wanted to be with him, so I suffered through the rest of the holes by just sitting in the cart and smiling. OK, so I bore easily. By the time our rental car loomed into view, I would happily give up golf for life. My husband out-guessed me and suggested that he could golf anytime. He wanted to spend time with me.

Abe and I hit several of the "hot spots" in the International Bazaar (bizarre would have been a better word). I reiterate my dislike for the nightclub scene. They blared the music too damned loud. I did like a club called the Bahama Mama and we returned there several times. I liked it because it seemed to cater to people of our tastes. Traditional steel drum music wafted at a decent volume through the open, airy club. It seemed right out of a travel brochure, music and all. People could get up and dance to the island rhythms, talk, hit on others or just get intoxicated. I tried one, repeat one, of the island's classic and famous rum drinks, the Bahama Mama. As I don't drink, and a natural result of my foolishness, Box poured me into our hotel room that night. I don't enjoy how silly I get when I drink. My antics after only one deceptively sweet and pretty drink stirred up the island gossip mill. What happened to truth in advertising? And no, I won't tell you what I did.

If you left the tourist traps of Freeport behind, Grand Bahama took on a wonderful and unassuming small town air. We hit the touron traps as well, but the "outside" part of the Bahamas held more spectacular sights. Box and I visited the Garden of the Groves, Lucayan National Park, Old Freeport, toured a rum factory (boy, but do they stink!), and even wound up on a couple of "private" beaches where "clothing optional" should have been "clothing prohibited." Through it all, no matter how lovely the place, no matter how exciting a time I had, my husband's presence magnified it—MY husband. We could have walked through hell itself and I think I would have had a good time. Grand Bahama definitely occupied a spot on the far side of purgatory from hell. I enjoyed it enough that I later returned. Let me repeat—my husband!

We traveled to most of the places we wanted to go on motor scooters we rented. They burned wood-alcohol, if you can believe it. We did have to remember to ride on the left side of the road as the Bahamas had at one time been a British Colony. Soon we learned that the buses were timely and went everywhere you could possibly want to go. If a bus didn't have a destination on its route, it probably wasn't worth the trip. Box and I found this out for certain when we went down the length of the island to Sweeting's Cay. Nice enough place, but it wasn't that used to tourists. The locals didn't really appreciate us interloping. We stayed only long enough for a quick bite to eat and to refill our fuel tanks.

Garden of the Groves proved to be a nice way-station in the middle of our trip. The quiet and serene botanical garden gave us a rest from the human pressure of Greater Los Angeles and even from the tourists of Freeport. Box and I spent most of a day there, just languidly moving around, sitting and kissing in the quiet of a stand of tropical and sub-tropical trees. A tiny rundown chapel in the park surrounded by huge palm trees almost made me wish we had married there instead of the bayou, but only for a brief moment. The skiff wedding had been too idyllic.

Box and I traipsed through the mangrove swamps on constructed wooden paths of Grand Lucayan Park. The term swamp seemed a bit deceptive. Neither the water level nor the vegetation justified that soggy moniker. Typically the ground off the wooden slatted paths just squished a tiny bit of water under the weight of a step. At one point we did pass one tiny pond, with some colorful fish and ducks and a sluggish stream.

Box and I trekked to a surprise at our destination—a nearly deserted horse-shoe beach covered in white sand with the consistency of flour. The water shimmered a crystalline teal close to the beach and a deeper azure blue out farther. The bay formed by the beach cradled three twenty-meter rock outcroppings some two hundred meters offshore. The beauty of the place stole away my rationality. Box (my husband!) and I were on that beach alone.

Box and I spent the rest of the day there, long past the setting of the sun. We played in the water, snorkeled, rested lazily in the shade of a row of palms, and ate a packed lunch. As brilliant shades of a fuscia and ochre sunset faded across the ocean, Box and I made love. That beach, which has no name to the best of my knowledge, was the most peaceful place I've ever been. If there is a God, he sleeps there at night.

Our time in this "life away" all too soon came to an end. Box and I made a smart decision (this time). We gave away our cruise ship tickets and flew back from Freeport. No more ships for this girl.

Work awaited us both at home. It would have been all too easy to just chuck it all and let the world find its own way. Box and I had enough money to live comfortably for the rest of our lives. Ah, hell, let's be honest: we could have lived rich for the rest of our lives. Each time I thought about asking Box to chuck it all, I would remember that burned little girl, Susan Miller, with her hard, blackened flesh flaking off in oozing clumps. I couldn't do it. Someone had to provide for these people, even if it was me.

I wasn't chained to the School and I still had fun over those years, but at the same time I never worked harder in my life—the work of the righteous. I believed. And any time that I forgot, all I had to do was to stroll over to JFK Surgical Hospital and take a walk through the ward. In Margaret's own words, it was enough to make the guilties go away. I miss her, the old crusty bat.

I made several more changes to the School, other than the ones I've already noted. A big alteration was who supplied us with our standard requirements, catering, laundry service, etc. I always considered that the biggest hole in our security. Besides, what did the Chinese family, who ran our laundry, really know about being pregnant at the School? Not much. Did they know how much it hurt to put on an unsoftened bra over tender nipples? No. Did they know how the soft, starched sheets burned our skins? Nope. What about the reactions some of the girls had to the soaps they used? Not a clue. I announced to the girls that we would begin the practice of taking services from companies of girls who'd lived in the School before any others. I was clear that we would not let it change the service in any way (except for the better), but they would get preferential treatment.

What a difference it made. Our laundry contract changed in less than a pair of months as two Eights decided to go into business together and set up a laundry almost immediately after being released from the hospital. They made a great deal of money off of us. In fact, I think they have spread out and own three different shops providing services for six hospitals, four nursing homes and a jail. But the School got them started. All the girls thanked me for the comfort they provided. I think I was well on my way to being crowned Queen of the Pasadena. There would be no more chaffing clothes and bed-linens. No more yellowed pillowcases. No more blankets with holes in them.

The idea spread like wildfire. Soon our catering, food supplies, plumbing service (I hated to see our janitor, Mr. Diamond, go, but he confided in me that he was trying to come up with an excuse to retire anyway), company store, and ambulance services were all sourced to companies either owned by or co-owned by former clients. I even fielded suggestions for new services for the women. Most of them I rejected outright, but we did end up with a mini-gym, aerobics classes and a crafts coordinator.

The only problem I ever had with my policy was when I terminated my old catering contract. The owner of that company, a big black man named Jon Warles, insisted that he be kept on as our vendor. He threatened to go to the police if I didn't change my mind. I don't tolerate blackmailers. Mr. Nguyen received my first call. I had a better working relationship with him than our other partners. I gave him every piece of information I had on Mr. Warles. The Pasadena chief of police got my second call and the third followed shortly to the LA chief of police. I told each of them rather succinctly that they might receive a phone call from a concerned citizen and that it had better get buried or the rather large contribution to their respective pensions would dry up.

I don't know exactly what happened to Mr. Warles. I am a good guesser, however. I'm not sure whether either of the police forces got to him first, or Mr. Nguyen's thugs did. I surmise that in either case, Mr. Warles could no longer speak, write, or convey any message about the School. Maybe his widow received a fat settlement check from his life insurance and then again, maybe not—as it would have depended on the method of execution (no pun intended).

Now some of you might think of me as a hypocrite because of this little incident. I do not place Mr. Warles's blood on anyone's hands but my own. I'm not kidding myself. I killed him as certainly as if I thrust the knife in his back myself. I guess I should die for that alone, but again it was a matter of relativity. Mr. W. could have disrupted the workings of the School, perhaps permanently.

This would have caused a great number of unnecessary deaths of the infirmed of the West Coast. Who has a greater need for life—a single, middle-aged, pompous male, or hundreds, maybe hundreds of thousands, of women, children and men? Once again, my answer to that question is quite clear. Exit one Mr. Warles.

I had plastic surgery to put me together in a way I liked more. By the time I got around to it, it didn't take as much as I thought. I had worked most of my weight off just by running the business at a breakneck pace and having no time for lunch. Just some touch-ups managed to put me to a point where I was happy. Box neither sanctioned nor opposed my glamorization program. He told me, "Girly, I've loved ya since ya had t'a balls ta asked my mom 'bout her name, so ya be doin' w'at ya want."

I think that over the five years that I ran the School, I spent around a million on clothes alone. Yikes. Just call me Clothes Horse Lizzy. I guess it was my one true vice. Neither drugs, booze, nor smoke tempted me . . . well, I did have one other vice, but that one I learned (Box was a patient teacher). Nothing could put me in a better mood than to go down and spend tens of thousands of dollars on a designer dress. I filled the special closet in my house. Did I tell you about my house? No, I guess I didn't.

Let's back up just a bit. I initially moved in with my husband and friend, Mr. Boxner, but I didn't care for the commute. It took a minimum of forty-five minutes, even in my near-ground Thunderbird. So, I bought a small building near the School and had it renovated. The building had been a small theater. The rundown exterior, graffiti and all, I left untouched. I wanted no attention drawn to me. I did, however, make it as invasion-proof as I could, and I didn't stop with passive defenses. Four times in the three years following its completion, I had to call on my partners, at some expense, to have a body removed from my home. Distasteful, but they always handled it discretely with a minimum of fuss.

I left the balcony and the workings of the theater intact. I even managed to gather quite a large collection of the old films/CDs it projected. It was a quaint little amusement which Box and I shared when we could find the time. The rest of the theater I converted into my home away from home. It held two huge bedrooms, two baths, a large sitting room, games, and a small but well-equipped kitchen. Both bedrooms I equipped with His and Hers closets. The master bedroom's Hers closet was larger than . . . Well, Box once joked that I needed a golf cart to get from one end to the other. I had already acquired a rather large wardrobe by the time the contractors completed the remodel and desperately needed a place to keep it. Come to think of it, I was a true clotheshorse. I rarely got to wear anything I bought more than once—when I tried it on.

Now don't read anything into the fact that I had two bedrooms. My marriage to Box was in no way one of convenience. We always slept in the same bed except when circumstances dictated otherwise. I learned to love sex. I must have been a cold fish on our wedding night, but Box never complained. He just kept teaching me. I'm a quick study, especially when it started feeling good. Then he could barely keep me out of bed. I'm firmly of the mind that the two old saws are correct. "The darker the berry, the sweeter the juice," and "Once you've had black you'll never go back." Yes, we played around and tried other people, but we never strayed from our marriage. I learned that as good as sex is, it's even better with someone you love. After some experimentation I couldn't see sleeping with anyone else, not when Box made me happy. Not that I tried to keep him out of any other woman's bed but I think in the end that Box was also of the same mind. I never learned of any "indiscretion" by my husband, other than those we mutually authorized.

Belonging to Box made for a wonderful five years.

I guess you pretty much know the rest. Box was killed when Bertion Enterprises was finally raided. I guess it had to happen someday. The governor of Southern California, one of my erstwhile partners, had ambitions to be president, even if he made a fortune off the School as one of the principles. He decided to call in the Southern California Secret Service.

The police the School had so liberally funded over the years were the first ones through the doors. I understand they were given the choice of joining or losing their careers. I understand their choice, just not their judgment. Had they come to us, we could have avoided all of the unpleasantness by being somewhere else (with one less partner in the loop). They made their choice and no longer have a host to bleed. Oh, well, that's all water under the bridge.

The SCSS stormed the building five hundred strong, augmented by nearly two hundred local cops. I never found out why they felt they needed so many officers. I can't see anyone feeling threatened by a woman eight months with child. The Ay-Dees weren't equipped to do anything but control the girls. They saw the handwriting on the wall and certainly didn't resist. I assume they did it to put on a show for the TriVid cameras, which followed them in on their "forced assault of our fortress of evil." That's a direct quotation from the six o'clock news.

Twenty of them sprinted the stairs to my office as six crashed through the skylight on rappelling lines. The first one to the door made the fatal mistake of pointing a gun at me. Box sat across the room from me, next to the door, when they burst through. I heard the man's arm shatter before Box hurtled him over the railing to the floor thirty feet below.

Gauss fire cut down Box almost immediately. Three hundred thousand tiny twisting metal slivers, propelled to insane speeds, reduced my husband into a red expanding cloud. He remained stoic to the very end. The remains of his body fell forward onto the carpeting of my office. Box's blood stained the uniforms of each and every man in an uneven pattern across their midriff.

I'd lost the one thing in this world that had any real value. Box, I love you. It's amazing what you remember when your life is torn apart.

One of the rapellers, an SS colonel cuffed me across the face. His distinctive multi-gold-toned grape leaf design of a Black Hills gold ring tore a furrow in my cheek. The smell of gun bluing and burnt metal permeated the room. I could see the "General Dynamics" manufacturer's stamp on the two-handed weapon of the officer nearest me. I could smell that one goon wore English Leather.

I grieved during my trial. Despite all Robert Kafka had been able to do, I wasn't allowed to attend Box's funeral. Even if hypocritical of me, I said many prayers to his soul and hope that now my time is coming, we will be reunited. God? Heaven? Heaven could be defined if I were with my husband and a chess board.

The papers and the TriVid called me the Baby Butcher. You couldn't possibly miss the show trial and you already know the results, so I won't bore you. My trial became the single most popular viewing and reading topic in history. Over eighty percent of the Earth's twenty billion kept track of the trial. It's a distinction of sorts. I don't recommend it for anyone who wants to keep living.

Here it is, the eve of my death. Do I feel remorse for what I did? Not really. No, that's not right. I don't feel remorse at all. I traded nearly sixteen thousand "not quite lives" for nearly three hundred thousand lives in progress. Which was worse? Letting ninety thousand die and two hundred thousand be as good as dead, or killing the sixteen? My society has given me their answer. I'm dying for my choice.

My conscience, or the part that suffices, says that perhaps I should feel a deep shame for my acts. I tell it to go to sleep in the graves of those roughly twenty thousand who will die each year because the School won't be there for them.

Am I afraid? Yes. I would avoid this if I could. Many people have said that I will meet my Maker and he will judge me. If so, what will he or she say? Am I credited for the lives I've saved, or only dinged for the lives I've taken? What form of Maker will I meet?

I don't know that this will ever see print anywhere or help even one person—other than myself. I learned to love myself a little more, especially in this, my lowest time. Something that hasn't been exactly true since I was born. Now I see I am an amalgamation of my experiences and I cherish them all.

November 3, 2050

Father IronSky twirled his gray pony-tail around in one hand and the rosary in the other. His eyes bored into mine and I knew he was trying to find a way through my will. "Why can't you see that what you did was erroneous? I can't save you unless you repent."

"Because I didn't do anything wrong. Until you see that then it is impossible for you to save me or anyone." The beads of the rosary clicked in agitation.

"But you killed, my child."

"I am not your child, Father. I am a grown woman who made a decision. Neither you, nor anyone, will convince me that I was wrong. Yes, I killed. Is the butcher sinning when he kills a cow to feed a hundred people? Is the farmer a murderer when he gleans the wheat in the field to feed thousands? What about the fisherman, Father? Paul, an apostle, was a fisherman. Did his genocide of fish make him a sinner or did it feed your Catholic masses on Friday? No, I don't think so.

"Father, murder is in the eye of the beholder. I took only the lives that were already lost to save others. No, Father. I will meet God or the gods I find with my conscious, if not my deeds, free of guilt. I butchered one to save many. I murdered to spare thousands. I caused genocide of unwanted biological refuse to return life to hundreds of thousands. I will not sully my mind by second-guessing myself because some archaic law of the land says I am wrong." My voice vented the forcefulness of the emotions that railed within me. I might be wrong but my heart was and is finally right with my head. Father IronSky sat quietly, his nervous habit not even having the will to move his beads. Defeat wrote itself over his aged face. He took four very deep breaths before speaking.

"I cannot save or forgive you then, my child."

"I never asked to be saved, Father. And as for your forgiveness, I would never have even considered it."

"I will pray for you, Elizabeth."

"If you wish, Father IronSky. If your God really runs the universe then your prayers will not matter." The aged man stood. As he shuffled slowly and tiredly away, like a man carrying the sins Jesus supposedly bore, I realized I had added to the years in his heart.

The warden, a squirrelly little cauc with a dark purple birthmark covering the right side of his face, appeared as if from nowhere after the priest slipped out of sight. I had never met the warden but his very presence gave me the creeps.

"Good day, sir. May I help you? Please pull up a chair."

"You are very polite for a murderer who is going to die this afternoon," the man said with something of a lisp. The tone of his remark indicated that he regarded me one step above rubbish, or maybe not even that high.

"Well, sir, as little as I can say about my parents, they did manage to teach me manners, which is more than I can say for yours." The man glowered at me for a few seconds without speaking.

"Mrs. Elizabeth Boxner, I am here to allow you to choose a last meal and your manner of death. However, if you wish to be snotty, I will make sure that your execution is the most painful method I have at my disposal."

"You, sir, were the first to be impolite. I was merely allowing you to reap what you sowed. I think I would like deep-fried conch in beer batter with cocktail sauce, steamed fresh broccoli with plenty of butter, and baked freshly-earthed, red baby potatoes with sour cream and chives." I thought he would burst a blood vessel.

"Ma'am," he said as coldly as a Minnesota winter, "if it weren't for the media and the personal attentions of the governor himself, I would gladly burn you at the stake for your crimes, but for your rudeness I am tempted to let you live." I even lifted an eyebrow at that one. "Oh, yes. You would have fun here in the general population. You would probably last about as long as a child molester usually does. I think the last one made a record twenty-one days. Three weeks of hell, she lived through. That bitch lived through beatings, stabbings, broken ribs, broomstick rapes, a nipple cut off, her vagina sewed shut with jute and many more things that would give you nightmares.

"Yes, I think I would enjoy that very much. Unfortunately, you have two guardian angels at the moment. All I can do is let you choose a painless method of death."

"Well, I love you, too, Warden. I guess I will choose lethal injection as being the lesser of the evils." I said this much more calmly than I felt, but I wasn't going to let this weasel feel my fear.

"May you rot in hell, Mrs. Boxner."

I am going to finish this as I haven't much time left. The conch was as good as I remember it and the broccoli was superb. I offer my compliments to the warden's chef.

I don't know what else to add. I have something like a poem I wrote last night. I guess I really don't fear death anymore. I'm actually rather numb. I've used up my tears and my emotions. I don't know if my leaving this world makes it a better or a worse place. I would like to hope I have made some positive impact. Ninety thousand lives is the population of a decent Midwestern town. I hope it was worth the price we paid.

Legacy

To the passage of time, most people slip away unnoticed
without even acknowledging their presence.
Lives with the same value, on the ken of man,
as a covey of arctic terns or a school of sea shrimp.
These poor and pitiful souls contribute nothing
save perhaps a handful of equally worthless "begats."

Then merciless history perceives a few shining souls
producing minute works of praiseworthy or heinous note.
Flaring briefly and hotly, immolating and martyring themselves
to bring their existence to the mind of the almighty
in the form of a group of masterful symphonies of the mind,
or mass depravities which terrifyingly consume "begats."

Finally there are the tiny and few children of an age
permanently fixed with the eye of the future.
Unable to escape the critical judgment of any era,
their souls naked to every prying eye.
Each inexorably linked to the destinies they write
either epic sagas of evil or songs of purest love.

Who will ever forget names like Marilyn Monroe,
Hitler, Bach, De Sade, Martin Luther King, Jr.,
Genghis Khan, Pasture, Manson, Tesla, Oswald, Mother Teresa,
Dahlmer, Nobel, Capone, JFK, Stalin, Clara Barton, and David Koresh.
Each life stamped, for good or ill, with the seal of permanence,
their deeds recorded by forever in sickening or magnificent detail.

Will my life be so recorded in that exalted company?
For purest righteousness or darkest villainy I know not.
Engraved in the bodies of a hundred thousand,
and seared into the hearts of the millions who touch them,
Living in their "begats" for the one or two in a generation
who radically change the course of our pathetic existence.

My words, my deeds, my loves, my hates will live on,
my life will live beyond me in the millions I have nurtured,
in the minds of those I have healed with my gangrenous touch,
hurting to heal, maiming to protect, killing to cure.
The giddy laughs, unbearable sorrows, tense dramas,
sweaty sex, and impressive deeds of those I have loved.

I live not only in the tainted flesh of my oft-bloated body.
Oh, how I love my sweet unsullied boy, Richard,
Innocent to the wickeds of this horrific world
and the pains of my tortured and abused soul.
But I will also be carried forever in the touch and words,
of the lifeless thousands my life has reborn with new hope.

I have to get this in because Father IronSky (in his vestments for last rites), the warden, and three armed guards are coming for me. I go to die.

But in the end, I fooled everyone. I will continue to live. I told Dr. Rob to spare my seventh pregnancy. When Margaret Fox died and Box agreed to marry me, for sentimental reasons I had the child adopted by a wonderful family who have no connection to the School. They agreed to allow me to remain in Richard's life, but I guess that is no longer possible. I've made arrangements for the financial wellbeing of Richard and his adoptive parents. I have also left some of my writings for my son for when he is old enough to understand. I hope this missive will also make its way to him. I'm counting on Peggy for that one last favor (and a large bank account can be a powerful inducement).

Despite all the people I have saved, I think I would trade it all for one loud, raining Thursday afternoon early during my first pregnancy, Anita and I coming up with a new game to kill time with Box due in the afternoon, my mind unburdened by babies or death. I miss my innocence. May God have the mercy on my son's soul that he never had on mine.

Epilogue

Father Peter IronSky
Westside Frisco
Catholic Church
6334 New Bayside Drive
West Frisco, CA 96111

5 November, 2050

Cardinal Gandari
Palace of Justice
Mail Stop PJ14-620
Vatican City, Pluto

Cardinal Gandari,

Under cover of separate messenger I am enclosing the last words of Elizabeth Zimmer-Boxner, AKA the Baby Butcher. I obtained the only copy, despite the comments on the last few pages. I think this work should be evaluated by the "Steering Committee on Morals." This work is clearly subversive. I don't think I can state with enough vehemence how strongly I feel the need for it to be sealed in the Papal Library under the strongest of quarantines.

Elizabeth remained remorseless to the end and deemed her acts as kind of a cosmic benevolence to both the children she killed and the people who received the dead children's mortal flesh. A work of this kind cannot be released upon the general public as it might induce more borderline souls to follow in her footsteps, creating additional dead infants and lost souls.

It is also clear that Southern California's Governor Edwin Cuan is within the plot of the "Wayward School for Girls," and should be immediately denounced and excommunicated. I understand that the media has already begun to descend on him like vultures on a dying lion upon the release of Elizabeth's time-bomb to the press; however, I think we should remove any association with Mr. Cuan.

In addition, with this letter I will tender my resignation as a priest within the Catholic Church. I have served forty faithful years to my God and the Holy Church. I regret that I have to take this step, but I have fallen and can no longer perform my duties as a messenger of the Catholic Word and Faith.

I have failed to even convince Elizabeth that she had committed a wrong to God. I have failed to maintain the confession of my sins. But worst of all, I have sinned in believing that Elizabeth Zimmer-Boxner may have been right. In her own words, "The greatest good for the greatest number."

(signed) Doctor Peter IronSky

cc: Richard Boxner

file

File Addendum: Father Munchi Gandari (translated from Latin)

1) It is with a heavy heart that I approve the resignation of Father Peter IronSky. His loss of faith should not detract from the good works he has done. I approve full pension benefits and rights of a retiring member of our order.

2) I also heartily approve of sealing these records in the Eyes Only Papal Library. Access shall be limited to the Papal staff for a minimum of fifty years, at which time it shall once again be reviewed for reclassification.

3) Serious attempts have been made to find the whereabouts of Richard Zimmer-Boxner. I believe that no such person exists. It may have been the madness of her last days that Elizabeth Zimmer created the fantasy of a son. Elizabeth was quite intelligent and thus a doubt remains about this; however, I feel confident that the matter is closed and no other copies or other communications of this document exist.

4) All records of this issue will be sealed with it for the entire fifty-year period.

(signed) Cardinal Munchi Gandari
Dated: 1 April 2051

Author's Note

The day I knew I'd been successful as a writer was when, twenty years ago, a woman reading the second draft of this novel said, "There is no way a man wrote this book" followed quickly by, "You are one sick bastard."

Probing into the first statement I was informed that this book took the quintessential female aspect of pregnancy and recorded it fair and true, both in physical and emotional manifestations. Also, she added that the feelings brought on by rape and abandonment landed spot on. I have been told that as someone who had a good upbringing in a solid family and obviously as a man who couldn't have borne a child, I had not only overcome my own limitations and placed myself in the head of another "alien" person, but had done it so well as to be undetectable as anything but a woman. As such, at one time I considered publishing it under a feminine pen name.

In spite of the compliments above, Wayward School nearly never saw print. My closest advisors have all counseled me not to publish this book (see the dedication). I can paraphrase everyone's comment in a quote from my best critic and father, "It is the best written book I'd never read." The earlier readers of this book all said the same thing, in short: well written but too gritty and dark. I was disappointed, feeling this was one of the best works I'd ever written (and still do).

I know it is odd that an author would give you quotes about people who didn't like his book, but I feel it is important to share before I continue. I decided that it would never be published unless I got so famous (hah) that I could print any ole bit of trash and have it bought. So *Wayward School* was aborted (pun intended) into a drawer where it languished.

But *Wayward* wouldn't leave me alone. Like any child it wanted attention. It wanted to grow. It needed love, too. Every so often I'd mention the concept to a person at one of my shows. To my surprise they wanted it—overwhelmingly so. So I asked more and more, including some pregnant women, and out of about one hundred only got a single person who said that it didn't sound like something they would read.

So where was the disconnect? The only thing I could think of was that my sample readers and advisors just weren't the right demographics. So I decided to take a chance. It was time for *Wayward School* to be born (pun continued).

So before you burn me in effigy or put a contract out on my life, I have to say that I don't advocate anything in this book. While I am definitely pro-choice I can't say that I want us to go around creating babies for parts or parts from babies. I am following along with my fellow brethren in the Sci Fi community by answering a "what if" question. That question that came to my twisted mind was, "What could we do with all the unwanted pregnancies to reduce overpopulation and unloved children in families?" Whoops!

Never get an author thinking over weighty issues.

However the medical profession is making my book obsolete before my eyes. There are stem cell printings of skin, bone, and other organs. Between that and other tissue-growing techniques on the verge (or already here), the concepts of this book will be passé and ridiculous long before the dates I've specified. I will admit to a cheat in this book . . . I say that printing tissue causes cancer. I have no such data or belief but I needed a viable reason why it wasn't used.

However this is a story of good and evil and what choices we make or are forced into. I hope that I've made you think about your own.

Oh, and as an aside, the woman who claimed I was a sick bastard chose to date me and eventually marry me anyway (and remains married to me over twenty years later).

Other Works Published by TANSTAAFL Press

Novels by Tom Gondolfi

An Eighty Percent Solution – CorpGov Chronicles: Book One

In a world where corporations suborn governments as a part of good business practice and unregistered humans can be killed without penalty, Tony Sammis, a midlevel corporate functionary, finds himself unwittingly a pawn in a guerilla war between a powerful cabal of business leaders and an elusive but deadly underground movement. His final solution to the biological terror unleashed mirrors Tony's own twisted sense of justice.

Thinking Outside the Box – CorpGov Chronicles: Book Two

Winning one war doesn't seem to be enough. Tony Sammis and the Green Action Militia are once again thrust into the center of a conflict that will change the lives of everyone in the solar system. This time they are allies with the fledgling CorpGov and even the United States government against the ravages of the corrupt Metropolitan Police force. The GAM and their allies are fighting a losing war with few soldiers and even fewer weapons. Behind the scenes, a humble and unsuspected power block lurks with its own axe to grind.

Self-interest, romance, freedom, and a lust for power simmer together in this chaotic soup of tension, intrigue, assassination, and war.

The Bleeding Edge – CorpGov Chronicles: Book Three

Tony Sammis and Nanogate lead a patchwork alliance that includes the nascent CorpGov, Green Action Militia, the president of the United States, the Pacific Northwest Mob, most of the megacorps and the United Brotherhood of Bodyguards. The war the CorpGov alliance knows they can't win has begun, but they are no longer fighting to win. Tony and Nanogate know they may not survive, but they intend to deliver the most grievous wounds they can. The most dangerous animal is one with no hope.

Toy Wars

Flung to a remote world, a semi-sentient group of robotic mining factories arrive with their programming hashed. They can only create animated toys instead of normal mining and fighting machines. One of these factories, pushed to the edge of extinction by the fratricidal conflict, attempts a desperate gamble. Infusing one of its toys with the power of sentience begins the quest of a 2-meter-tall purple teddy bear and his pink polka-dotted elephant companion. They must cross an alien world to find and enlist the aid of mortal enemies to end the genocide before Toy Wars claims their family—all while asking the immortal question, "Why am I?"

Toy Reservations

Isp, toyanity's religious zealot, returns at the head of a massive new Army of the Humans. He openly announces his intent to replace President Quixote's government with a theocracy. With most of his toys modified to peacetime purposes, Don Quixote must make a horrific decision for the very soul of his people.

Novels by Bruce Graw

Demon Holiday

Torval, Demon Third Class, Layer Four Hundred Twelve of the Eighth Circle of Hell, has been in the business of chastising sinners longer than he can remember. Delivering punishment is the only job he's ever known—the only job he's ever wanted. After Torval witnesses something unexpected, his demonic Overseer demands that he take time off to resolve this personal crisis. And so, Torval, the demon, finds himself sent on vacation . . .to Earth, the proving ground of souls!

Demon Ascendant

Torval, Demon Third Class, Layer Four Hundred Twelve of the Eighth Circle of Hell, on vacation to Earth has managed to find another demon, dated a woman and inadvertently explored some of the sins of humankind: greed, gluttony, and lust. Through all this, his biggest struggle involves deciding if he wants his holiday to end or to continue forever.

Lady Hornet

Elizabeth Fontaine is a lonely, ordinary young woman in a world where superheroes struggle daily against evil. To fill the empty void within her soul, she becomes a hero fangirl, following every super's event, subscribing to multiple fanzines, and never missing the daily superhero talk shows...until one day, fate grants her the opportunity to leave behind her boring, dreary life and become what she's always dreamed of...a superheroine! Elizabeth learns the hard way the meaning of the phrase, "Caveat Emptor!"—let the buyer beware!

The Faerie of Central Park

The last of her kind in New York City, Tillianita tends the land and beasts as best she can, reluctantly obeying her departed father's warning to avoid humans at all costs. A freak accident casts her out of the relative safety of Central Park. Lost and alone with a broken wing, she wonders if she'll ever see her home again. On his own for the first time in his life, college freshman Dave Thompson isn't sure he'll ever fit in. When he stumbles upon an extremely realistic fairy doll, he thinks perhaps it might make a good present for a future date until he discovers that it's not a doll at all. His find turns not only his life upside down but also expands his narrow view of the world.

Novels by Stephanie L. Weippert

Sweet Secrets

At seven, Michael is mysteriously transported to a world where magic is done by cooking. He's tested and taken as a student in the premier magic school on the planet. His fellow students can make cookies that fly and chocolate turtles that actually walk. Michael is told he has more power than any of them.

But his stepfather, Brad, has been charged with watching his stepson Michael for the first time. When the boy disappears before his eyes, Brad panics. Within hours he is on an adventure tracking his son alongside an enigmatic chef. He has to get Michael home before his Mother finds out he's gone or there is going to be hell to pay.

Road to Chaos

Robert Thompson is a vain, egotistical actor bent on making his mark on Hollywood. On his way to an important audition that may make his career, another car crashes into his. The other car is totaled but his land yacht is barely dented. The other driver, in a fit of lunacy, insists that they get in his car and drive away before the chaos mathamagic police find them. Robert scoffs. Magic is for rubes and what in this crazy man's delusions does chaos or math have to do with it?

Robert clings to his beliefs until he finds out that the other driver is his long-lost cousin, the magic police tries to kill them both, and his cousin Eric teleports them to Tibet. Robert finds himself bounced around the globe on a mixed attempt to both evade the brutal mathamagic goon squad and clear Eric's name, all the while hoping that he can return to salvage his real life of movies.

**Enter the... apocalyptic anthology series from
TANSTAAFL Press – edited by Thomas Gondolfi**

Enter the Apocalypse

Thirty-two authors from all over the world have created a wide range of apocalypses for your reading pleasure. Within the pages of this anthology, you will find exceptional works focusing on hungry zombies, virulent viruses, nuclear missiles, malevolent fey, vindictive aliens, challenging crustaceans, and more — each of these maelstroms creating massive disturbances within human society.

While works of holocausts tend toward a uniform darkness, Enter the Apocalypse contains a number of catastrophes that are humorous enough to cause hysterics and others that are so black as to cause the devil himself to shrink away.

Enter the Aftermath

Continuing the theme started with Enter the Apocalypse, TANSTAAFL Press brings you another anthology of the end of mankind as we know it. In this volume writers were asked to explore the height or burnout of a disaster. Thirty-eight international authors offer dominating warlocks, ironic phone calls, thoughtless kaiju, frozen ecology, survival mutations, misbehaving aliens, and even two disparate takes on artificial intelligence - just to name a few. Enter the Aftermath provides insights into all humanity and even some non-homosapiens that we anthropomorphize. Come inside and enjoy the darkness and humor woven by our storytellers.

Enter the Rebirth

Every reaction, no matter how violent, always reaches some equilibrium state. This final anthology shares stories of what the new normal looks like after the end of days.

11202891R00127

Made in the USA
San Bernardino, CA
07 December 2018